# GREAT black magic STORIES

# GREAT
# black
# magic
# STORIES

**Edited by**
## Michel
## Parry

**Taplinger Publishing Company** | **New York**

Published in the United States in 1977 by
TAPLINGER PUBLISHING CO., INC.
New York, New York

Library of Congress Cataloging in Publication Data
Main entry under title:

Great black magic stories.

    CONTENTS: Campbell, R. Potential.—Wheatley, D. The snake
—Boucher, A. They bite. [etc.]
    1. Magic—Fiction. I. Parry, Michel.
PZ1.G7953    1977    [PN6071.M155]    808.83'1    77-76574
ISBN 0-8008-3618-9

# CONTENTS

# ACKNOWLEDGEMENTS

The Editor would like to extend his sincere thanks and appreciation to the following authors, agents, and publishers for permission to reprint copyright material. Every effort has been made to trace the copyright holders of these stories. In the event of any accidental infringement of copyright, the Editor and Publisher offer their apologies and will undertake to make the necessary corrections in future editions.

"Potential" by Ramsey Campbell. From *Demons by Daylight*. Copyright © 1973 by Ramsey Campbell. Reprinted by permission of the author and Arkham House Publishers.

"The Snake" by Dennis Wheatley. From *Gunmen, Gallants and Ghosts*. Copyright 1943 by Dennis Wheatley. Reprinted by permission of the author, and Messers. Brook Richlieu, Ltd., and A. P. Watt and Son.

"They Bite" by Anthony Boucher. Copyright 1943 by Anthony Boucher. Reprinted by permission of Curtis Brown, Ltd., and Mrs. Phyllis White.

"The Vixen" by Aleister Crowley. Reprinted from *The Equinox* by permission of John Symonds and Kenneth Grant, the Outer Head of the Ordo Templi Orientis.

" 'He Cometh and He Passeth By' " by H. R. Wakefield. Copyright 1928 by H. R. Wakefield. Reprinted by permission of The Estate of H. R. Wakefield.

"The Invoker of the Beast" by Feodor Sologub, translated by John Cournos. From *The Old House and Other Stories*. Reprinted by permission, of Martin Secker, Publishers.

"Witch War" by Richard Matheson. Copyright 1951 by Better Publications, for *Startling Stories*. Reprinted by permission of Harold Matson Co., Inc.

"Nasty" by Fredric Brown. Copyright © 1961 by Fredric Brown. Reprinted by permission of Mrs. Elizabeth C. Brown and agents for The Estate of Fredric Brown, Scott Meredith Literary Agency, Inc., 845 Third Avenue, New York, N.Y. 10022.

"The New People" by Charles Beaumont. Copyright © 1958 by Charles Beaumont. Reprinted by permission of Harold Matson Co., Inc.

"In the Valley of the Sorceress" by Sax Rohmer. Reprinted by permission of Collier Associates and Methuen & Co., Ltd., and The Estate of Sax Rohmer.

"The Hand of Glory" by Seabury Quinn. Copyright 1933 by the Popular Fiction Publishing Company, for *Weird Tales*. Reprinted by permission of Margaret Quinn and Kirby McCauley.

# INTRODUCTION

Why Black Magic stories? Why not pure wholesome *White* Magic stories? The fact of the matter is – the devil has all the best stories!

Recent years have seen a remarkable resurgence of interest in magic, astrology, witchcraft, and occult subjects generally, accompanied by a popular demand for films like *Rosemary's Baby* and *The Exorcist*, and for stories of fantasy wherein magic is almost mundane and warlocks and demons as commonplace as the mailman.

Why should magic continue to fascinate us, citizens of the Space Age? The contributing factors are many, but undoubtedly the dominant personality behind the Magical Revival is the man whose name has become synonymous with Black Magic – Aleister Crowley. Crowley died in 1947 but, like a long-dead star whose signals still reach us, his influence continues to be felt. (The Beatles may have had a hand in this by including his picture on the sleeve of their *Sergeant Pepper's Lonely Hearts Club Band* L.P.) It is only fitting that this collection of Black Magic stories should include a contribution by the *Master Theiron*, or Great Beast of Revelations, as Crowley styled himself. Crowley's tale of *The Vixen*, a story that the Marquis de Sade would surely have relished, is representative of a semi-serious desire on Crowley's part to shock and outrage less questing souls, a tendency that was to earn him the label of the 'Wickedest Man in the World'. The same inclination is exhibited by Black Magician Oscar Clinton, the villain of H. R. Wakefield's *He Cometh and He Passeth by*. This is hardly surprising

9

since, in fact, Clinton is nothing more than an effective caricature of Crowley himself* Other contributors in these pages with more than a passing interest in the actual practice of magic are the creator of the insidious Dr Fu Manchu, Sax Rohmer (who, like Crowley, was a member of the famous magical secret society, the Order of the Golden Dawn), and Madame Helena Petrovna Blavatsky, the Russian medium and spiritualist who founded the Theosophical Society and is remembered as the foremost female occultist of modern times.

The rest of our contributors are not magicians but writers, writers who are amongst the very best in England, the United States, and Russia to have put their talent into the writing of supernatural stories. There is, for instance, Dennis Wheatley, who, for thirty years, has thrilled readers with novels such as *The Devil Rides Out*. When that masterpiece of Satanic intrigue was filmed, chosen to write the script was Richard Matheson, represented here by *Witch War*. His own recently filmed novel, *Hell House*, is an excellent testimonial to the impressive extent of Mr Matheson's knowledge of the Black Arts.

Then there are names such as Anthony Boucher, Charles Beaumont, Frederic Brown, and Ramsey Campbell. When one considers the devilish visions conjured up by these writers, the mastery with which, in turn, they captivate, enthrall, and terrify the reader ... then the distinction between writer and magician does not seem so great after all.

Here then are stories in which you are invited to make pacts with demons, join strange covens, romp with witches, offer up blood-sacrifices, and participate in exotic – and erotic – rituals. And all, if you heed the Warning

---

* Crowley was a boon to novelists looking for a real-life model on which to base their sundry Satanists and Black Magicians. Other 'fictional' Crowleys include Oliver Haddo in Somerset Maugham's *The Magician*, Hugo Astley in Dion Fortune's *The Winged Bull*, Caradoc Cunningham in Colin Wilson's *Man Without a Shadow*, and the villain of Sax Rohmer's *Salute to Bazarada*, Servius Jerome.

printed elsewhere, without any risk of personal danger whatsoever.

The Devil Himself couldn't offer a better deal than that!

*Michel Parry*

# POTENTIAL

## by Ramsey Campbell

On the poster outside the Cooperative Hall, forming from the stars twined in the foliage, Charles had read: 'BRICHESTER'S FIRST BE-IN – FREE FLOWERS AND BELLS!' But in the entrance hall, beyond the desk where a suspicious muscle-man accepted his ten shillings, two girls were squabbling over the last plastic bell. Searching in the second cardboard carton, Charles found a paper flower whose petals were not too dog-eared, whose wire hooked into his buttonhole without snapping. 'Bloody typical,' a boy said next to him. 'I'm going to write to the *International Times* about this.'

He meant it wasn't a true love-in, Charles supposed, fumbling with terminology. He'd once bought the *International Times*, the underground newspaper, but the little he had understood he hadn't liked. Uneasily he watched the crowds entering the ballroom. Cloaks, shawls, boys with hair like dark lather, like tangled wire: Charles adjusted his 'Make Love Not War' badge, conscious of its incongruity against his grey office suit. He glanced up at the names of groups above the ballroom door: the Titus Groans, the Faveolate Colossi. 'OK, guys and gals, we've got a fabulously faveolate evening ahead for you,' he muttered in faint parody. 'Come on,' said the boy at his side, 'let's go in.'

Through the entrance Charles could see swaying figures merged by chameleon lights and hear drums like subterranean engines; as they entered the guitars screamed, a spotlight plunged through his eyes to expand inside his skull. 'Let me adjust,' he said to his companion: anything to gain time. Threads of joss-smoke curled into his nostrils, sinuous as the hands of a squatting girl,

Indian-dancing for an encircling intent audience. A middle-aged man left the circle, which closed, and wandered ill at ease: A reporter, Charles thought. He searched the vast ballroom; groups of thirteen-year-old girls dancing, multicoloured spotlights painting faces, projectors spitting images of turbulent liquid on the walls, on the stage the Faveolate Colossi lifting guitars high in a faintly obscene gesture. 'Ready?' asked the boy at his side.

They danced towards two girls: sixteen, perhaps, or younger. A crimson light found Charles; when it moved away his face stayed red. Each time he moved his foot it was dragged down by a sense of triviality; he thought of the file left on his desk last night, to be dealt with on Monday morning. He sensed the reporter watching him from the shadows. The music throbbed to silence. The two girls glared at Charles and walked away. 'Not much cop, anyway,' said his companion – but then he seemed to see someone he knew: he vanished in the murk.

On the balcony above the ballroom a girl wearily blew bubbles through the shafts of coloured light. They settled, bursting when they touched floor or flesh: Charles saw his life. 'Are you a flower person?' a voice asked: it was the reporter, twirling a paper flower.

'No less so than you, I should think.' Charles felt cheated: the boys with flowers behind their ears, the girls dancing together like uneasy extras in a musical, the jagged lances of sound, the lights excruciating as the dazzle of scraped tin, gave him nothing: less than the fragments he'd retained from books on philosophy.

'I'm not one – Good Lord, no. I'm just searching.'

Charles sensed sympathy. 'You're not a reporter?'

'Never have been. Is that what I look like? No wonder they've all been watching me.'

'Then why are you here?'

'For the same reason as you,' the other said. 'Searching.'

Charles supposed that was true. He stared about: at the far end from the stage a bar had been given over to lemonade. 'Let me stand you a drink,' the other said.

At the bar Charles saw that the man's hands were trembling; he'd torn the paper petals from the wire. Charles couldn't walk away; he searched for distraction. On stage the leader of the Titus Groans was staggering about, hands covering his eyes, crying 'Oswald, Kennedy, James Dean, Marilyn Monroe – The speakers round the ballroom squealed and snorted. 'Kill, kill!' screamed the Titus Groan, setting fire to a cardboard amplifier. Charles glanced away, at caped figures in a corner. 'Sons of Dracula,' he muttered in a weak Karloff parody. The other laughed. 'You're a good mimic,' he said. Charles thought of the office: moments when he'd felt the conversation move away from him and improvised an imitation to hold attention. He stared at the figures smoking gravely in the corner, until he saw the flash of a packet of Woodbines.

'If someone had given you LSD or hashish, would you have accepted?' the other asked, sipping a Coke and belching.

'I don't know. Perhaps.' Something to set him apart from the people at the office, though they'd never know: he hadn't even dared to wear his badge among them.

'You feel empty. You're looking for something to fill you, to expand your mind as they'd say.' The man's hands were shaking again: the glass jangled on the bar.

'Ja, iss right, Herr Doktor,' but it didn't work. 'I suppose you're right,' Charles said.

The Titus Groan was casting flowers into the crowd. Suddenly Charles wanted one – then immediately he didn't: it was trivial. Girls scrambled for the flowers; as they converged they changed from red to green. 'Gerroff!' yelled one. 'I think' – Charles said. 'I know,' the other agreed. 'Let's leave.'

In the entrance hall the pugilist behind the desk peered at them suspiciously. 'By the way, my name's Cook,' the man mentioned. 'Charles,' Charles said.

They emerged into the main street; behind the blue lamps the moon was choked by clouds. A passing couple eyed Charles's flower and 'Make Love Not War' and shook their heads, tut-tut. 'I know you bought that badge for the occasion,' Cook remarked. 'You might as well take it off.'

'I do believe in it, you know,' Charles said.

'Of course,' Cook said. 'We all do.'

Tomorrow Charles might say: 'Last night I met a philosopher' – but once he'd claimed as his own a description of a robbery told him by a friend, only to be taunted by his neighbour at the office: 'Yes, I saw that too. Last week on TV, wasn't it?' Two boys passed, tinkling with beads and bells. Charles was about to offer Cook a drink: he'd formed vague friendships at the office thus. But Cook was struggling to speak.

'I wonder –' he mumbled. The moon fought back the clouds, like an awakening face. 'I don't know you very well, but still – you seem sympathetic ... Look, I'll tell you. I'm meeting some friends of mine who are experimenting with the mind, let's say. Trying to realize potential. It sounds dramatic, but maybe they can help you find yourself.' His head shook; he looked away.

He was nervous, Charles could see: it was as if he'd drained Charles's unease into himself, leaving Charles the power to calm him. 'I'll try anything once,' Charles said. Blinded by the lamps like photofloods, the moon shrank back into the clouds.

They walked towards a side street where Cook's car was parked. In the unreal light the shops rose to Victorian façades, annihilating time. Charles wondered what they'd give him: LSD, lights, hypnosis? In the Be-In the pounding sound and leaping lights had reminded him somehow of brainwashing. He didn't like the idea of hypnosis: he wanted to be aware of his actions, to preserve his identity. Perhaps he'd simply watch the others.

Down a side street, on a stage of light from a pub door, two men fought. Charles couldn't look away. 'I thought so,' Cook said. 'You're one of us.'

In the next street Cook's car waited, its headlights dull like great blind eyes. 'I hope you're not too perfect,' Cook mumbled, unlocking the door. 'They can't abandon me, not now. No, I'm just suspicious by nature, I know that.' Savagely he twisted the ignition key, and shuddered. 'They're in Severnford,' he said.

Darkness spread again over the last house like decay, and the road dipped. As they swept over 'a rise Charles saw the distant Severn: a boat drifted quietly and vanished. Hills were lit like sleeping colossi; over them the moon bounced absurdly before the clouds closed. Suddenly Cook stopped the car. The darkness hid his face, but Charles could make out his hands working on the wheel. Cook rolled the window down. 'Look up there,' he said, pointing an unsteady finger at a gap in the clouds exposing the universe, a lone far frosty star. 'Infinity. There must be something in all that to fill us.'

In Severnford they pulled up near the wharf. The streets were lit by gas-lamps, reflected flickering in windows set in dark moist stone. 'We'll walk from here,' Cook said.

They crossed an empty street of shops. On the corner of an alley Cook stopped before a window: socks, shirts, skirts, bags of sweets, tins of Vim, along the front of the pane a line of books like a frieze. 'Do you read science fiction?' Cook asked.

'Not much,' Charles said. 'I don't read much.' Not fiction, anyway, and retained little.

'You should read Lovecraft.' Next to the tentacled cover a man fought off a razor, hands flailing, eyes pleading with the camera: Cook almost gripped Charles's arm, then flinched away. They entered the alley. Two dogs scrabbling at dustbins snarled and ran ahead. In a lighted window, above the broken glass which grew from the alley wall, someone played a violin.

Beyond the houses at the end of the alley ran the Severn. The boat had gone; tranquil lights floated against the current. Gas-lamps left the windows of the houses dark and gaping, shifted shadows behind the broken leaning doors. 'Over here,' Cook said, clearing his throat.

'Here?' Cook had headed for a disused pub, its dim window autographed in dust. Charles wavered: was

Cook perhaps alone? Why had he lured him here? Then Charles looked up; behind the sign – THE RIVERSIDE – nailed across the second storey, he glimpsed the bright edge of a window and heard a hint of voices, mixed with some sound he couldn't place. Cook was swallowed by the lightless doorway; the two dogs ran out whimpering. Charles followed his guide.

Beer-bottles were piled in pyramids on the bar, held together by Sellotape; in the topmost candles flared, their flames flattened and leapt, briefly revealing broken pump-handles on the bar-top like ancient truncheons, black mirrors from which Charles' face sprang surprised, two crates behind the bar cloaked in sacking. POLICE ARE PEOPLE TOO was painted on a glass partition; for a moment it appeared like the answer of an oracle. 'Oh, the police know about this,' Cook said, catching Charles's eye. 'They're used to it by now, they don't interfere. Upstairs.'

Beyond the bar a dark staircase climbed; as they mounted past a large unseen room, through whose empty window glimmered the Severn, the voices hushed, giving way to the sound which worried Charles. Cook knocked twice on a panelled door. A secret society, thought Charles, wondering. The door opened.

Sound rushed out. Charles's first thought was of the Be-In: a united shriek of violins, terrifying. Inside the long room faces turned to him. 'Take off your shoes,' Cook said, leaving his own in the row at the door, padding on to the fur which carpeted the flat.

Charles complied uneasily, postponing the moment when he must look up. When he did they were still watching: but not curious, clearly eager to know him. He felt accepted; for the first time he was wanted for himself, not a desperately mimicked image. The young man in black who had opened the door circled him, shoulder-length ringlets swaying, and took his hand. 'I'm Smith,' he said. 'You're in my flat.'

Cook hurried forward. 'This is Charles,' he stuttered.

'Yes, yes, Cook, he'll tell us his name when he's ready.'

Cook retreated, almost tripping over someone prone on

the fur. Charles surveyed; boys with hair they shook back from their faces, girls already sketched on by experience, in a corner an old couple whose eyes glittered as if galvanized – writers, perhaps. They weren't like the people at the office; he felt they could give him something he sought. Against the walls two speakers shrieked; several of the listeners lay close, crawling closer. 'What's that?' Charles asked.

'Penderecki. *Threnody for the Victims of Hiroshima.*'

Charles watched the listeners: in the violins the imaginative might hear the screams of the victims, in the pizzicati the popping of scorched flesh. Near one speaker *Beyond Belief* protected a veneer from a pub ashtray; next to it lay *New Worlds Speculative Fiction, We Pass From View, Le Sadisme au Cinema,* an *International Times* and a pile of Ultimate Press pornography, above which, mute, stared Mervyn Peake's Auschwitz sketches. 'Smoke?' Smith asked, producing a gold cigarette-case.

'No thanks,' Charles said; when he knew them better he'd try the marihuana, if that was what it was.

'I will,' Cook interrupted, taking a black cigarette.

The violins died. 'Time?' someone suggested.

'I'll make sure.' Smith turned to Charles apologetically: 'We don't use words unless they're meaningful.' He padded to a corner and opened a door which Charles hadn't noticed; beyond it light blazed as at the Be-In. Charles thought he heard voices whispering, and a metal sound. He glanced about, avoiding the faces; outside the window loomed the back of the pub sign. A wall hid the river from him, but he could still see the quiet boat in the moonlight. He wished they'd speak instead of watching him; but perhaps they were waiting for him to declare himself. He wished Cook wouldn't stand at the bookcase, his shivering back aware of Charles.

Smith appeared, closing the door. The faces turned from Charles to him. 'Charles has come to find himself,' he said. 'In there, Charles.'

They stood up and surrounded the door, leaving a path for Charles. They were eager – too eager; Charles hesitated. He'd wanted to be part of something, not alone and acted upon. But Smith smiled deprecatingly; the fur lulled Charles's nerves like a childhood blanket. He started forward. 'Wait,' Smith said. He stared at Cook, still trembling before the bookcase. 'Cook,' he called, 'you want to participate. You be guide.'

'I feel sick,' said Cook's back.

'You don't want to leave us after so long.'

Cook shuddered and whirled to face them. He looked at Charles, then away. 'All right,' he whispered, 'I'll help him.' Beckoned by Smith, he preceded Charles into the other room.

Charles almost turned and ran, he couldn't have said why; but he was inhibited against rejecting people he'd just met. He strode past the eyes into the blazing light.

At first he didn't see the girl. There was so much in the way: cameras on splayed tripods, blind blinding spotlights climbed by cords like Lovecraft tentacles, in the centre of the floor a rack of knives and razors and sharp instuments, carefully arranged. He heard what must be the whimper of a dog on the wharf. Suddenly he peered through the twined cords and thrust Cook aside. A girl was tied to the wall. Her arms were crucified high. She was naked.

The jigsaw fitted – *International Times*, pornography, the cameras, pornographic films – but Charles felt no revulsion, simply anger: he'd come so far for this. Then a glimpse of crimson drew his eye to the gap where the girl's left little finger should have been. Unbelieving, he stared at the floor, at the pattern of crimson tracing the agonized flurry of her hand.

'Make your choice,' Cook said.

Slowly Charles turned, sick with hatred. Cook had retreated to the door; over his shoulder the others craned for a better view. 'Make your choice,' Cook repeated, indicating the rack of knives: his voice trembled, and the girl looked back and whimpered. 'Let what is in you be you. Release your potential, your power.'

Charles couldn't look at the girl; if he did he'd be

19

sick. He could feel her pleading with him. He approached the rack; his stockinged feet clung to the floor as in a nightmare. He touched a knife; its blade mutilated his reflection, its edge was razor sharp. He clutched the handle and glanced with prickling eyes towards the door. It wouldn't work: too far to run. He struggled to remove the knife from the rack.

'Go on, Cook, help him,' Smith said. The girl sobbed. Cook turned about, trembling. 'Cook,' Smith said.

Cook sidled towards Charles, his eyes appealing like a dog's as they linked the girl and Charles: Charles was his nightmare. Almost at the rack, Cook stood shaking and glared towards the girl. 'My God!' he cried. 'You haven't –'

'My wife?' Smith called. 'Not even I.'

The knife slid from the rack and was at once in Cook's stomach. Yet Charles saw the blade flash on Cook's face, flayed not so much by terror as by knowledge. Cook fell on the knife. Charles closed his eyes. Blindly he wiped his hands on his jacket. At last he faced them, and almost knew what Cook had known. They were watching him with a new expression: worship.

Behind him he heard movement. He had to turn. The girl was pulling her hands free of the cords, flexing her little finger which had been hidden in her palm, wiping off the crimson paint on a cloth from the floor. As she passed Charles she stretched out her hand to touch him, but at the last moment lowered her eyes and knelt before Cook's body. Smith joined her and they linked hands. The others followed and knelt, the old couple sinking slowly as their charge was drained. They turned up their faces to Charles, waiting.

You made this happen! he might have shouted to defeat them. You staged this, you invented it! It means nothing.

And all he'd done had been to perform their script – But his hand had held the knife, his hand still felt it plunge, his hand displayed the blade beneath which they cowered. Within him something woke and swelled, tearing him open, drawing him into itself. They saw; they knew. The girl stretched out her hands towards him, and they chorused a name.

At once it was outside his body, no longer part of him. For a moment he was filled by the innocence of oblivion. Then, finally, he knew. He felt what they had called forth sucking him out like an oyster, converting him into itself, the pain as his molecules ripped asunder as if his fingers were being wrenched loose. He cried out once. Then blood fountained from his mouth.

They moved whispering through the flat, eyes averted. Two of them supported Cook's body to his car. 'In the hills, remember,' Smith whispered.

He returned to the studio, head bowed. 'The river?' someone asked, pointing to the dry grey shape on the floor.

'It's nothing now,' Smith said. 'It won't be recognized. The front door.'

They gathered up the husk and piled it into a paper carrier, where it rasped, hollow. Someone took the bag down through the pub. The candles had guttered. He threw the contents of the bag into the street beneath the gas-lamps, and the dogs converged snarling to fight. Then he rejoined the others, as reverently they raised their eyes to what filled the flat, and waited for it to speak.

# THE SNAKE

## by Dennis Wheatley

I didn't know Carstairs at all well, mind you, but he was our nearest neighbour and a stranger to the place. He'd asked me several times to drop in for a chat, and that weekend I'd been saddled with a fellow called Jackson.

He was an engineer who had come over from South America to report on a mine my firm were interested in. We hadn't got much in common and the talk was getting a bit thin, so on the Sunday evening I thought I'd vary the entertainment by looking up Carstairs and taking Jackson with me.

Carstairs was pleased enough to see us; he lived all on his own but for the servants. What he wanted with a big place like that I couldn't imagine, but that was his affair. He made us welcome and we settled down in comfortable armchairs to chat.

It was one of those still summer evenings with the scent of the flowers drifting in through the open windows, and the peace of it all makes you think for the moment that the city, on Monday morning, is nothing but a rotten bad dream.

I think I did know in a vague way that Carstairs had made his money mining, but when, or where, I hadn't an idea. Anyhow, he and young Jackson were soon in it up to the neck, talking technicalities. That never has been my end of the business. I was content to lend them half an ear while I drank in the hush of the scented twilight; a little feller was piping away to his mate for all he was worth in the trees at the bottom of the garden.

It was the bat started it; you know how they flit in on a summer's night through the open windows, absolutely silently, before you are aware of them. How they're here one moment – and there the next, in and out of the shadows while you flap about with a newspaper like a helpless fool. They're unclean things, of course, but harmless enough, yet never in my life have I seen a big man so scared as Carstairs.

'Get it out!' he yelled. 'Get it out,' and he buried his bald head in the sofa cushions.

I think I laughed, anyhow I told him it was nothing to make a fuss about, and switched out the light.

The bat zigzagged from side to side once or twice, and then flitted out into the open as silently as it had come.

Carstairs's big red face had gone quite white when he peeped out from beneath his cushions. 'Has it gone?' he asked in a frightened whisper.

'Of course it has,' I assured him. 'Don't be silly – it might have been the devil himself from the fuss you made!'

'Perhaps it was,' he said seriously. As he sat up I could see the whites of his rather prominent eyes surrounding the blue pupil – I should have laughed if the man hadn't been in such an obvious funk.

'Shut the windows,' he said sharply, as he moved over to the whisky and mixed himself a pretty stiff drink. It seemed a sin on a night like that, but it was his house, so Jackson drew them to.

Carstairs apologized in a half-hearted sort of way for making such a scene, then we settled down again.

In the circumstances it wasn't unnatural that the talk should turn to witchcraft and things like that.

Young Jackson said he'd heard some pretty queer stories in the forests of Brazil, but that didn't impress me, because he looked a good half-dago himself, for all his English name, and dagoes always believe in that sort of thing.

Carstairs was a different matter; he was as British as could be, and when he asked me seriously if I believed in Black Magic I didn't laugh, but told him just as seriously that I did not.

'You're wrong then,' he declared firmly, 'and I'll tell

you this, I shouldn't be sitting here if it wasn't for Black Magic.'

'You can't be serious,' I protested.

'I am,' he said. 'For thirteen years I roamed the Union of South Africa on my uppers, a "poor white", if you know what that means. If you don't – well, it's hell on earth. One rotten job after another with barely enough pay to keep body and soul together, and between jobs not even that, so that at times you'd even lower yourself to chum up to a black for the sake of a drink or a bit of a meal. Never a chance to get up in the world, and despised by natives and whites alike – well, I suppose I'd be at it still but that I came up against the Black Art, and that brought me big money. Once I had money I went into business. That's twenty-two years ago – I'm a rich man now, and I've come home to take my rest.'

Carstairs evidently meant every word he said, and I must confess I was impressed. There was nothing neurotic about him, he was sixteen stone of solid, prosaic Anglo-Saxon; in fact, he looked just the sort of chap you'd like to have with you in a tight corner. That's why I'd been so surprised when he got in such a blue funk about the bat.

'I'm afraid I'm rather an unbeliever,' I admitted, 'but perhaps that's because I've never come up against the real thing – won't you tell us some more about it?'

He looked at me steadily for a moment with his round, blue eyes. 'All right,' he said, 'if you like; help yourself to another peg, and your friend too.'

We refilled our glasses and he went on: 'When I as good as said just now, "that bat may be the devil in person", I didn't mean quite that. Maybe there are people who can raise the devil – I don't know, anyhow I've never seen it done; but there is a power for evil drifting about the world – suffused in the atmosphere, as you might say, and certain types of animals seem to be sensitive to it – they pick it up out of the ether just like a wireless receiving set.

'Take cats – they're uncanny beasts; look at the way

they can see in the dark; and they can do more than that; they can see things that we can't in broad day. You must have seen them before now, walk carefully round an object in a room that simply wasn't there.

'These animals are harmless enough in themselves, of course, but where the trouble starts is when they become used as a focus by a malignant human will. However, that's all by the way. As I was telling you, I'd hiked it up and down the Union for thirteen years, though it wasn't the Union in those days. From Durban to Damaraland, and from the Orange River to Matabel, fruit farmer, miner, salesman, wagoner, clerk – I took every job that offered, but for all the good I'd done myself I might as well have spent my time on the Breakwater instead.

'I haven't even made up my mind today which is the tougher master – the Bible-punching Dutchman, with his little piping voice, or the whisky-sodden South African Scot.

'At last I drifted into Swaziland; that's on the borders of Portuguese East, near Lourenço Marques and Delagoa Bay. As lovely a country as you could wish to see; it's all been turned into native reserve now, but in those days there was a handful of white settlers scattered here and there.

'Anyhow, it was there in a saloon at Mbabane that I met old Benny Isaacsohn, and he offered me a job. I was down and out, so I took it, though he was one of the toughest-looking nuts that I'd ever come across. He was a bigger man than I am, with greasy black curls and a great big hook of a nose. His face was as red as a turkey cock, and his wicked black eyes were as shifty as sin. He said his store-keeper had died on him sudden, and the way he said it made me wonder just what had happened to that man.

'But it was Benny or picking up scraps from a native kraal – so I went along with him there and then.

'He took me miles up country to his famous store – two tins of sardines and a dead rat were about all he had in it, and of course I soon tumbled to it that trading honest wasn't Benny's real business. I don't doubt he'd sized me up and reckoned I wouldn't be particular. I was careful not to be too curious, because I had a sort of idea that that was what my predecessor had died of.

'After a bit he seemed to get settled in his mind about me, and didn't take much trouble to conceal his little games. He was doing a bit of gun-running for the natives from over the Portuguese border and a handsome traffic in illicit booze. Of course all our customers were blacks; there wasn't another white in a day's march except for Rebecca – Benny's old woman.

'I kept his books for him; they were all fake, of course. Brown sugar meant two dummy bullets out of five, and white, three, I remember; the dummies were cardboard painted to look like lead – cartridges come cheaper that way! Anyhow, Benny knew his ledger code all right.

'He didn't treat me badly on the whole; we had a shindy one hot night soon after I got there and he knocked me flat with one blow from his big red fist. After that I used to go and walk it off if I felt my temper getting the best of me –and it did at times when I saw the way he used to treat those niggers. I'm not exactly squeamish myself, but the things he used to do would make you sick.

'When I got into the game, I found that gun-running and liquor weren't the end of it. Benny was a money-lender as well – that's where he over-reached himself and came up aginst the Black Art.

'Of the beginnings of Benny's dealing with Umtonga, the witch-doctor, I know nothing. The old heathen would come to us now and again all decked out in his cowrie shells and strings of leopards' teeth, and Benny always received him in state. They'd sit drinking glass for glass of neat spirit for hours on end until Umtonga was carried away dead drunk by his men. The old villain used to sell off the surplus virgins of his tribe to Benny, and Benny used to market them in Portuguese East, to-gether with the wives of the poor devils who were in his clutches and couldn't pay the interest on their debts.

'The trouble started about nine months after I'd settled there; old Umtonga was a spender in his way, and there began to be a shortage of virgins in the tribe, so he started to borrow on his own account and then he couldn't pay. The interviews weren't so funny then – he began to go away sober and shaking his big black stick.

'That didn't worry Benny. He'd been threatened by people before, and he told Umtonga that if he couldn't raise enough virgins to meet his bill he'd better sell off a few of his wives himself.

'I was never present at the meetings, but I gathered a bit from what old Benny said in his more expansive moments, and I'd picked up enough Swazi to gather the gist of Umtonga's views when he aired them at parting on the stoep.

'Then one day Umtonga came with three women – it seemed that they were the equivalent of the original debt, but Benny had a special system with regard to his loans. Repayment of capital was nothing like enough – and the longer the debt was outstanding the greater the rate of interest became. By that time he wanted about thirty women, and good ones at that, to clear Umtonga off his books.

'The old witch-doctor was calm and quiet; contrary to custom, he came in the evening and he did not stay more than twenty minutes. The walls were thin, so I heard most of what went on – he offered Benny the three women – or death before the morning.

'If Benny had been wise he would have taken the women, but he wasn't. He told Umtonga to go to the devil – and Umtonga went.

'His people were waiting for him outside, about a dozen of them, and he proceeded to make a magic. They handed him a live black cock and a live white cock, and Umtonga sat down before the stoep and he killed them in a curious way.

'He examined their livers carefully, then he began to rock backwards and forwards on his haunches, and in his old cracked voice he sang a weird, monotonous chant.

The others lay down flat on the ground and wriggled round him one after the other on their bellies. They kept that up for about half an hour and then the old wizard began to dance. I can see his belt of monkey tails swirling about him now, as he leapt and spun. You wouldn't have thought that lean old savage had the strength in him to dance like that.

'Then all of a sudden he seemed to have a fit – he went absolutely rigid and fell down flat. He dropped on his face, and when his people turned him over we could see he was frothing at the mouth. They picked him up and carried him away.

'You know how the night comes down almost at once in the tropics. Umtonga started his incantation in broad daylight, and it didn't take so very long, but by the time he'd finished it was dark as pitch, with nothing but the Southern Cross and the Milky Way to light the hidden world.

'In those places most people still act by Nature's clock. We had the evening meal, old Rebecca, Benny, and I; he seemed a bit preoccupied, but that was no more than I would have been in the circumstances. Afterwards he went into his office room to see what he'd made on the day, as he always did, and I went off to bed.

'It was the old woman roused me about two o'clock – it seems she'd dropped off to sleep, and awoke to find that Benny had not come up to bed.

'We went along through the shanty, and there he was with his eyes wide and staring, gripping the arms of his office chair and all hunched up as though cowering away from something.

'He had never been a pretty sight to look at, but now there was something fiendish in the horror on his blackened face, and of course he'd been dead some hours.

'Rebecca flung her skirts over her head, and began to wail fit to bring the house down. After I'd got her out of the room, I went back to investigate – what could have killed Benny Isaacsohn? I was like you in those days – I didn't believe for a second that that toothless old fool

28

Umtonga had the power to kill from a distance.

'I made a thorough examination of the room, but there was no trace of anybody having broken in, or even having been there. I had a good look at Benny – it seemed to me he'd died of apoplexy or some sort of fit, but what had brought it on? He'd seen something, and it must have been something pretty ghastly.

'I didn't know then that a week or two later I was to see the same thing myself.

'Well, we buried Benny the next day – there was the usual kind of primitive wake, with the women howling and the men getting free drinks – half Africa seemed to have turned up; you know how mysteriously news travels in the black man's country.

'Umtonga put in an appearance; he expressed neither regret nor pleasure, but stood looking on. I didn't know what to make of it. The only evidence against him was the mumbo-jumbo of the night before, and no sane European could count that as proof of murder. I was inclined to think that the whole thing was an amazing coincidence.

'When the burying was over he came up to me. "Why you no kill house-boys attend Big Boss before throne of Great Spirit?" he wanted to know.

'I explained that one killing in the house was quite enough at a time. Then he demanded his stick, said he had left it behind in Benny's office the night before.

'I was pretty short with him, as you can imagine, but I knew the old ruffian's stick as well as I knew my own hairbrush; so I went in to get it.

'There it was lying on the floor – a four-foot snake stick. I dare say you've seen the sort of thing I mean; they make them shorter for Europeans. They are carved out of heavy wood, the snake's head is the handle, the tail the ferrule. Between, there are from five to a dozen bands; little markings are carved all down it to represent the scales. Umtonga's was a fine one – quite thin, but as heavy as lead. It was black, and carved out of ebony, I imagine. Not an ounce of give in it, but it would have

29

made a splendid weapon. I picked it up and gave it to him without a word.

'For about ten days I saw no more of him. Old Rebecca stopped her wailing, and got down to business. Benny must have told her about most of his deals that mattered, for I found that she knew pretty much how things stood. It was agreed that I should carry on as a sort of manager for her, and after a bit we came to the question of Umtonga. I suggested that the interest was pretty hot, and that the man might be really dangerous. Wouldn't it be btter to settle with him for what we could get? But she wouldn't have it; you would have thought I was trying to draw her eye-teeth when I suggested forgoing the interest! She fairly glared at me.

' "What is it to do with you?" she screamed. "I need money, I have the future of my – er – myself to think of. Send a boy with a message that you want to see him, and when he comes – make him pay."

'Well, there was nothing to do but to agree; the old shrew was worse than Benny in some ways. I sent a boy the following morning, and the day after Umtonga turned up.

'I saw him in Benny's office while his retinue waited outside; I was sitting in Benny's chair – the chair he'd died in – and I came to the point at once.

'He sat there for a few minutes just looking at me; his wizened old face was like a dried-up fruit that had gone bad. His black boot-button eyes shone with a strange malignant fire, then he said very slowly, "You – very brave young Baas."

' "No," I said, "just businesslike, that's all."

' "You know what happen to old Baas – he die – you want to go Great Spirit yet?"

'There was something evil and powerful in his steady stare; it was horribly disconcerting, but I wouldn't give in to it, and I told him I didn't want anything except his cash that was due, or its equivalent.

' "You forget business with Umtonga?" he suggested. "You do much good business, other mens. You no forget,

Umtonga make bad magic – you die."

'Well, it wasn't my business – it was the old woman's. I couldn't have let him out if I'd wanted to – so there was only one reply, the same as he'd got from Benny.

'I showed him Benny's gun, and told him that if there were any monkey tricks I'd shoot on sight. His only answer was one of the most disdainful smiles I've ever seen on a human face. With that he left me and joined his bodyguard outside.

'They then went through the same abracadabra with another black cock and another white cock – wriggled about on their bellies, and the old man danced till he had another fit and was carried away.

'Night had fallen in the meantime, and I was none too easy in my mind. I thought of Benny's purple face and staring eyes.

'I had supper with the old hag, and then I went to Benny's room. I like my tot, but I'd been careful not to take it; I meant to remain stone cold sober and wide-awake that night.

'I had the idea that one of Umtonga's people had done something to Benny, poisoned his drink perhaps.

'I went over his room minutely, and after I'd done, there wasn't a place you could have hidden a marmoset. Then I shut the windows carefully, and tipped up a chair against each so that no one could get in without knocking it down. If I did drop off, I was bound to wake at that. I turned out the light so that they should have no target for a spear or an arrow, and then I sat down to wait.

'I never want another night like that as long as I live; you know how you can imagine things in the darkness – well, what I didn't imagine in those hours isn't worth the telling.

'The little noises of the veldt came to me as the creepings of the enemy – half a dozen times I nearly lost my nerve and put a bullet into the blacker masses of the shadows that seemed to take on curious forms, but I was pretty tough in those days and I stuck it out.

'About eleven o'clock the moon came up; you would have thought that made it better, but it didn't. It added a new sort of terror – that was all. You know how eerie moonlight can be; it is unnatural somehow, and I believe there's a lot in what they say about there being evil in the moon. Bright bars of it stood out in rows on the floor, where it streamed in silent and baleful through the slats in the jalousies. I found myself counting them over and over again. It seemed as if I were becoming mesmerized by that cold, uncanny light. I pulled myself up with a jerk.

'Then I noticed that something was different about the desk in front of me. I couldn't think what it could be – but there was something missing that had been there a moment before.

'All at once I realized what it was, and the palms of my hands became clammy with sweat. Umtonga had left his stick behind again – I had picked it up off the floor when I searched the office and leant it against the front of the desk; the top of it had been there before my eyes for the last three hours in the semi-darkness – standing up stiff and straight – and now it had disappeared.

'It couldn't have fallen, I should have heard it – my eyes must have been starting out of my head. A ghastly thought had come to me – just supposing that stick was not a stick?

'And then I saw it – the thing was lying straight and still in the moonlight, with its eight to ten wavy bands, just as I'd seen it a dozen times before; I must have dreamed I propped it against the desk – it must have been on the floor all the time, and yet I knew deep down in me that I was fooling myself and that it had moved of its own accord.

'My eyes never left it – I watched, holding my breath to see if it moved – but I was straining so that I couldn't trust my eyesight. The bright bars of moonlight on the floor began to waver ever so slightly, and I knew that my sight was playing me tricks; I shut my eyes for a moment – it was the only thing to do – and when I opened them again the snake had raised its head.

'My vest was sticking to me, and my face was dripping wet. I knew now what had killed old Benny – I knew, too, why his face had gone black. Umtonga's stick was no stick at all, but the deadliest snake in all Africa – a thing that can move like lightning, can overtake a galloping horse, and kill its rider, so deadly that you're stiff within four minutes of its bite – I was up against a black mamba.

'I had my revolver in my hand, but it seemed a stupid, useless thing – there wasn't a chance in a hundred that I could hit it. A shotgun's the only thing that's any good; with that I might have blown its head off, but the guns weren't kept in Benny's room, and like a fool I'd locked myself in.

'The brute moved again as I watched it; it drew up its tail with a long slithering movement. There could be no doubt now; Umtonga was a super snake-charmer, and he'd left this foul thing behind to do his evil work.

'I sat there petrified, just as poor Benny must have done, wondering what in Heaven's name I could do to save myself, but my brain simply wouldn't work.

'It was an accident that saved me. As it rose to strike, I slipped in my attempt to get to my feet and kicked over Benny's wicker waste-paper basket; the brute went for that instead of me. The force with which they strike is tremendous – it's like the blow from a hammer or the kick of a mule. Its head went clean through the side of the basket and there it got stuck; it couldn't get its head out again.

'As luck would have it, I had been clearing out some of Benny's drawers that day, and I'd thrown away a whole lot of samples of quartz; the basket was about a third full of them and they weigh pretty heavy; a few had fallen out when it fell over, but the rest were enough to keep the mamba down.

'It thrashed about like a gigantic whip-lash, but it couldn't free its head, and I didn't waste a second; I started heaving ledgers on its tail. That was the end of the business as far as the mamba was concerned – I'd got it pinned down in half the time it took you to drive out that bat. Then I took up my gun again. "Now, my beauty," I thought, "I've got you where I want you, and I'll just quietly blow your head off – I'm going to have a damn fine pair of shoes out of your skin."

'I knelt down to the job and levelled my revolver; the snake struck twice, viciously, in my direction, but it couldn't get within a foot of me and it no more than jerked the basket either time.

'I looked down the barrel of the pistol within eighteen inches of its head, and then a very strange thing happened – and this is where the Black Magic comes in.

'The moonlit room seemed to grow dark about me, so that the baleful light faded before my eyes – the snake's head disappeared from view – the walls seemed to be expanding and the queer, acrid odour of the native filled my nostrils.

'I knew that I was standing in Umtonga's hut, and where the snake had been a moment before I saw Umtonga sleeping – or in a trance, if you prefer it. He was lying with his head on the belly of one of his women as is the custom of the country, and I stretched out a hand towards him in greeting. It seemed that, although there was nothing there, I had touched something – and then I realized with an appalling fear that my left hand was holding the waste-paper basket in which was the head of the snake.

'There was a prickling sensation on my scalp, and I felt my hair lifting – stiff with the electricity that was streaming from my body. With a tremendous effort of will-power I jerked back my hand. Umtonga shuddered in his trance – there was a thud, and I knew that the snake had struck in the place where my hand had been a moment before.

'I was half-crazy with fear, my teeth began to chatter, and it came to me suddenly that there was an icy wind blowing steadily upon me. I shivered with the deadly cold – although in reality it was a still, hot night. The

34

wind was coming from the nostrils of the sleeping Umtonga full upon me; the bitter coldness of it was numbing me where I stood, I knew that in another moment I should fall forwards on the snake.

'I concentrated every ounce of will-power in my hand that held the gun – I could not see the snake, but my eyes seemed to be focused upon Umtonga's forehead. If only my frozen finger could pull the trigger – I made a supreme effort, and then there happened a very curious thing.

'Umtonga began to talk to me in his sleep – not in words, you understand, but as spirit talks to spirit. He turned and groaned and twisted where he lay. A terrible sweat broke out on his forehead and round his skinny neck. I could see him as clearly as I can see you – he was pleading with me not to kill him, and in that deep, silent night, where space and time had ceased to exist, I knew that Umtonga and the snake were one.

'If I killed the snake, I killed Umtonga. In some strange fashion he had suborned the powers of evil, so that when at the end of the incantation he fell into a fit, his malignant spirit passed into the body of his dread familiar.

'I suppose I ought to have killed that snake and Umtonga too, but I didn't. Just as it is said that a drowning man sees his whole life pass before him at the moment of death – so I saw my own. Scene after scene out of my thirteen years of disappointment and failure flashed before me – but I saw more than that.

'I saw a clean, tidy office in Jo'burg, and I was sitting there in decent clothes. I saw this very house as you see it from the drive – although I'd never seen it in my life before – and I saw other things as well.

'At that moment I had Umtonga in my power, and he was saying as clearly as could be – 'All these things will I give unto you – if only you will spare my life.'

'Then the features of Umtonga faded. The darkness lightened and I saw again the moonlight streaming through the slats of old Benny's office – and the mamba's head!

'I put the revolver in my pocket, unlocked the door, and locking it again behind me, went up to bed.

'I slept as though I'd been on a ten-day forced march, I was so exhaused; I woke late, but everything that had happened in the night was clear in my memory – I knew I hadn't dreamed it. I loaded a shotgun and went straight to Benny's office.

'There was the serpent still beside the desk – its head thrust through the wicker basket and the heavy ledgers pinning down its body. It seemed to have straightened out, though, into its usual form, and when I knocked it lightly with the barrel of the gun it remained absolutely rigid. I could hardly believe it to be anything more than a harmless piece of highly polished wood, and yet I knew that it had a hideous, hidden life, and after that I left it very carefully alone.

'Umtonga turned up a little later, as I felt sure he would; he seemed very bent and old. He didn't say very much, but he spoke again about his debt, and asked if I would not forgo some part of it – he would pay the whole if he must, but it would ruin him if he did. To sell his wives would be to lose authority with his tribe.

'I explained that it wasn't my affair, but Rebecca's; she owned everything now that Benny was dead.

'He seemed surprised at that; natives don't hold with women owning property. He said he'd thought that the business was mine and all I had to do was to feed Rebecca till she died.

'Then he wanted to know if I would have helped him had that been the case. I told him that extortion wasn't my idea of business, and with that he seemed satisfied; he picked up his terrible familiar and stumped away without another word.

'The following week I had to go into Mbabane for stores. I was away a couple of nights and when I got back Rebecca was dead and buried; I heard the story from the house-boys. Umtonga had been to see her on the evening that I left. He'd made his magic again before the stoep, and they'd found her dead and black in the morning. I asked if by any chance he'd left his stick behind him, although I knew the answer before I got it – "Yes, he'd come back for it the following day."

'I started in to clear up Benny's affairs, and board by board to pull the shanty down. Benny didn't believe in banks and I knew there was a hoard hidden somewhere. It took me three weeks, but I found it. With that, and a reasonable realization of what was outstanding, I cleared up a cool ten thousand. I've turned that into a hunded thousand since, and so you see that it was through the Black Art that I came to be sitting here.'

As Carstairs came to the end of the story, something made me turn and look at Jackson; he was glaring at the elder man, and his dark eyes shone with a fierce light in his sallow face.

'Your name's not Carstairs,' he cried suddenly in a harsh voice. 'It's Thompson – and mine is Isaacsohn. *I* am the child that you robbed and abandoned.'

Before I could grasp the full significance of the thing he was on his feet – I saw the knife flash as it went home in Carstair's chest, and the young Jew shrieked, 'You fiend – you paid that devil to kill my mother.'

# THEY BITE

## by Anthony Boucher

There was no path, only the almost vertical ascent. Crumbled rock for a few yards, with the roots of sage finding their scanty life in the dry soil. Then jagged outcroppings of crude crags, sometimes with accidental footholds, sometimes with overhanging and untrustworthy branches of greasewood, sometimes with no aid to climbing but the leverage of your muscles and the ingenuity of your balance.

The sage was as drably green as the rock was drably brown. The only colour was the occasional rosy spikes of a barrel cactus.

Hugh Tallant swung himself up on to the last pinnacle. It had a deliberate, shaped look about it – a petrified fortress of Lilliputians, a Gibraltar of pygmies. Tallant perched on its battlements and unslung his field-glasses.

The desert valley spread below him. The tiny cluster of buildings that was Oasis, the exiguous cluster of palms that gave name to the town and shelter to his own tent and to the shack he was building, the dead-ended highway leading straightforwardly to nothing, the oiled roads diagramming the vacant blocks of an optimistic subdivision.

Tallant saw none of these. His glasses were fixed beyond the oasis and the town of Oasis on the dry lake. The gliders were clear and vivid to him, and the uniformed men busy with them were as sharply and minutely visible as a nest of ants under glass. The training school was more than usually active. One glider in particular, strange to Tallant, seemed the focus of attention. Men would come and examine it and glance back at the older models in comparison.

Only the corner of Tallant's left eye was not preoccupied with the new glider. In that corner something moved, something little and thin and brown as the earth. Too large for a rabbit, much too small for a man. It darted across that corner of vision, and Tallant found gliders oddly hard to concentrate on.

He set down the bifocals and deliberately looked about him. His pinnacle surveyed the narrow, flat area of the crest. Nothing stirred. Nothing stood out against the sage and rock but one barrel of rosy spikes. He took up the glasses again and resumed his observations. When he was done, he methodically entered the results in the little black notebook.

His hand was still white. The desert is cold and often sunless in winter. But it was a firm hand, and as well trained as his eyes, fully capable of recording faithfully the designs and dimensions which they had registered so accurately.

Once his hand slipped, and he had to erase and redraw, leaving a smudge that displeased him. The lean, brown thing had slipped across the edge of his vision again. Going towards the east edge, he would swear, where that set of rocks jutted like the spines on the back of a stegosaur.

Only when his notes were completed did he yield to curiosity, and even then with cynical self-approach. He was physically tired, for him an unusual state, from this daily climbing and from clearing the ground for his shack-to-be. The eye muscles play odd nervous tricks. There could be nothing behind the stegosaur's armour.

There was nothing. Nothing alive and moving. Only the torn and half-plucked carcass of a bird, which looked as though it had been gnawed by some small animal.

It was halfway down the hill – hill in Western terminology, though anywhere east of the Rockies it would have been considered a sizeable mountian – that Tallant again had a glimpse of a moving figure.

But this was no trick of a nervous eye. It was not little

nor thin nor brown. It was tall and broad and wore a loud red-and-black lumberjacket. It bellowed,'Tallant!' in a cheerful and lusty voice.

Tallant drew near the man and said, 'Hello.' He paused and added, 'Your advantage, I think.'

The man grinned broadly. 'Don't know me? Well, I daresay ten years is a long time, and the California desert ain't exactly the Chinese ricefields. How's stuff? Still loaded down with Secrets for Sale?'

Tallant tried desperately not to react to that shot, but he stiffened a little. 'Sorry. The prospector get-up had me fooled. Good to see you again, Morgan.'

The man's eyes had narrowed. 'Just having my little joke,' he smiled. 'Of course you wouldn't have no serious reason for mountain climbing around a glider school, now, would you? And you'd kind of need field-glasses to keep an eye on the pretty birdies.'

'I'm out here for my health.' Tallant's voice sounded unnatural even to himself.

'Sure, sure. You were always in it for your health. And come to think of it, my own health ain't been none too good lately. I've got me a little cabin way to hell-and-gone around here, and I do me a little prospecting now and then. And somehow it just strikes me, Tallant, like maybe I hit a pretty good lode today.'

'Nonsense, old man. You can see –'

'I'd sure hate to tell any of them Army men out at the field some of the stories I know about China and the kind of men I used to know out there. Wouldn't cotton to them stories a bit, the Army wouldn't. But if I was to have a drink too many and get talkative-like –"

'Tell you what,' Tallant suggested brusquely. 'It's getting near sunset now, and my tent's chilly for evening visits. But drop around in the morning and we'll talk over old times. Is rum still your tipple?'

'Sure is. Kind of expensive now, you understand –'

'I'll lay some in. You can find the place easily – over by the oasis. And we ... we might be able to talk about your prospecting, too.'

Tallant's thin lips were set firm as he walked away.

The bartender opened a bottle of beer and plunked it on the damp-circled counter. 'That'll be twenty cents,' he said, then added as an afterthought, 'Want a glass? Sometimes tourists do.'

Tallant looked at the others sitting at the counter – the red-eyed and unshaven old man, the flight sergeant unhappily drinking a Coke – it was after Army hours for beer – the young man with the long, dirty trench-coat and the pipe and the new-looking brown beard – and saw no glasses. 'I guess I won't be a tourist,' he decided.

This was the first time Tallant had had a chance to visit the Desert Sport Spot. It was as well to be seen around in a community. Otherwise people begin to wonder and say. 'Who is that man out by the oasis? Why don't you ever see him any place?'

The Sport Spot was quiet that night. The four of them at the counter, two Army boys shooting pool, and a half-dozen of the local men gathered about a round poker table, soberly and wordlessly cleaning a construction worker whose mind seemed more on his beer than on his cards.

'You just passing through?' the bartender asked sociably.

Tallant shook his head. 'I'm moving in. When the Army turned me down for my lungs, I decided I better do something about it. Heard so much about your climate here I thought I might as well try it.'

'Sure thing,' the bartender nodded. 'You take up until they started this glider school, just about every other guy you meet in the desert is here for his health. Me, I had sinus, and look at me now. It's the air.'

Tallant breathed the atmosphere of smoke and beer suds, but did not smile. 'I'm looking forward to miracles.'

'You'll get 'em. Whereabouts you staying?'

'Over that way a bit. The agent called it "the old Carker place".'

Tallant felt the curious listening silence and frowned.

41

The bartender had started to speak and then thought better of it. The young man with the beard looked at him oddly. The old man fixed him with red and watery eyes that had a faded glint of pity in them. For a moment, Tallant felt a chill that had nothing to do with the night air of the desert.

The old man drank his beer in quick gulps and frowned as though trying to formulate a sentence. At last he wiped beer from his bristly lips and said, 'You wasn't aiming to stay in the adobe, was you?'

'No. It's pretty much gone to pieces. Easier to rig me up a little shack than try to make the adobe liveable. Meanwhile I've got a tent.'

'That's all right, then, mebbe. But mind you don't go poking around that there adobe.'

'I don't think I'm apt to. But why not? Want another beer?'

The old man shook his head reluctantly and slid from his stool to the ground. 'No thanks. I don't rightly know as I –'

'Yes?'

'Nothing. Thanks all the same.' He turned and shuffled to the door.

Tallant smiled. 'But why should I stay clear of the adobe?' he called after him.

The old man mumbled.

'What?'

'They bite,' said the old man, and went out shivering into the night.

The bartender was back at his post. 'I'm glad he didn't take that beer you offered him,' he said. 'Along about this time in the evening I have to stop serving him. For once he had the sense to quit.'

Tallant pushed his own empty bottle forwards. 'I hope I didn't frighten him away.'

'Frighten? Well, mister, I think maybe that's just what you did do. He didn't want beer that sort of came, like you might say, from the old Carker place. Some of the old-timers here, they're funny that way.'

Tallant grinned. 'Is it haunted?'

'Not what you'd call haunted, no. No ghosts there that I ever heard of.' He wiped the counter with a cloth and seemed to wipe the subject away with it.

The flight sergeant pushed his Coke bottle away, hunted in his pocket for nickels, and went over to the pinball machine. The young man with the beard slid onto his vacant stool. 'Hope old Jake didn't worry you,' he said.

Tallant laughed. 'I suppose every town has its deserted homestead with a grisly tradition. But this sounds a little different. No ghosts, and they bite. Do you know anything about it?'

'A little,' the young man said seriously. 'A little. Just enough to –'

Tallant was curious. 'Have one on me and tell me about it.'

The flight sergeant swore bitterly at the machine.

Beer gurgled through the beard. 'You see,' the young man began, 'the desert's so big you can't be alone in it. Ever notice that? It's all empty and there's nothing in sight, but there's always something moving over there where you can't quite see it. It's something very dry and thin and brown, only when you look around it isn't there. Ever see it?'

'Optical fatigue –' Tallant began.

'Sure. I know. Every man to his own legend. There isn't a tribe of Indians hasn't got some way of accounting for it. You've heard of the Watchers? And the twentieth-century white man comes along, and it's optical fatigue. Only in the nineteenth century things weren't quite the same, and there were the Carkers.'

'You've got a special localized legend?'

'Call it that. You glimpse things out of the corner of your mind, same like you glimpse lean, dry things out of the corner of your eye. You encase 'em in solid circumstance and they're not so bad. That is known as the Growth of Legend. The Folk Mind in Action. You take the Carkers and the things you don't quite see, and you put 'em together. And they bite.'

Tallant wondered how long that beard had been absorbing beer. 'And what were the Carkers?' he prompted politely.

'Ever hear of Sawney Bean? Scotland – reign of James First, or maybe the Sixth, though I think Roughead's wrong on that for once. Or let's be more modern – ever hear of the Benders? Kansas in the 1870s? No? Ever hear of Procrastes? Or Polyphemus? Or Fee-fi-fo-fum?

There are ogres, you know. They're no legend. They're fact, they are. The inn where nine guests left for every ten that arrived, the mountain cabin that sheltered travellers from the snow, sheltered them all winter till the melting spring uncovered their bones, the lonely stretches of road that so many passengers travelled halfway – you'll find 'em everywhere. All over Europe and pretty much in this country too before communications became what they are. Profitable business. And it wasn't just the profit. The Benders made money sure; but that wasn't why they killed all their victims as carefully as a kosher butcher. Sawney Bean got so he didn't give a damn about the profit; he just needed to lay in more meat for the winter.

'And think of the chances you'd have at an oasis.'

'So these Carkers of yours were, as you call them, ogres?'

'Carkers, ogres – maybe they were Benders. The Benders were never seen alive, you know, after the townpeople found those curiously butchered bodies. There's a rumour they got this far west. And the time checks pretty well. There wasn't any town here in the eighties. Just a couple of Indian families, last of a dying tribe living on at the oasis. They vanished after the Carkers moved in. That's not so surprising. The white race is a sort of super-ogre, anyway. Nobody worried about them. But they used to worry about why so many travellers never got across this stretch of desert. The travellers used to stop over at the Carkers', you see, and somehow they often never got any farther. Their wagons'd be found maybe fifteen miles beyond in the desert. Sometimes they found the bones, too, parched and white. Gnawed-looking, they said sometimes.'

'And nobody ever did anything about these Carkers?'

'Oh, sure. We didn't have King James Sixth – only I still think it was First – to ride up on a great white horse for a gesture, but twice Army detachments came here and wiped them all out.'

'Twice? One wiping-out would do for most families.' Tallant smiled.

'Uh-uh. That was no slip. They wiped out the Carkers twice because, you see, once didn't do any good. They wiped 'em out and still travellers vanished and still there were gnawed bones. So they wiped 'em out again. After that they gave up, and people detoured the oasis. It made a longer, harder trip, but after all–'

Tallant laughed. 'You mean to say these Carkers were immortal?'

'I don't know about immortal. They somehow just didn't die very easy. Maybe, if they were the Benders – and I sort of like to think they were – they learned a little more about what they were doing out here on the desert. Maybe they put together what the Indians knew and what they knew, and it worked. Maybe whatever they made their sacrifices to understood them better out here than in Kansas.'

'And what's become of them – aside from seeing them out of the corner of the eye?'

'There's forty years between the last of the Carker history and this new settlement at the oasis. And people won't talk much about what they learned here in the first year or so. Only that they stay away from that old Carker adobe. They tell some stories – The priest says he was sitting in the confessional one hot Saturday afternoon and thought he heard a penitent come in. He waited a long time and finally lifted the gauze to see was anybody there. Something was there, and it bit. He's got three fingers on his right hand now, which looks funny as hell when he gives a benediction.'

45

Tallant pushed their two bottles towards the bartender. 'That yarn, my young friend, has earned another beer. How about it, bartender? Is he always as cheerful like this, or is this just something he's improvized for my benefit?'

The bartender set out the fresh bottles with great solemnity. 'Me, I wouldn't've told you all that myself, but then, he's a stranger too and maybe don't feel the same way we do here. For him it's just a story.'

'It's more comfortable that way,' said the young man with the beard, and he took a firm hold on his beer bottle.

'But as long as you've heard that much,' said the bartender, 'you might as well – It was last winter, when we had that cold spell. You heard funny stories that winter. Wolves coming into prospectors' cabins just to warm up. Well, business wasn't so good. We don't have a licence for hard liquor, and the boys don't drink much beer when it's that cold. But they used to come in anyway because we've got that big oil burner.

'So one night there's a bunch of 'em in here – old Jake was here, that you was talking to, and his dog Jigger – and I think I hear somebody else come in. The door creaks a little. But I don't see nobody, and the poker game's going, and we're talking just like we're talking now, and all of a sudden I hear a kind of a noise like *crack*! over there in that corner behind the juke box near the burner.

'I go over to see what goes and it gets away before I can see it very good. But it was little and thin and it didn't have no clothes on. It must've been damned cold that winter.'

'And what was the cracking noise?' Tallant asked dutifully.

'That? That was a bone. It must've strangled Jigger without any noise. He was a little dog. It ate most of the flesh, and if it hadn't cracked the bone for the marrow it could've finished. You can still see the spots over there. The blood never did come out.'

46

There had been silence all through the story. Now suddenly all hell broke loose. The flight sergeant let out a splendid yell and began pointing excitedly at the pinball machine and yelling for his payoff. The construction worker dramatically deserted the poker game, knocking his chair over in the process, and announced lugubriously that these guys here had their own rules, see?

Any atmosphere of Carker-inspired horror was dissipated. Tallant whistled as he walked over to put a nickel in the juke box. He glanced casually at the floor. Yes, there was a stain, for what that was worth.

He smiled cheerfully and felt rather grateful to the Carkers. They were going to solve his blackmail problem very neatly.

Tallant dreamed of power that night. It was a common dream with him. He was a ruler of the new American Corporate State that would follow the war; and he said to this man, 'Come!' and he came, and to that man, 'Go!' and he went, and to his servants, 'Do this!' and they did it.

Then the young man with the beard was standing before him, and the dirty trench-coat was like the robes of an ancient prophet. And the young man said, 'You see yourself riding high, don't you? Riding the crest of the wave – the Wave of the Future, you call it. But there's a deep, dark undertow that you don't see, and that's a part of the Past. And the Present and even your Future. There is evil in mankind that is blacker even than your evil, and infinitely more ancient.'

And there was something in the shadows behind the young man, something little and lean and brown.

Tallant's dream did not disturb him the following morning. Nor did the thought of the approaching interview with Morgan. He fried his bacon and eggs and devoured them cheerfully. The wind had died down for a change, and the sun was warm enough so that he could strip to the waist while he cleared land for his shack. His machete glinted brilliantly as it swung through the air

47

and struck at the roots of the brush.

When Morgan arrived his full face was red and sweating.

'It's cool over there in the shade of the adobe,' Tallant suggested. 'We'll be more comfortable.' And in the comfortable shade of the adobe he swung the machete once and clove Morgan's full, red, sweating face in two.

It was so simple. It took less effort than uprooting a clump of sage. And it was so safe. Morgan lived in a cabin way to hell-and-gone and was often away on prospecting trips. No one would notice his absence for months, if then. No one had any reason to connect him with Tallant. And no one in Oasis would hunt for him in the Carker-haunted adobe.

The body was heavy, and the blood dripped warm on Tallant's bare skin. With relief he dumped what had been Morgan on the floor of the adobe. There were no boards, no flooring. Just the earth. Hard, but not too hard to dig a grave in. And no one was likely to come poking around in this taboo territory to notice the grave. Let a year or so go by, and the grave and the bones it contained would be attributed to the Carkers.

The corner of Tallant's eye bothered him again. Deliberately he looked about the interior of the adobe.

The little furniture was crude and heavy, with no attempt to smooth down the strokes of the ax. It was held together with wooden pegs or half-rotted thongs. There were age-old cinders in the fireplace, and the dusty shards of a cooking jar among them.

And there was a deeply hollowed stone, covered with stains that might have been rust, if stone rusted. Behind it was something like a man and something like a lizard, and something like the things that flit across the corner of the eye.

Curious now, Tallant peered about further. He penetrated to the corner that the one unglassed window lighted but dimly. And there he let out a choking gasp. For a moment he was rigid with horror. Then he smiled and all but laughed aloud.

This explained everything. Some curious individual had seen this, and from his accounts had burgeoned the whole legend. The Carkers had indeed learned something from the Indians, but that secret was the art of embalming.

It was a perfect mummy. Either the Indian art had shrunk bodies, or this was that of a ten-year-old boy. There was no flesh. Only skin and bone and taut, dry stretches of tendon between. The eyelids were closed; the sockets looked hollow under them. The nose was sunken and almost lost. The scant lips were tightly curled back from the long and very white teeth, which stood forth all the more brilliantly against the deep-brown skin.

It was a curious little trove, this mummy. Tallant was already calculating the chances for raising a decent sum of money from an interested anthropologist – murder can produce such delightfully profitable chance by-products – when he noticed the infinitesimal rise and fall of the chest.

The Carker was not dead. It was sleeping.

Tallant did not dare stop to think beyond the instant. This was no time to pause to consider if such things were possible in a well-ordered world. It was no time to reflect on the disposal of the body of Morgan. It was a time to snatch up your machete and get out of here.

But in the doorway he halted. There, coming across the desert, heading for the adobe, clearly seen this time, was another – a female.

He made an involuntary gesture of indecision. The blade of the machete clanged ringingly against the adobe wall. He heard the dry shuffling of a roused sleeper behind him.

He turned fully now, the machete raised. Dispose of this nearer one first, then face the female. There was no room even for terror in his thoughts, only for action.

The lean brown shape darted at him avidly. He moved lightly away and stood poised for its second charge. It shot forward again. He took one step back, machete arm raised, and fell headlong over the corpse of Morgan. Before he could rise, the thin thing was upon him. Its sharp teeth had met through the palm of his left hand.

The machete moved swiftly. The thin dry body fell headless to the floor. There was no blood.

The grip of the teeth did not relax. Pain coursed up Tallant's left arm – a sharper, more bitter pain than you would expect from the bite. Almost as though venom –

He dropped the machete, and his strong white hand plucked and twisted at the dry brown lips. The teeth stayed clenched, unrelaxing. He sat bracing his back against the wall and gripped the head between his knees. He pulled. His flesh ripped, and blood formed dusty clots on the dirt floor. But the bite was firm.

His world had become reduced now to that hand and that head. Nothing outside mattered. He must free himself. He raised his aching arm to his face, and with his own teeth he tore at that unrelenting grip. The dry flesh crumbled away in desert dust, but the teeth were locked fast. He tore his lip against their white keenness, and tasted in his mouth the sweetness of blood and something else.

He staggered to his feet again. He knew what he must do. Later he could use cautery, a tourniquet, see a doctor with a story about a Gila monster – their heads grip too, don't they? – but he knew what he must do now.

He raised the machete and struck again.

His white hand lay on the brown floor, gripped by the white teeth in the brown face. He propped himself against the adobe wall, momentarily unable to move. His open wrist hung over the deeply hollowed stone. His blood and his strength and his life poured out before the little figure of sticks and clay.

The female stood in the doorway now, the sun bright on her thin brownness. She did not move. He knew that she was waiting for the hollow stone to fill.

# THE VIXEN

## by Aleister Crowley

Patricia Fleming threw the reins to a groom, and ran up the steps into the great house, her thin lips white with rage.

Lord Eyre followed her heavily. 'I'll be down in half an hour,' she laughed merrily, 'tell Dawson to bring you a drink!' Then she went straight through the house, her girlish eyes the incarnation of a curse.

For the third time she had failed to bring Geoffrey Eyre to her feet. She looked into her hat; there in the lining was the talisman that she had tested – and it had tricked her.

What do I need? she thought. Must it be blood?

She was a maiden of the pure English strain; brave, gay, honest, shrewd – and there was not one that guessed the inmost fire that burnt her. For she was but a child when the Visitor came.

The first of the Visits was in a dream. She woke choking; the air – clear, sweet, and wholesome as it blew through the open window from the Chilterns – was fouled with a musty stench. And she woke her governess with a tale of a tiger.

The second Visit was again at night. She had been hunting, was alone at the death, had beaten off the hounds. That night she heard a fox bark in her room. She spent a sleepless night of terror; in the morning she found the red hairs of a fox upon her pillow.

The third Visit was nor in sleep nor waking.

But she tightened her lips, and would have veiled the hateful gleam in her eyes.

It was that day, though, that she struck a servant with her riding-whip.

She was so sane that she knew exactly wherein her madness lay; and she set all her strength not to conquer but to conceal it.

Two years later, and Patricia Fleming, the orphan heiress of Carthwell Abbey, was the county toast, Diana of the Chilterns.

Yet Geoffrey Eyre evaded her. His dog's fidelity and honesty kept him true to the little north-country girl that three months earlier had seduced his simplicity. He did not even love her; but she had made him think so for an hour; and his pledged word held him.

Patricia's open favour only made him hate her because of its very seduction. It was really his own weakness that he hated.

Patricia ran, tense and angry, through the house. The servants noticed it. The mistress has been crossed, they thought, she will go to the chapel and get ease. Praising her.

True, to the chapel she went; locked the door, dived behind the altar, struck a secret panel, came suddenly into a priest's hiding-hole, a room large enough to hold a score of men if need be.

At the end of the room was a great scarlet cross, and on it, her face to the wood, her wrists and ankles swollen over the whip lashes that bound her, hung a naked girl, big-boned, voluptuous. Red hair streamed over her back.

'What, Margaret! so blue?' laughed Patricia.

'I am cold,' said the girl upon the cross, in an indifferent voice.

'Nonsense, dear!' answered Patricia, rapidly divesting herself of her riding-habit. 'There is no hint of frost; we had a splendid run, and a grand kill. You shall be warm yet, for all that.'

This time the girl writhed and moaned a little.

Patricia took from an old wardrobe a close-fitting suit of fox fur, and slipped it on her slim white body.

'Did I make you wait, dear?' she said, with a curious leer. 'I am the keener for the sport, be sure!'

She took the faithless talisman from her hat. It was a

little square of vellum, written upon in black. She took a hairpin from her head, pierced the talisman, and drove the pin into the girl's thigh.

'They must have blood,' said she. 'Now see how I will turn the blue to red! Come! don't wince: you haven't had it for a month.'

Then her ivory arm slid like a serpent from the furs, and with the cutting whip she struck young Margaret between the shoulders.

A shriek rang out: its only echo was Patricia's laugh, childlike, icy, devilish.

She struck again and again. Great weals of purple stood on the girl's back; froth tinged with blood came from her mouth, for she had bitten her lips and tongue in agony.

Patricia grew warm and rosy – exquisitely beautiful. Her bare breasts heaved; her lips parted; her whole body and soul seemed lapped in ecstasy.

'I wish you were Geoffrey, girlie!' she panted.

Then the skin burst. Raw flesh oozed blood that dribbled down Margaret's back.

Still the fair maid struck and struck in the silence, until the tiny rivulets met and waxed great and touched the talisman. She threw the bloody whalebone into a corner, and went upon her knees. She kissed her friend; she kissed the talisman; and again kissed the girl, the warm blood staining her pure lips.

She took the talisman, and hid it in her bosom. Last of all she loosened the cords, and Margaret sank in a heap to the floor. Patricia threw furs over her and rolled her up in them; brought wine, and poured it down her throat. She smiled, kindly, like a sister.

'Sleep now awhile, sweetheart!' she whispered, and kissed her forehead.

It was a very demure and self-possessed little maiden that made dinner lively for poor Geoffrey, who was thinking over his mistake.

Patricia's old aunt, who kept house for her, smiled on the flirtation. It was not by accident that she left them alone sitting over the great fire. 'Poor Margaret has her rheumatism again,' she explained innocently; 'I must go and see how she is.' Loyal Margaret!

So it happened that Geoffrey lost his head. 'The ivy is strong enough' (she had whispered, ere their first kiss had hardly died). 'Before the moon is up, be sure!' and glided off just as the aunt returned.

Eyre excused himself; half a mile from the house he left his horse to his man to lead home, and ten minutes later was groping for Patricia in the dark.

White as a lily in body and soul, she took him in her arms.

Awaking as from death, he suddenly cried out, 'Oh God! What is it? Oh my God! my God! Patricia! Your body! Your body!'

'Yours!' she cooed.

'Why, you're all hairy!' he cried. 'And the scent! the scent!'

From without came sharp and resonant the yap of a hound as the moon rose.

Patricia put her hands to her body. He was telling the truth. 'The Visitor!' she screamed once with fright, and was silent. He switched the light on, and she screamed again.

There was a savage lust upon his face.

'This afternoon,' he cried, 'you called me a dog. I looked like a dog and thought like a dog; and, by God! I am a dog. I'll act like a dog then!'

Obedient to some strange instinct, she dived from the bed for the window.

But he was on her; his teeth met in her throat.

In the morning they found the dead bodies of both hound and fox – but how did that explain the wonderful elopement of Lord Eyre and Miss Fleming? For neither of them was ever seen again.

I think Margaret understands; in the convent which she rules today there hangs beside a blood-stained cutting-whip the silver model of a fox, with the inscription:

*'Patricia Margaritæ vulpis vulpem dedit.'*

# 'HE COMETH AND HE PASSETH BY'

## by H. R. Wakefield

Edward Bellamy sat down at his desk, untied the ribbon round a formidable bundle of papers, yawned and looked out of the window. On that glistening evening the prospect from Stone Buildings, Lincoln's Inn, was restful and soothing. Just below the motor mowing-machine placidly 'chug-chugged' as it clipped the finest turf in London. The muted murmurs from Kingsway and Holborn roamed in placidly. One sleepy pigeon was scratching its poll and ruffling its feathers in a tree opposite, two others – one coyly fleeing, the other doggedly in pursuit – strutted the greensward. 'A curious rite of courtship,' thought Bellamy, 'but they seem to enjoy it; more than I enjoy the job of reading this brief!'

Had these infatuated fowls gazed back at Mr Bellamy they would have seen a pair of resolute and trustworthy eyes dominating a resolute, nondescript face, one that gave an indisputable impression of kindliness, candour, and mental alacrity. No woman had etched lines upon it, nor were those deepening furrows ploughed by the higher exercise of the imagination marked thereon.

By his thirty-ninth birthday he had raised himself to the unchallenged position of the most brilliant junior at the Criminal Bar, though that is, perhaps, too flashy an epithet to describe that combination of inflexible integrity, impeccable common sense, perfect health, and tireless industry which was Edward Bellamy. A modest person, he attributed his success entirely to that 'perfect health', a view not lightly to be challenged by those who spend many of their days in those Black Holes of controversy, the Law Courts of London. And he had spent nine out of the last fourteen days therein. But the result had been a signal triumph, for the Court of Criminal Appeal had taken *his* view of Mr James Stock's motives, and had substituted ten years' penal servitude for a six-foot drop. And he was very weary – and yet here was this monstrous bundle of papers! He had just succeeded in screwing his determination to the sticking point when his telephone bell rang.

He picked up the receiver languidly, and then his face lightened.

'I know that voice. How are you, my dear Philip? Why, what's the matter? Yes, I'm doing nothing. Delighted! Brooks's at eight o'clock. Right you are!'

So Philip had not forgotten his existence. He had begun to wonder. His mind wandered back over his curious friendship with Franton. It had begun on the first morning of their first term at Univ., when they had both been strolling nervously about the quad. That it ever had begun was the most surprising thing about it, for superficially they had nothing in common. Philip, the best bat at Eton, almost too decorative, with a personal charm most people found irresistible, the heir to great possessions. He, the crude product of an obscure grammar school, destined to live precariously on his scholarships, gauche, shy, taciturn. In the ordinary way they would have graduated to different worlds, for the economic factor alone would have kept their paths all through their lives at Oxford inexorably apart. They would have had little more in common with each other than they had with their scouts. And yet they had spent a good part of almost every day together during term-time, and during every vacation he had spent some time at Franton Hall, where he had had first revealed to him those many and delicate refinements of life which only great wealth, allied with traditional taste, can secure. Why had it been so? He had eventually asked Philip.

'Because,' he replied, 'you have a first-class brain, I have a second or third. I have always had things made too easy for me. You have had most things made too hard. *Ergo,* you have a first-class character. I haven't. I feel a sense of respectful shame towards you, my dear Teddie, which alone would keep me trotting at your heels. I feel I can rely on you as on no one else. You are at once my superior and my complement. Anyway, it has happened, why worry? Analysing such things often spoils them, it's like over-rehearsing.'

And then the War – and even the Defence of Civilization entailed subtle social distinctions.

Philip was given a commission in a regiment of cavalry (with the best will in the world Bellamy never quite understood the privileged role of the horse in the higher ranks of English society); he himself enlisted in a line regiment, and rose through his innate common sense and his unflagging capacity for finishing a job to the rank of Major, D.S.O. and bar, and a brace of wound-stripes. Philip went to Mesopotamia and was eventually invalided out through the medium of a gas-shell. His right lung seriously affected, he spent from 1917 to 1924 on a farm in Arizona.

They had written to each other occasionally – the hurried flippant, shadow-of-death letters of the time, but somehow their friendship had dimmed and faded and become more than a little pre-War by the end of it, so that Bellamy was not more than mildly disappointed when he heard casually that Philip was back in England, yet had had but the most casual, damp letter from him.

But there had been all the old cordiality and affection in his voice over the telephone – and something more – not so pleasant to hear.

At the appointed hour he arrived in St James's Street, and a moment later Philip came up to him.

'Now, Teddie,' he said, 'I know what you're thinking, I know I've been a fool and the rottenest sort of type to have acted as I have, but there is a kind of explanation.'

Bellamy surrendered at once to that absurd sense of delight at being in Philip's company, and his small resentment was rent and scattered. None the less he regarded him with a veiled intentness. He was looking tired and old -- forcing himself – there was something seriously the matter.

'My very dear Philip,' he said, 'you don't need to explain things to me. To think it is eight years since we met!'

'First of all let's order something,' said Philip. 'You have what you like, I don't want much, except a drink.' Whereupon he selected a reasonable collation for Bellamy and a dressed crab and asparagus for himself. But he drank two Martinis in ten seconds, and these were not the first – Bellamy knew – that he had ordered since five-thirty (there *was* something wrong).

For a little while the conversation was uneasily, stalely reminiscent. Suddenly Philip blurted out, 'I can't keep it any longer. You're the only really reliable, unswerving friend I've ever had. You will help me, won't you?'

'My dear Philip,' said Bellamy, touched. 'I always have and always will be ready to do anything you want me to do and at any time – you know that.'

'Well, then, I'll tell you my story. First of all, have you ever heard of a man called Oscar Clinton?'

'I seem to remember the name. It is somehow connected in my mind with the nineties, raptures and roses, absinthe and poses; and the *other* Oscar. I believe his name cropped up in a case I was in. I have an impression he's a wrong 'un.'

'That's the man,' said Philip. 'He stayed with me for three months at Franton.'

'Oh,' said Bellamy sharply, 'how was that?'

'Well, Teddie, anything the matter with one's lungs affects one's mind – not always for the worse, however. I know that's true, and it affected mine. Arizona is a moon-dim region, very lovely in its way and stark and old, but I had to leave it. You know I was always a sceptic, rather a wooden one, as I remember; well, that ancient, lonely land set my lung-polluted mind working. I used to stare and stare into the sky. One is brought right up against the vast enigmas of time and space and eternity when one lung is doing the work of two, and none too well at that.'

Edward realized under what extreme tension Philip

had been living, but felt that he could establish a certain control over him. He felt more in command of the situation and resolved to keep that command.

'Well,' continued Philip, filling up his glass, 'when I got back to England I was so frantically nervous that I could hardly speak or think. I felt insane, unclean – mentally. I felt I was going mad and could not bear to be seen by anyone who had known me – that is why I was such a fool as not to come to you. You have your revenge! I can't tell you, Teddie, how depression roared through me! I made up my mind to die, but I had a wild desire to know to what sort of place I should go. And then I met Clinton. I had rushed up to London one day just to get the inane anodyne of noise and people, and I suppose I was more or less tight, for I walked into a club of sorts called the "Chorazin" in Soho. The door-keeper tried to turn me out, but I pushed him aside, and then someone came up and led me to a table. It was Clinton.

'Now there is no doubt he had great hypnotic power. He began to talk, and I at once felt calmer and started to tell him all about myself. I talked wildly for an hour, and he was so deft and delicate in his handling of me that I felt I could not leave him. He has a marvellous insight into abnormal mental – psychic – whatever you like to call them – states. Some time I'll describe what he looks like – he's certainly like no one else in the world.

'Well, the upshot was that he came down to Franton next day and stayed on. Now, I know that his motives were entirely mercenary, but none the less he saved me from suicide, and to a great extent gave back peace to my mind.

'Never could I have imagined such an irresistible and brilliant talker. Whatever he may be, he's also a poet, a profound philosopher, and amazingly versatile and erudite. Also, when he likes, his charm of manner carries one away. At least, in my case it did – for a time – though he borrowed £20 or more a week from me.

'And then one day my butler came to me, and with the hushed gusto appropriate to such revelations murmured that two of the maids were in the family way and that another had told him an hysterical little tale – floating in floods of tears – about how Clinton had made several attemps to force his way into her bedroom.

'Well, Teddie, that sort of thing is that sort of thing, but I felt such a performance couldn't possibly be justified, that taking advantage of a trio of rustics in his host's house was a dastardly and unforgivable outrage.

'Other people's morals are chiefly their own affair, but I had a personal responsibility towards these buxom victims – well, you can realize just how I felt.

'I had to speak about it to Clinton, and did so that night. No one ever saw him abashed. He smiled at me in a superior and patronizing way, and said he quite understood that I was almost bound to hold such feudal and socially primitive views, suggesting, of course, that my chief concern in the matter was that he had infringed my *droit de seigneur* in these cases. As for him, he considered it was his duty to disseminate his unique genius as widely as possible, and that it should be considered the highest privilege for anyone to bear his child. He had to his knowledge seventy-four offspring alive, and probably many more – the more the better for the future of humanity. But, of course, he understood and promised for the future – bowing to my rights and my prejudices – to allow me to plough my own pink and white pastures – and much more to the same effect.

'Though still under his domination, I felt there was more lust than logic in these specious professions, so I made an excuse and went up to London the next day. As I left the house I picked up my letters, which I read in the car on the way up. One was a three-page catalogue *raisonné* from my tailor. Not being as dressy as all that, it seemed unexpectedly grandiose, so I paid him a visit. Well, Clinton had forged a letter from me authorizing him to order clothes at my expense, and a lavish outfit had been provided.

'It then occurred to me to go to my bank to discover precisely how much I had lent Clinton during the last three months. It was £420. All these discoveries – telescoping – caused me to review my relationship with Clinton. Suddenly I felt it had better end. I might be medieval, intellectually costive, and the possessor of much scandalously unearned increment, but I could not believe that the pursuit and contemplation of esoteric mysteries necessarily implied the lowest possible standards of private decency. In other words, I was recovering.

'I still felt that Clinton was the most remarkable person I had ever met. I do to this day – but I felt I was unequal to squaring such magic circles.

'I told him so when I got back. He was quite charming, gentle, understanding, commiserating, and he left the next morning, after pronouncing some incantation whilst touching my forehead. I missed him very much. I believe he's the devil, but he's that sort of person.

'Once I had assured the prospective mothers of his children that they would not be sacked and that their destined contributions to the population would be a charge upon me – there is a codicil to my will to this effect – they brightened up considerably, and rather too frequently snatches of the Froth-Blowers' Anthem cruised down to me as they went about their duties. In fact, I had a discreditable impression that the Immaculate Third would have shown less lachrymose integrity had the consequence of surrender been revealed *ante factum*. Eventually a brace of male infants came to contribute their falsettos to the dirge – for whose appearance the locals have respectfully given me the credit. These brats have searching, calign eyes, and when they reach the age of puberty I should not be surprised if the birth statistics for East Surrey began to show remarkable – even a magical – rise.

'Oh, how good it is to talk to you, Teddie, and get it all off my chest! I feel almost light-hearted, as though my poor old brain had been curetted. I feel I can face and fight it now.

'Well, for the next month I drowsed and read and drowsed and read until I felt two-lunged again. And several times I almost wrote to you, but I felt such lethargy and yet such a certainty of getting quite well again that I put everything off. I was content to lie back and let that blessed healing process work its quiet kindly way with me.

'And then one day I got a letter from a friend of mine, Melrose, who was at the House when we were up. He is the Secretary of "Ye Ancient Mysteries', a dining club I joined before the War. It meets once a month and discusses famous mysteries of the past – the *Mary Celeste*, the 'McLachlan Case', and so on – with a flippant yet scholarly zeal; but that doesn't matter. Well, Melrose said that Clinton wanted to become a member, and had stressed the fact that he was a friend of mine. Melrose was a little upset, as he had heard vague rumours about Clinton. Did I think he was likely to be an acceptable member of the club?

'Well, what was I to say? On the one side of the medal were the facts that he had used my house as his stud-farm, that he had forged my name and sponged on me shamelessly. On the reverse was the fact that he was a genius and knew more about Ancient Mysteries than the rest of the world put together. But my mind was soon made up; I could not recommend him. A week later I got a letter – a charming letter, a most understanding letter, from Clinton. He realized, so he said, that I had been bound to give the secretary of the Ancient Mysteries the advice I had – no doubt I considered he was not a decent person to meet my friends. He was naturally disappointed, and so on.

'How the devil, I wondered, did he know – not only that I had put my thumbs down against him, but also the very reason for which I had put them down!

'So I asked Melrose, who told me he hadn't mentioned the matter to a soul, but had discreetly removed Clinton's name from the list of candidates for election. And no one should have been any the wiser; but how much wiser Clinton was!

'A week later I got another letter from him, saying that he was leaving England for a month. He enclosed a funny little paper pattern thing, an outline cut out with scissors with a figure painted on it, a beastly-looking thing. Like this!'

And he drew a quick sketch on the table-cloth.

Certainly it was unpleasant, thought Bellamy. It appeared to be a crouching figure in the posture of pursuit. The robes it wore seemed to rise and billow above its head. Its arms were long – too long – scraping the ground with curved and spiked nails. Its head was not quite human, its expression devilish and venomous. A horrid, hunting thing, its eyes encarnadined and infinitely evil, glowing animal eyes in the foul dark face. And those long vile arms – not pleasant to be in their grip. He hadn't realized Philip could draw as well as that. He straightened himself, lit a cigarette, and rallied his fighting powers. For the first time he realized, why, that Philip was in serious trouble! Just a rather beastly little sketch on a table-cloth. And now it was up to him!

'Clinton told me,' continued Philip, 'that this was a most powerful symbol which I should find of the greatest help in my mystical studies. I must place it against my forehead, and pronounce at the same time a certain sentence. And, Teddie, suddenly, I found myself doing so. I remember I had a sharp feeling of surprise and irritation when I found I had placarded this thing on my head and repeated this sentence.'

'What was the sentence?' asked Bellamy.

'Well, that's a funny thing,' said Philip. 'I can't remember it, and both the slip of paper on which it was written and the paper pattern had disappeared the next morning. I remember putting them in my pocket-book, but they completely vanished. And, Teddie, things haven't been the same since.' He filled his glass and emptied it, lit a cigarette, and at once pressed the life from it in an ash-tray and then lit another.

'Bluntly, I've been bothered, haunted perhaps is too strong a word – too pompous. It's like this. That same night I had read myself tired in the study, and about twelve o'clock I was glancing sleepily around the room when I noticed that one of the bookcases was throwing out a curious and unaccountable shadow. It seemed as if something was hiding behind the bookcase, and that this was that something's shadow. I got up and walked over to it, and it became just a bookcase shadow, rectangular and reassuring. I went to bed.

'As I turned on the light on the landing I noticed the same sort of shadow coming from the grandfather clock. I went to sleep all right, but suddenly found myself peering out of the window, and there was that shadow stretching out from the trees and in the drive. At first there was about that much of it showing,' and he drew a line down the sketch on the table-cloth, 'about a sixth. Well, it's been a simple story since then. Every night that shadow had grown a little. It is now almost all visible. And it comes out suddenly from different places. Last night it was on the wall beside the door into the Dutch garden. I never know where I'm going to see it next.'

'And how long has this been going on?' asked Bellamy.

'A month tomorrow. You sound as if you thought I was mad. I probably am.'

'No, you're as sane as I am. But why don't you leave Franton and come to London?'

'And see it on the wall of the club bedroom! I've tried that, Teddie, but one's as bad as the other. Doesn't it sound ludicrous? But it isn't to me.'

'Do you usually eat as little as this?' asked Bellamy.

' "And drink as much?" you were too polite to add. Well, there's more to it than indigestion, and it isn't incipient D.T. It's just I don't feel very hungry nowadays.'

Bellamy got that rush of tiptoe pugnacity which had won him so many desperate cases. He had had a Highland grandmother from whom he had inherited a powerful visualizing imagination, by which he got a fleeting yet authentic insight into the workings of men's minds. So now he knew in a flash how he would feel if Philip's ordeal had been his.

'Whatever it is, Philip,' he said, 'there are two of us now.'

64

'Then you do believe in it,' said Philip. 'Sometimes I can't. On a sunny morning with starlings chattering and buses swinging up Waterloo Place – then how can such things be? But at night I know they are.'

'Well,' said Bellamy after a pause, 'let us look at it coldly and precisely. Ever since Clinton sent you a certain painted paper pattern you've seen a shadowed reproduction of it. Now I take it he has – as you suggested – unusual hypnotic powers. He has studied mesmerism?'

'I think he's studied every bloody thing,' said Philip.

'Then that's a possibility.'

'Yes,' agreed Philip, 'it's a possibility. And I'll fight it, Teddie, now that I have you, but can you minister to a mind diseased?'

'Throw quotation to the dogs,' replied Bellamy. 'What one man has done another can undo – there's one for you.'

'Teddie,' said Philip, 'will you come down to Franton tonight?'

'Yes,' said Bellamy. 'But why?'

'Because I want you to be with me at twelve o'clock tonight when I look out from the study window and think I see a shadow flung on the flagstones outside the drawing-room window.'

'Why not stay up here for tonight?'

'Because I want to get it settled. Either I'm mad or – Will you come?'

'If you really mean to go down tonight I'll come with you.'

'Well, I've ordered the car to be here by nine-fifteen,' said Philip. 'We'll go to your rooms, and you can pack a suitcase and we'll be there by half past ten.' Suddenly he looked up sharply, his shoulders drew together and his eyes narrowed and became intent. It happened that at that moment no voice was busy in the dining-room of the Brooks's Club. No doubt they were changing over at the Power Station, for the lights dimmed for a moment. It seemed to Bellamy that someone was developing wavy, wicked little films far back in his brain, and a voice suddenly whispered in his ear with a vile sort of shyness: 'He cometh and he passeth by!'

As they drove down through the night they talked little. Philip drowsed and Bellamy's mind was busy. His preliminary conclusion was that Philip was neither mad not going mad, but that he was not normal. He had always been very sensitive and highly strung, reacting too quickly and deeply to emotional stresses – and this living alone and eating nothing – the worst thing for him.

And this Clinton. He had the reputation of being an evil man of power, and such persons' hypnotic influence was absurdly underrated. He'd get on his track.

'When does Clinton get back to England?' he asked.

'If he kept to his plans he'll be back about now,' said Philip sleepily.

'What are his haunts?'

'He lives near the British Museum in rooms, but he's usually to be found at the Chorazin Club after six o'clock. It's in Larn Street, just off Shaftesbury Avenue. A funny place with some funny members.'

Bellamy made a note of this.

'Does he know you know me?'

'No, I think not, there's no reason why he should.'

'So much the better,' said Bellamy.

'Why?' asked Philip.

'Because I'm going to cultivate his acquaintance.'

'Well, do look out, Teddie; he has a marvellous power of hiding the fact, but he's dangerous, and I don't want you to get into any trouble like mine.'

'I'll be careful,' said Bellamy.

Ten minutes later they passed the gates of the drive of Franton Manor, and Philip began glancing uneasily about him and peering sharply where the elms flung shadows. It was a perfectly still and cloudless night, with a quarter moon. It was just a quarter to eleven as they entered the house. They went up to the library on the first floor which looked out over the Dutch garden to the Park. Franton is a typical Georgian house with charming gardens and Park, but too big and lonely for one nervous

66

person to inhabit, thought Bellamy.

The butler brought up sandwiches and drinks, and Bellamy thought he seemed relieved at their arrival. Philip began to eat ravenously, and gulped down two stiff whiskies. He kept looking at his watch, and his eyes were always searching the walls.

'It comes, Teddie, even when it ought to be too light for shadows.'

'Now then,' replied the latter, 'I'm with you, and we're going to keep quite steady. It may come, but I shall not leave you until it goes and for ever.' And he managed to lure Philip on to another subject, and for a time he seemed quieter, but suddenly he stiffened, and his eyes became rigid and staring. 'It's there,' he cried, 'I know it!'

'Steady, Philip!' said Bellamy sharply. 'Where?'

'Down below,' he whispered, and began creeping towards the window.

Bellamy reached it first and looked down. He saw it at once, knew what it was, and set his teeth.

He heard Philip shaking and breathing heavily at his side.

'It's there,' he said, 'and it's complete at last!'

'Now, Philip,' said Bellamy, 'we're going down, and I'm going out first, and we'll settle the thing once and for all.'

They went down the stairs and into the drawing-room. Bellamy turned the light on and walked quickly to the French window and began to try to open the catch. He fumbled with it for a moment.

'Let me do it,' said Philip, and put his hand to the catch, and then the window opened and he stepped out.

'Come back, Philip!' cried Bellamy. As he said it the lights went dim, a fierce blast of burning air filled the room, the window came crashing back. Then through the glass Bellamy saw Philip suddenly throw up his hands and something huge and dark lean from the wall and envelop him. He seemed to writhe for a moment in its folds. Bellamy strove madly to thrust the window open, while his soul strive to withstand the mighty and evil power he felt was crushing him, and then he saw Philip flung down with awful force, and he could hear the foul, crushing thud as his head struck the stone.

And then the window opened and Bellamy dashed out into a quiet and scented night.

At the inquest the doctor stated he was satisfied that Mr Franton's death was due to a severe heart attack – he had never recovered from the gas, he said, and such a seizure was always possible.

'Then there are no particular circumstances about the case?' asked the Coroner.

The doctor hesitated. 'Well, there is one thing,' he said slowly. 'The pupils of Mr Franton's eyes were – well, to put it simply to the jury – instead of being round, they were drawn up so that they resembled half-moons – in a sense they were like the pupils in the eyes of a cat.'

'Can you explain that?' asked the Coroner.

'No, I have never seen a similar case,' replied the doctor. 'But I am satisfied the cause of death was as I have stated.'

Bellamy was, of course, called as a witness, but he had little to say.

*

About eleven o'clock on the morning after these events Bellamy rang up the Chorazin Club from his chambers and learned from the manager that Mr Clinton had returned from abroad. A little later he got a Sloane number and arranged to lunch with Mr Solan at the United Universities Club. And then he made a conscientious effort to estimate the chances in Rex v. Tipwinkle.

But soon he was restless and pacing the room. He could not exorcize the jeering demon which told him sniggeringly that he had failed Philip. It wasn't true, but it pricked and penetrated. But the game was not yet played out. If he had failed to save he might still avenge. He would see what Mr Solan had to say.

That personage was awaiting him in the smoking

room. Mr Solan was an original and looked it. Just five feet and two inches – a tiny body, a mighty head with a dominating forehead studded with a pair of thrusting frontal lobes. All this covered with a thick, greying thatch. Veiled, restless little eyes, a perky, tilted, little nose, and a very thin-lipped, fighting mouth from which issued the most curious, resonant, high, and piercing voice. This is a rough and ready sketch of one who is universally accepted to be the greatest living Oriental scholar – a mystic – once upon a time a Senior Wrangler, a philosopher of European repute, a great and fascinating personality, who lived alone, save for a brace of tortoiseshell cats and a housekeeper, in Chester Terrace, Sloane Square. About every six years he published a masterly treatise on one of his special subjects; otherwise he kept himself to himself with the remorseless determination he brought to bear upon any subject which he considered worth serious consideration, such as the Chess Game, the works of Bach, the paintings of Van Gogh, the poems of Housman, and the short stories of P. G. Wodehouse and Austin Freeman.

He entirely approved of Bellamy, who had once secured him substantial damages in a copyright case. The damages had gone to the Society for the Prevention of Cruelty to Animals.

'And what can I do for you, my dear Bellamy?' he piped, when they were seated.

'First of all, have you ever heard of a person called Oscar Clinton? Secondly, do you know anything of the practice of sending an enemy a painted paper pattern?'

Mr Solan smiled slightly at the first question, and ceased to smile when he heard the second.

'Yes,' he said, 'I have heard of both, and I advise you to have nothing whatsoever to do with either.'

'Unfortunately,' replied Bellamy, 'I have already had to do with both. Two night ago my best friend died – rather suddenly. Presently I will tell you how he died. But first of all, tell me something about Clinton.'

'It is characteristic of him that you know so little about

him,' replied Solan, 'for although he is one of the most dangerous and intellectually powerful men in the world he gets very little publicity nowadays. Most of the much-advertized Naughty Boys of the Nineties harmed no one but themselves – they merely canonized their own and each other's dirty linen, but Clinton was in a class by himself. He was – and no doubt still is – an accomplished corrupter, and he took, and no doubt still takes, a jocund delight in his hobby. Eventually he left England – by request – and went out East. He spent some years in a Tibetan monastery, and then some other years in less reputable places – his career is detailed very fully in a file in my study – and then he applied his truly mighty mind to what I may loosely call magic; for what I loosely call magic, my dear Bellamy, most certainly exists. Clinton is highly psychic, with great natural hypnotic power. He then joined an estoteric and little-known sect – Satanists – of which he eventually became High Priest. And then he returned to what we call civilization, and has since been "moved on" by the Civil Powers of many countries, for his forte is the extraction of money from credulous and timid individuals – usually female – by methods highly ingenious and peculiarly his own. It is a boast of his that he has never yet missed his revenge. He ought to be stamped out with the brusque ruthlessness meted out to a spreading fire in a Californian forest.

'Well, there is a short inadequate sketch of Oscar Clinton, and now about these paper patterns.'

*

Two hours later Bellamy got up to leave. 'I can lend you a good many of his books,' said Mr Solan, 'and you can get the rest at Lilley's. Come to me from four till six on Wednesdays and Fridays, and I'll teach you all I think essential. Meanwhile, I will have a watch kept upon him; but I want you, my dear Bellamy, to do nothing decisive till you are qualified. It would be a pity if the Bar were to be deprived of your great gifts prematurely.'

'Many thanks,' said Bellamy. 'I have now placed myself

in your hands, and I'm in this thing till the end – some end or other.'

Mr Plank, Bellamy's clerk, had no superior in his profession, one which is the most searching test of character and adaptability. Not one of the devious and manifold tricks of his trade was unpractised by him, and his income was £1,250 per annum, a fact which the Inland Revenue Authorities strongly suspected, but were quite unable to establish. He liked Mr Bellamy, personally well enough, financially very much indeed. It was not surprising, therefore, that many seismic recording instruments registered sharp shocks at four p.m. on 12 June 193—, a disturbance caused by the precipitous descent of Mr Plank's jaw when Mr Bellamy instructed him to accept no more briefs for him for the next three months. 'But,' continued that gentleman, 'here is a cheque which will, I trust, reconcile you to the fact.'

Mr Plank scrutinized the numerals and was reconciled.

'Taking a holiday, sir?' he asked.

'I rather doubt it,' replied Bellamy. 'But you might suggest to any inquisitive inquirers that that is the explanation.'

'I understand, sir.'

From then till midnight, with one short pause, Bellamy was occupied with a pile of exotically bound volumes. Occasionally he made a note on his writing-pad. When his clock struck twelve he went to bed and read *The Wallet of Kai-Lung* till he felt sleepy enough to turn out the light.

At eight o'clock the next morning he was busy once more with an exotically bound book, and making an occasional note on his writing-pad.

Three weeks later he was bidding a temporary farewell to Mr Solan, who remarked: 'I think you'll do now. You are an apt pupil; pleading has given you a command of convincing bluff, and you have sufficient psychic insight to make it possible for you to succeed. Go forth and prosper. At all times I shall be fighting for you. He will be there at nine tonight.'

At a quarter past that hour Bellamy was asking the door-keeper of the Chorazin Club to tell Mr Clinton that a Mr Bellamy wished to see him.

Two minutes later the official reappeared and led him downstairs into an ornate and gaudy cellar decorated with violence and indiscretion – the work, he discovered later, of a neglected genius who had died of neglected cirrhosis of the liver. He was led up to a table in the corner, where someone was sitting alone.

Bellamy's first impression of Oscar Clinton remained vividly with him till his death. As he got up to greet him he could see that he was physically gigantic – six foot five at least, with a massive torso – the build of a champion wrestler. Topping it was a huge, square, domed head. He had a white yet mottled face, thick, tense lips, the lower one protruding fantastically. His hair was clipped close, save for one twisted and oiled lock which curved down to meet his eyebrows. But what impressed Bellamy most was a pair of the hardest, most penetrating and merciless eyes – one of which seemed soaking wet and dripping slowly.

Bellamy 'braced his belt about him' – he was in the presence of a power.

'Well, sir,' said Clinton in a beautifully musical voice with a slight drawl, 'I presume you are connected with Scotland Yard. What can I do for you?'

'No,' replied Bellamy, forcing a smile, 'I'm in no way connected with that valuable institution.'

'Forgive the suggestion,' said Clinton, 'but during a somewhat adventurous career I have received so many unheralded visits from more or less polite police officials. What, then, is your business?'

'I haven't any, really,' said Bellamy. 'It's simply that I have long been a devoted admirer of your work, the greatest imaginative work of our time, in my opinion. A friend of mine mentioned casually that he had seen you going into this Club, and I could not resist taking the liberty of forcing, just for a moment, my company upon you.'

Clinton stared at him, and seemed not quite at his ease.

'You interest me,' he said at length. 'I'll tell you why. Usually I know decisively by certain methods of my own whether a person I meet comes as an enemy or a friend. These tests have failed in your case, and this, as I say, interests me. It suggests things to me. Have you been in the East?'

'No,' said Bellamy.

'And made no study of its mysteries?'

'None whatever, but I can assure you I come merely as a most humble admirer. Of course, I realize you have enemies – all great men have; it is the privilege and penalty of their pre-eminence, and I know you to be a great man.'

'I fancy,' said Clinton, 'that you are perplexed by the obstinate humidity of my left eye. It is caused by the rather heavy injection of heroin I took this afternoon. I may as well tell you I use all drugs, but am the slave of none. I take heroin when I desire to contemplate. But tell me – since you profess such an admiration for my books – which of them most meets with your approval?'

'That's a hard question,' replied Bellamy, 'but *A Damsel with a Dulcimer* seems to me exquisite.'

Clinton smiled patronizingly.

'It has merits,' he said, 'but is immature. I wrote it when I was living with a Bedouin woman aged fourteen in Tunis. Bedouin women have certain natural gifts' – and here he became remarkably obscene, before returning to the subject of his works; 'my own opinion is that I reached my zenith in *The Songs of Hamdonna*. Hamdonna was a delightful companion, the fruit of the raptures of an Italian gentleman and a Persian lady. She had the most naturally – the most brilliantly vicious mind of any woman I ever met. She required hardly any training. But she was unfaithful to me, and died soon after.'

'The *Songs* are marvellous,' said Bellamy, and he began quoting from them fluently.

Clinton listened intently. 'You have a considerable gift

73

for reciting poetry,' he said. 'May I offer you a drink? I was about to order one for myself.'

'I'll join you on one condition – that I may be allowed to pay for both of them – to celebrate the occasion.'

'Just as you like,' said Clinton, tapping the table with his thumb, which was adorned with a massive jade ring curiously carved. 'I always drink brandy after heroin, but you order what you please.'

It may have been the whisky, it may have been the pressing nervous strain or a combination of both, which caused Bellamy now to regard the mural decorations with a much modified sangfroid. Those distorted and tortured patches of flat colour, how subtly suggestive they were of something sniggeringly evil!

'I gave Valin the subject for those panels,' said Clinton. 'They are meant to represent an impression of the stages in the Black Mass, but he drank away his original inspiration, and they fail to do that majestic ceremony justice.'

Bellamy flinched at having his thoughts so easily read.

'I was thinking the same thing,' he replied; 'that unfortunate cat they're slaughtering deserved a less ludicrous memorial to its fate.'

Clinton looked at him sharply and sponged his oozing eye.

'I have made these rather flamboyant references to my habits purposely. Not to impress you, but to see *how* they impressed you. Had you appeared disgusted, I should have known it was useless to pursue our acquaintanceship. All my life I have been a law unto myself, and that is probably why the Law has always shown so much interest in me. I know myself to be a being apart, one to whom the codes and conventions of the herd can never be applied. I have sampled every so-called "vice", including every known drug. Always, however, with an object in view. Mere purposeless debauchery is not in my character. My Art, to which you have so kindly referred, must always come first. Sometimes it demands that I sleep with a negress, that I take opium or hashish; sometimes it dictates rigid asceticism, and I tell you, my friend, that if such an instruction came again tomorrow, as it has often come in the past, I could, without the slightest effort, lead a life of complete abstinence from drink, drugs, and women for an indefinite period. In other words, I have gained absolute control over my senses after the most exhaustive experiments with them. How many can say the same? Yet one does not know what life can teach till that control is established. The man of superior power – there are no such women – should not flinch from such experiments; he should seek to learn every lesson evil as well as good has to teach. So will he be able to extend and multiply his personality, but always he must remain absolute master of himself. And then he will have many strange rewards, and many secrets will be revealed to him. Some day, perhaps, I will show you some which have been revealed to me.'

'Have you absolutely no regard for what is called "morality"?' asked Bellamy.

'None whatever. If I wanted money I should pick your pocket. If I desired your wife – if you have one – I should seduce her. If someone obstructs me – something happens to him. You must understand this clearly – for I am not bragging – I do nothing purposelessly nor from what I consider a bad motive. To me "bad" is synonymous with "unnecessary". I do nothing unnecessary.'

'Why is revenge necessary?' asked Bellamy.

'A plausible question. Well, for one thing I like cruelty – one of my unpublished works is a defence of Super-Sadism. Then it is a warning to others, and lastly it is a vindication of my personality. All excellent reasons. Do you like my *Thus spake Eblas*?'

'Masterly,' replied Bellamy. 'The perfection of prose; but, of course, its magical significance is far beyond my meagre understanding.'

'My dear friend, there is only one man in Europe about whom that would not be equally true.'

'Who is that?' asked Bellamy.

Clinton's eyes narrowed venomously.

'His name is Solan,' he said. 'One of these days, per-haps –' and he paused. 'Well, now, if you like I will tell you some of my experiences.'

*

An hour later a monologue drew to its close. 'And now, Mr Bellamy, what is your role in life?'

'I'm a barrister.'

'Oh, so you *are* connected with the Law?'

'I hope,' said Bellamy, smiling, 'you'll find it possible to forget it.'

'It would help me to do so,' replied Clinton, 'if you would lend me ten pounds. I have forgotten my note-case – a frequent piece of negligence on my part – and a lady awaits me. Thanks very much. We shall meet again, I trust.'

'I was just about to suggest that you dined with me one day this week?'

'This is Tuesday,' said Clinton. 'What about Thursday?'

'Excellent. Will you meet me at the Gridiron about eight?'

'I will be there,' said Clinton, mopping his eye. 'Good-night.'

*

'I can understand now what happened to Franton,' said Bellamy to Mr Solan the next evening. 'He is the most fascinating and catholic talker I have met. He has a wicked charm. If half to which he lays claim is true he has packed ten lives into sixty years.'

'In a sense,' said Mr Solan, 'he has the best brain of any living man. He also has a marvellous histrionic sense and he is *deadly*. But he is vulnerable. On Thursday en-courage him to talk of other things. He will consider you an easy victim. You must make the most of the evening – it may rather revolt you – he is sure to be suspicious at first.'

*

'It amuses and reassures me,' said Clinton at 10. 15 on Thursday evening in Bellamy's room. 'to find you have a lively appreciation of obscenity.'

He brought out a snuff-box, an exquisite little masterpiece with an inexpressibly vile design enamelled on the lid, from which he took a pinch of white powder which he sniffed up from the palm of his hand.

'I suppose,' said Bellamy, 'that all your magical lore would be quite beyond me.'

'Oh yes, quite,' replied Clinton, 'But I can show you what sort of power a study of that lore has given me, by a little experiment. Turn round, look out of the window, and keep quite quiet till I speak to you.'

It was a brooding night. In the south-west the clouds made restless, quickly shifting patterns – the heralds of coming storm. The scattered sound of the traffic in Kingsway rose and fell with the gusts of the rising wind. Bellamy found a curious picture forming in his brain. A wide lonely waste of snow and a hill with a copse of fir-trees, out from which someone came running. Presently this person halted and looked back, and then out from the wood appeared another figure (of a shape he had seen before). And then the one it seemed to be pursuing began to run on, staggering through the snow, over which the Shape seemed to skim lightly and rapidly, and to gain on its quarry. Then it appeared as if the one in front could go no farther. He fell and rose again, and faced his pursuer. The Shape came swiftly on, and flung itself hideously on the one in front, who fell to his knees. The two seemed intermingled for a moment ...

'Well, said Clinton, 'and what did you think of that?'

Bellamy poured out a whisky and soda and drained it.

'Extremely impressive,' he replied. 'It gave me a feeling of great horror.'

'The individual whose rather painful end you have just witnessed once did me a disservice. He was found in a remote part of Norway. Why he chose to hide himself there is rather difficult to understand.'

'Cause and effect?' asked Bellamy, forcing a smile.

Clinton took another pinch of the white powder.

'Possibly a mere coincidence,' he replied. 'And now I must go, for I have a "date", as they say in America, with a rather charming and profligate young woman. Could you possibly lend me a little money?'

When he had gone Bellamy washed his person very thoroughly in a hot bath, brushed his teeth with zeal, and felt a little cleaner. He tried to read in bed, but between him and Mr Jacob's *Night-Watchman* a bestial and persistent phantasmagoria forced its way. He dressed again, went out and walked the streets till dawn.

Some time later Mr Solan happened to overhear a conversation in the club smoking-room.

'I can't think what's happened to Bellamy,' said one. 'He does no work and is always about with that incredible swine Clinton.'

'A kink somewhere, I suppose,' said another, yawning. 'Dirty streak probably.'

'Were you referring to Mr Edward Bellamy, a friend of mine?' asked Mr Solan.

'We were,' said one.

'Have you ever known him to do a discreditable thing?'

'Not till now,' said another.

'Or a stupid thing?'

'I'll give you that,' said one.

'Well,' said Mr Solan, 'you have my word for it that he has not changed,' and he passed on.

'Funny old devil that,' said one.

'Rather shoves the breeze up me,' said another. 'He seems to know something. I like Bellamy, and I'll apologize to him for taking his name in vain when I see him next. But that bastard Clinton! —'

*

'It will have to be soon,' said Mr Solan. 'I heard today that he will be given notice to quit any day now. Are you prepared to go through with it?'

'He's the devil incarate,' said Bellamy. 'If you knew

78

what I'd been through in the last month!'

'I have a shrewd idea of it,' replied Mr Solan. 'You think he trusts you completely?'

'I don't think he has any opinion of me at all, except that I lend him money whenever he wants it. Of course, I'll go through with it. Let it be Friday night. What must I do? Tell me exactly. I know that but for you I should have chucked my hand in long ago.'

'My dear Bellamy, you have done marvellously well, and you will finish the business as resolutely as you have carried it through so far. Well, this is what you must do. Memorize it flawlessly.'

*

'I will arrange it that we arrive at his rooms just about eleven o'clock. I will ring up five minutes before we leave.'

'I shall be doing my part,' said Mr Solan.

Clinton was in high spirits at the Café Royal on Friday evening.

'I like you, my dear Bellamy,' he observed, 'not merely because you have a refined taste in pornography and have lent me a good deal of money, but for a more suitable reason. You remember when we first met I was puzzled by you. Well, I still am. There is some psychic power surrounding you. I don't mean that you are conscious of it, but there is some very powerful inflence working for you. Great friends though we are, I sometimes feel that this power is hostile to myself. Anyhow, we have had many pleasant times together.'

'And,' replied Bellamy, 'I hope we shall have many more. It has certainly been a tremendous privilege to have been permitted to enjoy so much of your company. As for that mysterious power you refer to, I am entirely unconscious of it, and as for hostility – well, I hope I've convinced you during the last month that I'm not exactly your enemy.'

'You have, me dear fellow,' replied Clinton. 'You have been a charming and generous companion. All the same, there is an enigmatic side to you. What shall we do to-night?'

'Whatever you please,' said Bellamy.

'I suggest we go round to my rooms,' said Clinton, 'bearing a bottle of whisky, and that I show you another little experiment. You are now sufficiently trained to make it a success.'

'Just what I should have hoped for,' replied Bellamy enthusiastically. 'I will order the whisky now.' He went out of the grill-room for a moment and had a few words with Mr Solan over the telephone. And then he returned, paid the bill, and they drove off together.

Clinton's rooms were in a dingy street about a hundred yards from the British Museum. They were drab and melancholy, and contained nothing but the barest necessities and some books.

It was exactly eleven o'clock as Clinton took out his latch-key, and it was just exactly then that Mr Solan unlocked the door of a curious little room leading off from the study.

Then he opened a bureau and took from it a large book bound in plain white vellum. He sat down at a table and began a bizarre procedure. He took from a folder at the end of the book a piece of what looked like crumpled tracing paper, and, every now and again consulting the quarto, drew certain symbols upon the paper, while repeating a series of short sentences in a strange tongue. The ink into which he dipped his pen for this exercise was a smoky sullen scarlet.

Presently the atmosphere of the room became intense, and charged with suspense and crisis. The symbols completed. Mr Solan became rigid and taut, and his eyes were those of one passing into trance.

*

'First of all a drink, my dear Bellamy,' said Clinton.

Bellamy pulled the cork and poured out two stiff pegs. Clinton drank his off. He gave the impression of being not quite at his ease.

'Some enemy of mine is working against me tonight,'

he said. 'I feel an influence strongly. However, let us try the little experiment. Draw up your chair to the window, and do not look round till I speak.'

Bellamy did as he was ordered, and peered at a dark façade across the street. Suddenly it was as if wall after wall rolled up before his eyes and passed into the sky, and he found himself gazing into a long, faintly lit room. As his eyes grew more used to the dimness he could pick out a number of recumbent figures, apparently resting on couches. And then from the middle of the room a flame seemed to leap, and then another and another until there was a fiery circle playing round one of these figures, which slowly rose to its feet and turned and stared at Bellamy; and its haughty, evil face grew vast, till it was thrust, dazzling and fiery, right into his own. He put up his hands to thrust back its scorching menace – and there was the wall of the house opposite, and Clinton was saying, 'Well?'

'Your power terrifies me!' said Bellamy. 'Who was that One I saw?'

'The one you saw was myself,' said Clinton, smiling, during my third reincarnation, about 1750 B.C. I am the only man in the world who can perform that quite considerable feat. Give me another drink.'

Bellamy got up (it was time!). Suddenly he felt invaded by a mighty reassurance. His ghostly terror left him. Something irresistible was sinking into his soul, and he knew that at the destined hour the promised succour had come to sustain him. He felt thrilled, resolute, exalted.

He had his back to Clinton as he filled the glasses, and with a lightning motion he dropped a pellet into Clinton's which fizzled like a tiny comet down through the bubbles and was gone.

'Here's to many more pleasant evenings,' said Clinton. 'You're a brave man, Bellamy,' he exclaimed, putting the glass to his lips. 'For what you have seen might well appal the devil!'

'I'm not afraid because I trust you,' replied Bellamy.

'By Eblis, this is a strong one,' said Clinton, peering into his glass.

'Same as usual,' said Bellamy, laughing. 'Tell me something. A man I knew who'd been many years in the East told me about some race out there who cut out paper patterns and paint them and send them to their enemies. Have you ever heard of anything of the sort?'

Clinton dropped his glass on the table sharply. He did not answer for a moment, but shifted uneasily in his chair.

'Who was this friend of yours?' he asked, in a voice already slightly thick.

'A chap called Bond,' said Bellamy.

'Yes, I've heard of that charming practice. In fact, I can cut them myself.'

'Really, how's it done? I should be fascinated to see it.'

Clinton's eyes blinked, and his head nodded.

'I'll show you one,' he said, 'but it's dangerous, and you must be very careful. Go to the bottom drawer of that bureau and bring me the piece of straw paper you'll find there. And there are some scissors on the writing-table and two crayons in the tray.' Bellamy brought them to him.

'Now,' said Clinton, 'this thing, as I say, is dangerous. If I wasn't drunk I wouldn't do it. And why am I drunk?' He leaned back in his chair and put his hand over his eyes. And then he sat up and, taking the scissors, began running them with extreme dexterity round the paper. And then he made some marks with the coloured pencils.

The final result of these actions was not unfamiliar in appearance to Bellamy.

'There you are,' said Clinton. 'That, my dear Bellamy, is potentially the most deadly little piece of paper in the world. Would you please take it to the fireplace and burn it to ashes?'

Bellamy burnt a piece of paper to ashes.

Clinton's head had dropped into his hands.

'Another drink?' asked Bellamy.

'My God, no,' said Clinton, yawning and reeling in his chair. And then his head went down again. Bellamy went up to him and shook him. His right hand hovered a second over Clinton's coat pocket.

'Wake up,' he said, 'I want to know what would make that piece of paper actually deadly?'

Clinton looked up blearily at him and then rallied slightly.

'You'd like to know, wouldn't you?'

'Yes,' said Bellamy. 'Tell me.'

'Just repeating six words,' said Clinton, 'but I shall not repeat them.' Suddenly his eyes became intent and fixed on a corner of the room.

'What's that?' he asked sharply. 'There! there! there! in the corner.' Bellamy felt again the presence of a power. The air of the room seemed rent and sparking.

'That, Clinton,' he said, 'is the spirit of Philip Franton, whom you murdered.' And then he sprang at Clinton, who was staggering from his chair. He seized him and pressed a little piece of paper fiercely to his forehead.

'Now, Clinton,' he cried, 'say those words!'

And then Clinton rose to his feet, and his face was working hideously. His eyes seemed bursting from his head, their pupils stretched and curved, foam streamed from his lips. He flung his hands above his head and cried in a voice of agony:

'He cometh and he passeth by!'

And then he crashed to the floor.

*

As Bellamy moved towards the door the lights went dim, in from the window poured a burning wind, and then from the wall in the corner a shadow began to grow. When he saw it, swift icy ripples poured through him. It grew and grew, and began to lean down towards the figure on the floor. As Bellamy took a last look back it was just touching it. He shuddered, opened the door, closed it quickly, and ran down the stairs and out into the night.

# THE INVOKER OF THE BEAST

## by Feodor Sologub

It was quiet and tranquil, and neither joyous nor sad. There was an electric light in the room. The walls seemed impregnable. The window was overhung by heavy, dark-green draperies, even denser in tone than the green of the wallpaper. Both doors – the large one at the side, and the small one in the depth of the alcove that faced the window – were securely bolted. And there, behind them, reigned darkness and desolation in the broad corridor as well as in the spacious and cold reception-room, where melancholy plants yearned for their native soil.

Gurov was lying on the divan. A book was in his hands. He often paused in his reading. He meditated and mused during these pauses, and it was always about the same thing. Always about *them*.

They hovered near him. This he had noticed long ago. They were hiding. Their manner was importunate. They rustled very quietly. For a long time they remained invisible to the eye. But one day, when Gurov awoke rather tired, sad, and pale, and languidly turned on the electric light to dissipate the greyish gloom of an early winter morning – he espied one of them suddenly.

Small, grey, shifty, and nimble, *he* flashed by, and in the twinkling of an eye disappeared.

And thereafter, in the morning, or in the evening, Gurov grew used to seeing these small, shifty, house sprites run past him. This time he did not doubt that they would appear.

To begin with he felt a slight headache, afterwards a sudden flash of heat, then of cold. Then, out of the corner, there emerged the long, slender Fever with her ugly, yellow face and her bony dry hands; she lay down at his side, and embraced him, and fell to kissing him and to laughing. And these rapid kisses of the affectionate and cunning Fever, and these slow approaches of the slight headache were agreeable.

Feebleness spread itself over the whole body, and lassitude also. This too was agreeable. It made him feel as though all the turmoil of life had receded into the distance. And people also became far away, unimportant, even unnecessary. He preferred to be with these quiet ones, these house sprites.

Gurov had not been out for some days. He had locked himself in at home. He did not permit any one to come to him. He was alone. He thought about them. He awaited them.

*

This tedious waiting was cut short in a strange and unexpected manner. He heard the slamming of a distant door, and presently he became aware of the sound of unhurried footfalls which came from the direction of the reception-room, just behind the door of his room. Some-one was approaching with a sure and nimble step.

Gurov turned his head towards the door. A gust of cold entered the room. Before him stood a boy, most strange and wild in aspect. He was dressed in linen draperies, half nude, barefoot, smooth-skinned, sun-tanned, with black tangled hair, and dark, burning eyes. An amazingly perfect, handsome face; handsome to a degree which made it terrible to gaze upon its beauty. And it portrayed neither good nor evil.

Gurov was not astonished. A masterful mood took hold of him. He could hear the house sprites scampering away to conceal themselves.

The boy began to speak.

'Aristomarchon! Perhaps you have forgotten your pro-mise? Is this the way of valiant men? You left me when I was in mortal danger, you had made me a promise, which it is evident you did not intend to keep. I have sought for you such a long time! And here I have found you, living at your ease, and in luxury.'

Gurov fixed a perplexed gaze upon the half nude, handsome lad; and turgid memories awoke in his soul. Something long since submerged arose in dim outlines and tormented his memory, which struggled to find a solution to the strange apparition; a solution, moreover, which seemed so near and so intimate.

And what of the invincibility of his walls? Something had happened round him, some mysterious transformation had taken place. But Gurov, engulfed in his vain exertions to recall something very near to him and yet slipping away in the tenacious embrace of ancient memory, had not yet succeeded in grasping the nature of the change that he felt had taken place. He turned to the wonderful boy.

'Tell me, gracious boy, simply and clearly, without unnecessary reproaches, what had I promised you, and when had I left you in a time of mortal danger? I swear to you, by all the holies, that my conscience could never have permitted me such a mean action as you reproach me with.'

The boy shook his head. In a sonorous voice, suggestive of the melodious outpouring of a stringed instrument, he said: 'Aristomarchon, you always have been a man skilful with words, and not less skilful in matters requiring daring and prudence. If I have said that you left me in a moment of mortal danger I did not intend it as a reproach, and I do not understand why you speak of your conscience. Our projected affair was difficult and dangerous, but who can hear us now; before whom, with your craftily arranged words and your dissembling ignorance of what happened this morning at sunrise, can you deny that you had given me a promise?'

The electric light grew dim. The ceiling seemed to darken and to recede into height. There was a smell of grass; its forgotten name, once, long ago, suggested something gentle and joyous. A breeze blew. Gurov raised himself, and asked: 'What sort of an affair had we two contrived? Gracious boy, I deny nothing. Only I don't know what you are speaking of. I don't remember.'

Gurov felt as though the boy were looking at him, yet not directly. He felt also vaguely conscious of another presence no less unfamiliar and alien than that of this curious stranger, and it seemed to him that the unfamiliar form of this other presence coincided with his own form. An ancient soul, as it were, had taken possession of Gurov and enveloped him in the long-lost freshness of its vernal attributes.

It was growing darker, and there was increasing purity and coolness in the air. There rose up in his soul the joy and ease of pristine existence. The stars glowed brilliantly in the dark sky. The boy spoke.

'We had undertaken to kill the Beast. I tell you this under the multitudinous gaze of the all-seeing sky. Perhaps you were frightened. That's quite likely too! We had planned a great, terrible affair, that our names might be honoured by future generations.'

Soft, tranquil, and monotonous was the sound of a stream which purled its way in the nocturnal silence. The stream was invisible, but its nearness was soothing and refreshing. They stood under the broad shelter of a tree and continued the conversation begun at some other time.

Gurov asked: 'Why do you say that I had left you in a moment of mortal danger? Who am I that I should be frightened and run away?'

The boy burst into a laugh. His mirth had the sound of music, and as it passed into speech his voice still quavered with sweet, melodious laughter.

'Aristomarchon, how cleverly you feign to have forgotten all! I don't understand what makes you do this, and with such a mastery that you bring reproaches against yourself which I have not even dreamt of. You had left me in a moment of mortal danger because it had to be, and you could not have helped me otherwise than by forsaking me at the moment. You will surely not remain stubborn in your denial when I remind you of the words of the Oracle?'

Gurov suddenly remembered. A brilliant light, as it were, unexpectedly illumined the dark domain of things forgotten. And in wild ecstasy, in a loud and joyous voice, he exclaimed: '*One* shall kill the Beast!'

The boy laughed. And Aristomarchon asked: 'Did you kill the Beast, Timarides?'

'With what?' exclaimed Timarides. 'However strong my hands are, I was not one who could kill the Beast with a blow of the fist. We, Aristomarchon, had not been prudent and we were unarmed. We were playing in the sand by the stream. The Beast came upon us suddenly and he laid his paw upon me. It was for me to offer up my life as a sweet sacrifice to glory and to a noble cause; it was for you to execute our plan. And while he was tormenting my defenceless and unresisting body, you, fleet-footed Aristomarchon, could have run for your lance, and killed the now blood-intoxicated Beast. But the Beast did not accept my sacrifice. I lay under him, quiescent and still, gazing into his bloodshot eyes. He held his heavy paw on my shoulder, his breath came in hot, uneven gasps, and he sent out low snarls. Afterwards, he put out his huge, hot tongue and licked my face; then he left me.'

'Where is he now?' asked Aristomarchon.

In a voice strangely tranquil and strangely sonorous in the quiet arrested stillness of the humid air, Timarides replied: 'He followed me. I do not know for how long I have been wandering until I found you. He followed me. I led him on by the smell of my blood. I do not know why he has not touched me until now. But here I have enticed him to you. You had better get the weapon which you had hidden so carefully and kill the Beast, while I in my turn will leave you in the moment of mortal danger, eye to eye with the enraged creature. Here's luck to you, Aristomarchon!'

As soon as he uttered these words Timarides started to run. For a short time his cloak was visible in the darkness, a glimmering patch of white. And then he disappeared. In the same instant the air resounded with the savage

88

bellowing of the Beast, and his ponderous tread became audible. Pushing aside the growth of shrubs there emerged from the darkness the huge, monstrous head of the Beast, flashing a livid fire out of its two enormous, flaming eyes. And in the dark silence of nocturnal trees the towering ferocious shape of the Beast loomed ominously as it approached Aristomarchon.

Terror filled Aristomarchon's heart.

'Where is the lance?' was the thought that quickly flashed across his brain.

And in that instant, feeling the fresh night breeze on his face, Aristomarchon realized that he was running from the Beast. His ponderous springs and his spasmodic roars resounded closer and closer behind him. And as the Beast came up with him a loud cry rent the silence of the night. The cry came from Aristomarchon, who, recalling then some ancient and terrible words, pronounced loudly the incantation of the walls.

And thus enchanted the walls erected themselves around him . . .

*

Enchanted, the walls stood firm and were lit up. A dreary light was cast upon them by the dismal electric lamp. Gurov was in his usual surroundings.

Again came the nimble Fever and kissed him with her yellow, dry lips, and caressed him with her dry, bony hands, which exhaled heat and cold. The same thin volume, with its white pages, lay on the little table beside the divan where, as before, Gurov rested in the caressing embrace of the affectionate Fever, who showered upon him her rapid kisses. And again there stood beside him, laughing and rustling, the tiny house sprites.

Gurov said loudly and indifferently: 'The incantation of the walls!'

Then he paused. But in what consisted this incantation? He had forgotten the words. Or had they never existed at all?

The little, shifty, grey demons danced round the

slender volume with its ghostly white pages, and kept on repeating with their rustling voices: 'Our walls are strong. We are in the walls. We have nothing to fear from the outside.'

In their midst stood one of them, a tiny object like themselves, yet different from the rest. He was all black. His mantle fell from his shoulders in folds of smoke and flame. His eyes flashed like lightning. Terror and joy alternated quickly.

Gurov spoke: 'Who are you?'

The black demon answered: 'I am the Invoker of the Beast. In one of your long-past existences you left the lacerated body of Timarides on the banks of a forest stream. The Beast had satisfied himself on the beautiful body of your friend; he had gorged himself on the flesh that might have partaken of the fullness of earthly happiness; a creature of superhuman perfection had perished in order to gratify for a moment the appetite of the ravenous and ever insatiable Beast. And the blood, the wonderful blood, the sacred wine of happiness and joy, the wine of superhuman bliss – what had been the fate of this wonderful blood? Alas! The thirsty, ceaselessly thirsty Beast drank of it to gratify his momentary desire, and is thirsty anew. You had left the body of Timarides, mutilated by the Beast, on the banks of the forest stream; you forgot the promise you had given your valorous friend, and even the words of the ancient Oracle had not banished fear from your heart. And do you think that you are safe, that the beast will not find you?'

There was austerity in the sound of his voice. While he was speaking the house sprites gradually ceased their dance; the little, grey house sprites stopped to listen to the Invoker of the Beast.

Gurov then said in reply: 'I am not worried about the Beast! I have pronounced eternal enchantment upon my walls and the Beast shall never penetrate hither, into my enclosure.'

The little grey ones were overjoyed, their voices tinkled with merriment and laughter; having gathered round, hand in hand, in a circle, they were on the point of bursting forth once more into dance, when the voice of the Invoker of the Beast rang out again, sharp and austere.

'But I am here. I am here because I have found you. I am here because the incantation of the walls is dead. I am here because Timarides is waiting and importuning me. Do you hear the gentle laugh of the brave, trusting lad? Do you hear the terrible bellowing of the Beast?'

From behind the wall, approaching nearer, could be heard the fearsome bellowing of the Beast.

'The Beast is bellowing behind the wall, the invincible wall!' exclaimed Gurov in terror. 'My walls are enchanted for ever, and impregnable against foes.'

Then spoke the black demon, and there was an imperious ring in his voice: 'I tell you, man, the incantation of the walls is dead. And if you think you can save yourself by pronouncing the incantation of the walls, why then don't you utter the words?'

A cold shiver passed down Gurov's spine. The incantation! He had forgotten the words of the ancient spell. And what mattered it? Was not the ancient incantation dead – dead?

Everything about him confirmed with irrefutable evidence the death of the ancient incantation of the walls – because the walls, and the light and the shade which fell upon them, seemed dead and wavering. The Invoker of the Beast spoke terrible words. And Gurov's mind was now in a whirl, now in pain, and the affectionate Fever did not cease to torment him with her passionate kisses. Terrible words resounded, almost deadening his senses – while the Invoker of the Beast grew larger and larger, and hot fumes breathed from him, and grim terror. His eyes ejected fire, and when at last he grew so tall as to screen off the electric light, his black cloak suddenly fell from his shoulders. And Gurov recognized him – it was the boy Timarides.

'Will you kill the Beast?' asked Timarides in a sonorous voice. 'I have enticed him, I have led him to you, I have destroyed the incantation of the walls. The cowardly gift of inimical gods, the incantation of the walls, had turned into naught my sacrifice, and had saved you from your action. But the ancient incantation of the walls is dead – be quick, then, to take hold of your sword and kill the Beast. I have been a boy – I have become the Invoker of the Beast. He had drunk of my blood, and now he thirsts anew; he had partaken also of my flesh, and he is hungry again, the insatiable, pitiless Beast. I have called him to you, and you, in fulfilment of your promise, may kill the Beast. Or die yourself.'

He vanished. A terrible bellowing shook the walls. A gust of icy moisture blew across to Gurov.

The wall facing the spot where Gurov lay opened, and the huge, ferocious, and monstrous Beast entered. Bellowing savagely, he approached Gurov and laid his ponderous paw upon his breast. Straight into his heart plunged the pitiless claws. A terrible pain shot through his whole body. Shifting his blood-red eyes the Beast inclined his head towards Gurov and, crumbling the bones of his victim with his teeth, began to devour his yet-palpitating heart.

# WITCH WAR

## by Richard Matheson

Seven pretty little girls sitting in a row. Outside, night, pouring rain – war weather. Inside, toasty warm. Seven overalled little girls chatting. Plaque on the wall saying: P.G. CENTRE.

Sky clearing its throat with thunder, picking and dropping lint lightning from immeasurable shoulders. Rain hushing the world, bowing the trees, pocking earth. Square building, low, with one wall plastic.

Inside, the buzzing talk of seven pretty little girls.

'So I says to him – "Don't give me *that*, Mr High and Mighty." So he says, "Oh yeah?" And I says, "Yeah!"'

'Honest, will I ever be glad when this thing's over. I saw the cutest hat on my last furlough. Oh, *what* I wouldn't give to wear it!'

'You too? Don't I *know* it! You just can't get your hair right. Not in *this* weather. Why don't they let us get rid of it?'

'*Men!* They make me sick.'

Seven gestures, seven postures, seven laughters ringing thin beneath thunder. Teeth showing in girl giggles. Hands tireless, painting pictures in the air.

P.G. Centre. Girls. Seven of them. Pretty. Not one over sixteen. Curls. Pigtails. Bangs. Pouting little lips – smiling, frowning, shaping emotion on emotion. Sparkling young eyes – glittering, twinkling, narrowing, cold or warm.

Seven healthy young bodies restive on wooden chairs. Smooth adolescent limbs. Girls – pretty girls – seven of them.

\*

An Army of ugly shapeless men, stumbling in mud, struggling along pitch-black muddy road.

Rain a torrent. Buckets of it thrown on each exhausted man. Sucking sound of great boots sinking into oozy yellow-brown mud, pulling loose. Mud dripping from heels and soles.

Plodding men – hundreds of them – soaked, miserable, depleted. Young men bent over like old men. Jaws hanging loosely, mouths gasping at black wet air, tongues lolling, sunken eyes looking at nothing, betraying nothing.

Rest.

Men sink down in the mud, fall on their packs. Heads thrown back, mouths open, rain splashing on yellow teeth. Hands immobile – scrawny heaps of flesh and bone. Legs without motion – khaki lengths of worm-eaten wood. Hundreds of useless limbs fixed to hundreds of useless trunks.

In back, ahead, beside rumble trucks and tanks and tiny cars. Thick tires splattering mud. Fat treads sinking, tearing at mucky slime. Rain drumming wet fingers on metal and canvas.

Lightning flashbulbs without pictures. Momentary burst of light. The face of war seen for a second – made of rusty guns and turning wheels and faces staring.

Blackness. A night hand blotting out the brief storm glow. Windblown rain flitting over fields and roads, drenching trees and trucks. Rivulets of bubbly rain tearing scars from the earth. Thunder, lightning.

A whistle. Dead men resurrected. Boots in sucking mud again – deeper, closer, nearer. Approach to a city that bars the way to a city that bars the way to a ...

*

An officer sat in the communication room of the P.G. Centre. He peered at the operator, who sat hunched over the control board, phones over his ears, writing down a message.

The officer watched the operator. They are coming, he

thought. Cold, wet, and afraid they are marching at us. He shivered and shut his eyes.

He opened them quickly. Visions fill his darkened pupils – of curling smoke, flaming men, unimaginable horrors that shape themselves without word or pictures.

'Sir,' said the operator, 'from advance observation post. Enemy forces sighted.'

The officer got up, walked over to the operator and took the message. He read it, face blank, mouth parenthesized. 'Yes,' he said.

He turned on his heel and went to the door. He opened it and went into the next room. The seven girls stopped talking. Silence breathed on the walls.

The officer stood with his back to the plastic window. 'Enemies,' he said. 'Two miles away. Right in front of you.'

He turned and pointed out the window. 'Right out there. Two miles away. Any questions?'

A girl giggled.

'Any vehicles?' another asked.

'Yes. Five trucks, five small command cars, two tanks.'

'That's too easy,' laughed the girl, slender fingers fussing with her hair.

'That's all,' said the officer. He started from the room. 'Go to it,' he added and, under his breath, 'Monsters!'

He left.

'Oh, me,' sighed one of the girls, 'Here we go again.'

'What a bore,' said another. She opened her delicate mouth and plucked out chewing gum. She put it under her chair seat.

'At least it stopped raining,' said a redhead, tying her shoelaces.

The seven girls looked around at each other. *Are you ready?* said their eyes. *I'm ready, I suppose.* They adjusted themselves on the chairs with girlish grunts and sighs. They hooked their feet around the legs of their chairs. All gum was placed in storage. Mouths were tightened into prudish fixity. The pretty little girls made ready for the game.

95

Finally they were silent on their chairs. One of them took a deep breath. So did another. They all tensed their milky flesh and clasped fragile fingers together. One quickly scratched her head to get it over with. Another sneezed prettily.

'Now,' said a girl on the right end of the row.

Seven pairs of beady eyes shut. Seven innocent little minds began to picture, to visualize, to transport.

Lips rolled into thin gashes, faces drained of colour, bodies shivered passionately. Their fingers twitching with concentration, seven pretty little girls fought a war.

*

The men were coming over the rise of a hill when the attack came. The leading men, feet poised for the next step, burst into flame.

There was no time to scream. Their rifles slapped down into the muck, their eyes were lost in fire. They stumbled a few steps and fell, hissing and charred, into the soft mud.

Men yelled. The ranks broke. They began to throw up their weapons and fire at the night. More troops puffed incandescently, flared up, were dead.

'Spread out!' screamed an officer as his gesturing fingers sprouted flame and his face went up in licking yellow heat.

The men looked everywhere. Their dumb terrified eyes searched for an enemy. They fired into the fields and woods. They shot each other. They broke into flopping runs over the mud.

A truck was enveloped in fire. Its driver leaped out, a two-legged torch. The truck went bumping over the road, turned, wove crazily over the field, crashed into a tree, exploded and was eaten up in blazing light. Black shadows flitted in and out of the aura of light around the flames. Screams rent the night.

Man after man burst into flame, fell crashing on his face in the mud. Spots of searing light lashed the wet darkness – screams – running coals, spluttering, glowing, dying – incendiary ranks – trucks cremated – tanks blowing up.

*A little blonde, her body tense with repressed excitement. Her lips twitch, a giggle hovers in her throat. Her nostrils dilate. She shudders in giddy fright. She imagines, imagines..*

A soldier runs headlong across a field, screaming, his eyes insane with horror. A gigantic boulder rushes at him from the black sky.

His body is driven into the earth, mangled. From the rock edge, fingertips protrude.

The boulder lifts from the ground, crashes down again, a shapeless trip hammer. A flaming truck is flattened. The boulder flies again to the black sky.

*A pretty brunette, her face a feverish mask. Wild thoughts tumble through her virginal brain. Her scalp grows taut with ecstatic fear. Her lips draw back from clenching teeth. A gasp of terror hisses from her lips. She imagines, imagines...*

A soldier falls to his knees. His head jerks back. In the light of burning comrades, he stares dumbly at the white-foamed wave that towers over him.

It crashes down, sweeps his body over the muddy earth, fills his lungs with salt water. The tidal wave roars over the field, drowns a hundred flaming men, tosses their corpses in the air with thundering whitecaps.

Suddenly the water stops, flies into a million pieces, and disintegrates.

*A lovely little redhead, hands drawn under her chin in tight bloodless fists. Her lips tremble, a throb of delight expands her chest. Her white throat contracts, she gulps in a breath of air. Her nose wrinkles with dreadful joy. She imagines, imagines...*

A running soldier collides with a lion. He cannot see in the darkness. His hands strike wildly at the shaggy mane. He clubs with his rifle butt.

A scream. His face is torn off with one blow of thick claws. A jungle roar billows in the night.

A red-eyed elephant tramples wildly through the mud,

picking up men in its thick trunk, hurling them through the air, mashing them under driving black columns.

Wolves bound from the darkness, spring, tear at throats. Gorillas scream and bounce in the mud, leap at falling soldiers.

A rhinoceros, leather skin glowing in the light of living torches, crashes into a burning tank, wheels, thunders into blackness, is gone.

Fangs – claws – ripping teeth – shrieks – trumpeting – roars. The sky rains snakes.

*

Silence. Vast brooding silence. Not a breeze, not a drip of rain, not a grumble of distant thunder. The battle is ended.

Grey morning mist rolls over the burned, the torn, the drowned, the crushed, the poisoned, the sprawling dead.

Motionless trucks – silent tanks, wisps of oily smoke still rising from their shattered hulks. Great death covering the field. Another battle in another war.

Victory – everyone is dead.

The girls stretched languidly. They extended their arms and rotated their round shoulders. Pink lips grew wide in pretty little yawns. They looked at each other and tittered in embarrassment. Some of them blushed. A few looked guilty.

Then they all laughed out loud. They opened more gum-packs, drew compacts from pockets, spoke intimately with schoolgirl whispers, with late-night dormitory whispers.

Muted giggles rose up flutteringly in the warm room.

'Aren't we awful?' one of them said, powdering her pert nose.

Later they all went downstairs and had breakfast.

# THE ENSOULED VIOLIN

## by Madame Blavatsky

In the year 1828, an old German, a music teacher, came
to Paris with his pupil and settled unostentatiously in
one of the quiet faubourgs of the metropolis. The first
rejoiced in the name of Samuel Klaus; the second answered to the more poetical appellation of Franz Stenio.
The younger man was a violinist, gifted, as rumour went,
with extraordinary, almost miraculous talent. Yet as he
was poor and had not hitherto made a name for himself
in Europe, he remained for several years in the capital of
France – the heart and pulse of capricious continental
fashion – unknown and unappreciated. Franz was a Styrian by birth, and, at the time of the event to be presently described, he was a young man considerably under
thirty. A philosopher and a dreamer by nature, imbued
with all the mystic oddities of true genius, he reminded
one of some of the heroes in Hoffmann's *Contes Fantas-
tiques*. His earlier existence had been a very unusual, in
fact, quite an eccentric one, and its history must be
briefly told – for the better understanding of the present
story.

Born of very pious country people, in a quiet burg
among the Styrian Alps; nursed 'by the native gnomes
who watched over his cradle'; growing up in the weird
atmosphere of the ghouls and vampires who play such a
prominent part in the household of every Styrian and
Slavonian in southern Austria; educated later, as a stu-
dent, in the shadow of the old Rhenish castles of Germany; Franz from his childhood had passed through
every emotional stage on the plane of the so-called 'supernatural'. He had also studied at one time the 'occult arts'
with an enthusiastic disciple of Paracelsus and Kunrath;

alchemy had few theoretical secrets for him; and he had dabbled in 'ceremonial magic' and 'sorcery' with some Hungarian Tziganes. Yet he loved above all else music, and above music – his violin.

At the age of twenty-two he suddenly gave up his practical studies in the occult, and from that day, though as devoted as ever in thought to the beautiful Grecian gods, he surrendered himself entirely to his art. Of his classic studies he had retained only that which related to the muses – Euterpe especially, at whose altar he worshipped – and Orpheus whose magic lyre he tried to emulate with his violin. Except his dreamy belief in the nymphs and the sirens, on account probably of the double relationship of the latter to the muses through Calliope and Orpheus, he was interested but little in the matters of this sublunary world. All his aspirations mounted, like incense, with the wave of the heavenly harmony that he drew from his instrument, to a higher and a nobler sphere. He dreamed awake, and lived a real though an enchanted life only during those hours when his magic bow carried him along the wave of sound to the Pagan Olympus, to the feet of Euterpe. A strange child he had ever been in his own home, where tales of magic and witchcraft grow out of every inch of the soil; a still stranger boy he had become, until finally he had blossomed into manhood, without one single characteristic of youth. Never had a fair face attracted his attention; not for one moment had his thoughts turned from his solitary studies to a life beyond that of a mystic Bohemian. Content with his own company, he had thus passed the best years of his youth and manhood with his violin for his chief idol, and with the gods and goddesses of old Greece for his audience, in perfect ignorance of practical life. His whole existence had been one long day of dreams, of melody and sunlight, and he had never felt any other aspirations.

How useless, but oh, how glorious those dreams! how vivid! and why should he desire any better fate? Was he not all that he wanted to be, transformed in a second of thought into one or another hero; from Orpheus, who held all nature breathless, to the urchin who piped away under the plane tree to the naiads of Calirrhoë's crystal fountain? Did not the swift-footed nymphs frolic at his beck and call to the sound of the magic flute of the Arcadian shepherd – who was himself? Behold, the Goddess of Love and Beauty herself descending from on high, attracted by the sweet-voiced notes of his violin! ... Yet there came a time when he preferred Syrinx to Aphrodite – not as the fair nymph pursued by Pan, but after her transformation by the merciful gods into the reed out of which the frustrated God of the Shepherds had made his magic pipe. For also, with time, ambition grows and is rarely satisfied. When he tried to emulate on his violin the enchanting sounds that resounded in his mind, the whole of Parnassus kept silent under the spell, or joined in heavenly chorus; but the audience he finally craved was composed of more than the gods sung by Hesiod, verily of the most appreciative *mélomanes* of European capitals. He felt jealous of the magic pipe, and would fain have had it at his command.

'Oh! that I could allure a nymph into my beloved violin!' – he often cried, after awakening from one of his day-dreams. 'Oh, that I could only span in spirit flight the abyss of Time! Oh, that I could find myself for one short day a partaker of the secret arts of the gods, a god myself, in the sight and hearing of enraptured humanity; and, having learned the mystery of the lyre of Orpheus, or secured within my violin a siren, thereby benefit mortals to my own glory.'

Thus, having for long years dreamed in the company of the gods of his fancy, he now took to dreaming of the transitory glories of fame upon this earth. But at this time he was suddenly called home by his widowed mother from one of the German universities where he had lived for the last year or two. This was an event which brought his plans to an end, at least so far as the immediate future was concerned, for he had hitherto drawn upon her alone for his meagre pittance, and his means were not sufficient for an independent life outside his native place.

His return had a very unexpected result. His mother, whose only love he was on earth, died soon after she had welcomed her Benjamin back; and the good wives of the burg exercised their swift tongues for many a month after as to the real causes of that death.

Frau Stenio, before Franz's return, was a healthy, buxom, middle-aged body, strong and hearty. She was a pious and a God-fearing soul too, who had never failed in saying her prayers, nor had missed an early mass for years during his absence. On the first Sunday after her son had settled at home – a day that she had been longing for and had anticipated for months in joyous visions, in which she saw him kneeling by her side in the little church on the hill – she called him from the foot of the stairs. The hour had come when her pious dream was to be realized, and she was waiting for him, carefully wiping the dust from the prayer-book he had used in his boyhood. But instead of Franz, it was his violin that responded to her call, mixing its sonorous voice with the rather cracked tones of the peal of the merry Sunday bells. The fond mother was somewhat shocked at hearing the prayer-inspiring sounds drowned by the weird, fantastic notes of the 'Dance of the Witches'; they seemed to her so unearthly and mocking. But she almost fainted upon hearing the definite refusal of her well-beloved son to go to church. He never went to church, he coolly remarked. It was loss of time; besides which, the loud peals of the old church organ jarred on his nerves. Nothing should induce him to submit to the torture of listening to that cracked organ. He was firm, and nothing could move him. To her supplications and remonstrances he put an end by offering to play for her a 'Hymn to the Sun' he had just composed.

From that memorable Sunday morning, Frau Stenio lost her usual serenity of mind. She hastened to lay her sorrows and seek for consolation at the foot of the confessional; but that which she heard in response from the stern priest filled her gentle and unsophisticated soul with dismay and almost with despair. A feeling of fear, a sense of profound terror, which soon became a chronic state wth her, pursued her from that moment; her nights became disturbed and sleepless, her days passed in prayer and lamentations. In her maternal anxiety for the salvation of her beloved son's soul, and for his *post-mortem* welfare, she made a series of rash vows. Finding that neither the Latin petition to the Mother of God written for her by her spiritual adviser, nor yet the humble supplications in German, addressed by herself to every saint she had reason to believe was residing in Paradise, worked the desired effect, she took to pilgrimages to distant shrines. During one of these journeys to a holy chapel situated high up in the mountains, she caught cold, amidst the glaciers of the Tyrol, and redescended only to take to a sick bed, from which she arose no more. Frau Stenio's vow had led her, in one sense, to the desired result. The poor woman was now given an opportunity of seeking out in *propria persona* the saints she had believed in so well, and of pleading face to face for the recreant son who refused adherence to them and to the Church, scoffed at monk and confessional, and held the organ in such horror.

Franz sincerely lamented his mother's death. Unaware of being the indirect cause of it, he felt no remorse; but selling the modest household goods and chattels, light in purse and heart, he resolved to travel on foot for a year or two, before settling down to any definite profession.

A hazy desire to see the great cities of Europe, and to try his luck in France, lurked at the bottom of this travelling project, but his Bohemian habits of life were too strong to be abruptly abandoned. He placed his small capital with a banker for a rainy day, and started on his pedestrian journey *via* Germany and Austria. His violin paid for his board and lodging in the inns and farms on his way, and he passed his days in the green fields and in the solemn silent woods, face to face with Nature, dreaming all the time as usual with his eyes open. During the three months of his pleasant travels to and fro, he never descended for one moment from Parnassus; but, as an alchemist transmutes lead into gold, so he transformed everything on his way into a song of Hesiod or Anacreon. Every evening, while fiddling for his supper and bed, whether on a green lawn or in the hall of a rustic inn, his fancy changed the whole scene for him. Village swains and maidens became transfigured into Arcadian shepherds and nymphs. The sand-covered floor was now a green sward; the uncouth couples spinning round in a measured waltz with the wild grace of tamed bears became priests and priestesses of Terpsichore; the bulky, cherry-cheeked and blue-eyed daughters of rural Germany were the Hesperides circling around the trees laden with the golden apples. Nor did the melodious strains of the Arcadian demi-gods piping on their syrinxes, and audible but to his own enchanted ear, vanish with the dawn. For no sooner was the curtain of sleep raised from his eyes than he would sally forth into a new magic realm of day-dreams. On his way to some dark and solemn pine-forest, he played incessantly, to himself and to everything else. He fiddled to the green hill, and forthwith the mountain and the moss-covered rocks moved forward to hear him the better, as they had done at the sound of the Orphean lyre. He fiddled to the merry-voiced brook, to the hurrying river, and both slackened their speed and stopped their waves, and, becoming silent, seemed to listen to him in an entranced rapture. Even the long-legged stork who stood meditatively on one leg on the thatched top of the rustic mill, gravely resolving unto himself the problem of his too-long existence, sent out after him a long and strident cry, screeching. 'Art thou Orpheus himself, O Stenio?'

It was a period of full bliss, of a daily and almost hourly exaltation. The last words of his dying mother, whispering to him of the horrors of eternal condemnation, had left him unaffected, and the only vision her warning evoked in him was that of Pluto. By a ready association of ideas, he saw the lord of the dark nether kingdom greeting him as he had greeted the husband of

Eurydice before him. Charmed with the magic sounds of his violin, the wheel of Ixion was at a standstill once more, thus affording relief to the wretched seducer of Juno, and giving the lie to those who claim eternity for the duration of the punishment of condemned sinners. He perceived Tantalus forgetting his never-ceasing thirst, and smacking his lips as he drank in the heaven-born melody; the stone of Sisyphus becoming motionless, the Furies themselves smiling on him, and the sovereign of the gloomy regions delighted, and awarding preference to his violin over the lyre of Orpheus. Taken *au sérieux*, mythology thus seems a decided antidote to fear, in the face of theological threats, especially when strengthened with an insane and passionate love of music; with Franz, Euterpe proved always victorious in every contest, aye, even with Hell itself!

But there is an end to everything, and very soon Franz had to give up uninterrupted dreaming. He had reached the university town where dwelt his old violin teacher, Samuel Klaus. When this antiquated musician found that his beloved and favourite pupil, Franz, had been left poor in purse and still poorer in earthly affections, he felt his strong attachment to the boy awaken with tenfold force. He took Franz to his heart, and forthwith adopted him as his son.

The old teacher reminded people of one of those grotesque figures which look as if they had just stepped out of some medieval panel. And yet Klaus, with his fantastic *allures* of a night-goblin, had the most loving heart, as tender as that of a woman, and the self-sacrificing nature of an old Christian martyr. When Franz had briefly narrated to him the history of his last few years, the professor took him by the hand, and leading him into his study simply said:

'Stop with me, and put an end to your Bohemian life. Make yourself famous. I am old and childless and will be your father. Let us live together and forget all save fame.'

And forthwith he offered to proceed with Franz to Paris, *via* several large German cities, where they would stop to give concerts.

In a few days Klaus succeeded in making Franz forget his vagrant life and its artistic independence, and re-awakened in his pupil his now dormant ambition and desire for worldly fame. Hitherto, since his mother's death, he had been content to receive applause only from the Gods and Goddesses who inhabited his vivid fancy; now he began to crave once more for the admiration of mortals. Under the clever and careful training of old Klaus his remarkable talent gained in strength and powerful charm with every day, and his reputation grew and expanded with every city and town wherein he made himself heard. His ambition was being rapidly realized; the presiding genii of various musical centres to whose patronage his talent was submitted soon proclaimed him *the one* violinist of the day, and the public declared loudly that he stood unrivalled by any one whom they had ever heard. These laudations very soon made both master and pupil completely lose their heads.

But Paris was less ready with such appreciation. Paris makes reputations for itself, and will take none on faith. They had been living in it for almost three years, and were still climbing with difficulty the artist's Calvary, when an event occurred which put and end even to their most modest expectations. The first arrival of Niccolo Paganini was suddenly heralded, and threw Lutetia into a convulsion of expectation. The unparalleled artist arrived, and – all Paris fell at once at his feet.

Now it is a well-known fact that a superstition born in the dark days of medieval superstition, and surviving almost to the middle of the present century, attributed all such abnormal, out-of-the-way talent as that of Paganini to 'supernatural' agency. Every great and marvellous artist had been accused in his day of dealings with the devil. A few instances will suffice to refresh the reader's memory.

Tartini, the great composer and violinist of the seventeenth century, was denounced as one who got his best inspirations from the Evil One, with whom he was, it was said, in regular league. This accusation was, of course, due to the almost magical impression he produced upon his audiences. His inspired performance on the violin secured for him in his native country the title of 'Master of Nations'. The *Sonate du Diable,* also called 'Tartini's Dream' – as everyone who has heard it will be ready to testify – is the most weird melody ever heard or invented: hence, the marvellous composition has become the source of endless legends. Nor were they entirely baseless, since it was he, himself, who was shown to have originated them. Tartini confessed to having written it on awakening from a dream, in which he had heard his sonata performed by Satan, for his benefit, and in consequence of a bargain made with his infernal majesty.

Several famous singers, even, whose exceptional voices struck the hearers with superstitious admiration, have not escaped a like accusation. Pasta's splendid voice was attributed in her day to the fact that, three months before her birth, the diva's mother was carried during a trance to heaven, and there treated to a vocal concert of seraphs. Malibran was indebted for her voice to St Cecilia, while others said she owed it to a demon who watched over her cradle and sung the baby to sleep. Finally, Paginini – the unrivalled performer, the mean Italian, who like Dryden's Jubal striking on the 'chorded shell' forced the throngs that followed him to worship the divine sounds produced, and made people say that 'less than a God, could not dwell within the hollow of his violin' – Paganini left a legend too.

The almost supernatural art of the greatest violin-player that the world has ever known was often speculated upon, never understood. The effect produced by him on his audience was literally marvellous, overpowering. The great Rossini is said to have wept like a sentimental German maiden on hearing him play for the first time. The Princess Elisa of Lucca, a sister of the great Napoleon, in whose service Paganini was, as director of her private orchestra, for a long time was unable to hear him play without fainting. In women he produced nervous fits and hysterics at his will; stout-hearted men he drove to frenzy. He changed cowards into heroes and made the bravest soldiers feel like so many nervous schoolgirls. Is it to be wondered at, then, that hundreds of weird tales circulated for long years about and around the mysterious Genoese, that modern Orpheus of Europe. One of these was especially ghastly. It was rumoured, and was believed by more people than would probably like to confess it, that the strings of his violin were made of *human intestines, according to all the rules and requirements of the Black Art.*

Exaggerated as this idea may seem to some, it has nothing impossible in it; and it is more than probable that it was this legend that led to the extraordinary events which we are about to narrate. Human organs are often used by the Eastern Black Magician, so-called, and it is an averred fact that some Bengali Tantrikas (reciters of *tantras,* or 'invocations to the demon', as a reverend writer has described them) use human corpses, and certain internal and external organs pertaining to them, as powerful magical agents for bad purposes.

However this may be, now that the magnetic and mesmeric potencies of hypnotism are recognized as facts by most physicians, it may be suggested with less danger than heretofore that the extraordinary effects of Paganini's violin-playing were not, perhaps, entirely due to his talent and genius. The wonder and awe he so easily excited were as much caused by his external appearance, 'which had something weird and demoniacal in it,' according to certain of his biographers, as by the inexpressible charm of his execution and his remarkable mechanical skill. The latter is demonstrated by his perfect imitaion of the flageolet, and his performance of long and magnificent melodies on the G string alone. In this performance, which many an artist has tried to copy without success, he remains unrivalled to this day.

It is owing to this remarkable appearance of his – termed by his friends eccentric, and by his too nervous victims, diabolical – that he experienced great difficulties in refuting certain ugly rumours. These were credited far more easily in his day than they would be now. It was whispered throughout Italy, and even in his own native town, that Paganini had murdered his wife, and, later on, a mistress, both of whom he had loved passionately, and both of whom he had not hesitated to sacrifice to his fiendish ambition. He had made himself proficient in magic arts, it was asserted, and has succeeded thereby in imprisoning the souls of his two victims in his violin – his famous Cremona.

It is maintained by the immediate friends of Ernst T. W. Hoffmann, the celebrated author of *Die Elixire des Teufels, Meister Martin*, and other charming and mystical tales, that Councillor Crespel, in the *Violin of Cremona*, was taken from the legend about Paganini. It is, as all who have read it know, the history of a celebrated violin, into which the voice and the soul of a famous diva, a woman whom Crespel had loved and killed, had passed, and to which was added the voice of his beloved daughter, Antonia.

Nor was this superstition utterly ungrounded, nor was Hoffmann to be blamed for adopting it, after he had heard Paganini's playing. The extraordinary facility with which the artist drew out of his instrument, not only the most unearthly sounds, but positively human voices, justified the suspicion. Such effects might well have startled an audience and thrown terror into many a nervous heart. Add to this the impenetrable mystery connected with a certain period of Paganini's youth, and the most wild tales about him must be found in a measure justifiable, and even excusable; especially among a nation whose ancestors knew the Borgias and the Medicis of Black Art fame.

*

In those pre-telegraphic days, newspapers were limited, and the wings of fame had a heavier flight than they have now.

Franz had hardly heard of Paganini; and when he did,

he swore he would rival, if not eclipse, the Genoese magician. Yes, he would either become the most famous of all living violinists, or he would break his instrument and put an end to his life at the same time.

Old Klaus rejoiced at such determination. He rubbed his hands in glee, and jumping about on his lame leg like a crippled satyr, he flattered and incensed his pupil, believing himself all the while to be performing a sacred duty to the holy and majestic cause of art.

Upon first setting foot in Paris, three years before, Franz had all but failed. Musical critics pronounced him a rising star, but had all agreed that he required a few more years' practice, before he could hope to carry his audiences by storm. Therefore, after a desperate study of over two years and uninterrupted preparations, the Styrian artist had finally made himself ready for his first serious appearance in the great Opera House where a public concert before the most exacting critics of the Old World was to be held; at this critical moment Paganini's arrival in the European metropolis placed an obstacle in the way of the realization of his hopes, and the old German professor wisely postponed his pupil's *début*. At first he had simply smiled at the wild enthusiasm, the laudatory hymns sung about the Genoese violinist, and the almost superstitious awe with which his name was pronounced. But very soon Paganini's name became a burning iron in the hearts of both the artists, and a threatening phantom in the mind of Klaus. A few days more, and they shuddered at the very mention of their great rival, whose success became with every night more unprecedented.

The first series of concerts was over, but neither Klaus nor Franz had as yet had an opportunity of hearing him and of judging for themselves. So great and so beyond their means was the charge for admission, and so small the hope of getting a free pass from a brother artist justly regarded as the meanest of men in monetary transactions, that they had to wait for a chance, as did many others. But the day came when neither master nor pupil could control their impatience any longer; so they pawned their watches, and with the proceeds bought two modest seats.

Who can describe the enthusiasm, the triumphs, of this famous, and at the same time fatal night! The audience was frantic; men wept and women screamed and fainted, while both Klaus and Stenio sat looking paler than two ghosts. At the first touch of Paginini's magic bow, both Franz and Samuel felt as if the icy hand of death had touched them. Carried away by an irresistible enthusiasm, which turned into a violent, unearthly mental torture, they dared neither look into each other's faces, nor exchange one word during the whole performance.

At midnight, while the chosen delegates of the Musical Societies and the Conservatory of Paris unhitched the horses, and dragged the carriage of the grand artist home in triumph, the two Germans returned to their modest lodging, and it was a pitiful sight to see them. Mournful and desperate, they placed themselves in their usual seats at the fire-corner, and neither for a while opened his mouth.

'Samuel!' at last exclaimed Franz, pale as death itself. 'Samuel – it remains for us now but to die! ..Do you hear me? ... We are worthless! We were two madmen to have ever hoped that any one in this world would ever rival ... him!'

The name of Paganini stuck in his throat, as in utter despair he fell into his armchair.

The old professor's wrinkles suddenly became purple. His little greenish eyes gleamed phosphorescently as, bending towards his pupil, he whispered to him in hoarse and broken tones:

'*Nein, nein!* Thou art wrong, my Franz! I have taught thee, and thou hast learned all of the great art that a simple mortal, and a Christian by baptism, can learn from another simple mortal. Am I to blame because these accursed Italians, in order to reign unequalled in the domain of art, have recourse to Satan and the diabolical effects of Black Magic?'

Franz turned his eyes upon his old master. There was a sinister light burning in those glittering orbs; a light telling plainly, that, to secure such a power, he, too, would not scruple to sell himself, body and soul, to the Evil One.

But he said not a word, and, turning his eyes from his old master's face, he gazed dreamily at the dying embers.

The same long-forgotten incoherent dreams, which, after seeming such realities to him in his younger days, had been given up entirely, and had gradually faded from his mind, now crowded back into it with the same force and vividness as of old. The grimacing shades of Ixion, Sisyphus, and Tantalus resurrected and stood before him, saying:

'What matters hell – in which thou believest not. And even if hell there be, it is the hell described by the old Greeks, not that of the modern bigots – a locality full of conscious shadows to whom thou canst be a second Orpheus.'

Franz felt that he was going mad, and, turning instinctively, he looked his old master once more right in the face. Then his bloodshot eye evaded the gaze of Klaus.

Whether Samuel understood the terrible state of mind of his pupil, or whether he wanted to draw him out, to make him speak, and thus to divert his thoughts, must remain as hypothetical to the reader as it is to the writer. Whatever may have been in his mind, the German enthusiast went on, speaking with a feigned calmness:

'Franz, my dear boy, I tell you that the art of the accursed Italian is not natural; that it is due neither to study nor to genius. It never was acquired in the usual, natural way. You need not stare at me in that wild manner, for what I say is in the mouth of millions of people. Listen to what I now tell you, and try to understand. You have heard the strange tale whispered about the famous Tartini? He died one fine Sabbath night, strangled by his familiar demon, who had taught him how to endow his violin with a human voice, by shutting up in it, by means of incantations, the soul of a young virgin. Paganini did more. In order to endow his instrument with the faculty of emitting human sounds, such as sobs, despairing cries, supplications, moans of love and fury – in short, the most heart-rending notes of the human voice – Paganini became the murderer not only of his wife and his mistress, but also of a friend, who was more tenderly attached to him than any other being on this earth. He then made the four chords of his magic violin out of the intestines of his last victim. This is the secret of his enchanting talent, of that overpowering melody, that combination of sounds, which you will never be able to master unless..

The old man could not finish the sentence. He staggered back before the fiendish look of his pupil, and covered his face with his hands.

Franz was breathing heavily, and his eyes had an expression which reminded Klaus of those of a hyena. His pallor was cadaverous. For some time he could not speak, but only gasped for breath. At last he slowly muttered:

'Are you in earnest?'

'I am, as I hope to help you.'

'And ... and do you really believe that had I only the means of obtaining human intestines for strings, I could rival Paganini?' asked Franz, after a moment's pause, and casting down his eyes.

The old German unveiled his face, with a strange look of determination upon it, softly answered:

'Human intestines alone are not sufficient for our purpose; they must have belonged to someone who had loved us well, with an unselfish holy love. Tartini endowed his violin with the life of a virgin; but that virgin had died of unrequited love for him. The fiendish artist had prepared beforehand a tube, in which he managed to catch her last breath as she expired, pronouncing his beloved name, and then he transferred this breath to his violin. As to Paganini, I have just told you his tale. It was with the consent of his victim, though, that he murdered him to get possession of his intestines.

'Oh, for the power of the human voice!' Samuel went

on, after a brief pause. 'What can equal the eloquence, the magic spell of the human voice? Do you think, my poor boy, I would not have taught you this great, this final secret, were it not that it throws one right into the clutches of him .. who must remain unnamed at night?' he added, with a sudden return to the superstitions of his youth.

Franz did not answer, but with a calmness awful to behold, he left his place, took down his violin from the wall where it was hanging, and, with one powerful grasp of the chords, he tore them out and flung them into the fire.

Samuel suppressed a cry of horror. The chords were hissing upon the coals, where, among the blazing logs, they wriggled and curled like so many living snakes.

'By the witches of Thessaly and the dark arts of Circe!' he exclaimed, with foaming mouth and his eyes burning like coals; 'by the Furies of Hell and Pluto himself, I now swear, in thy presence, O Samuel, my master, never to touch a violin again until I can string it with four human chords. May I be accursed for ever and ever if I do!' He fell senseless on the floor, with a deep sob, that ended like a funeral wail; old Samuel lifted him up as he would have lifted a child, and carried him to his bed. Then he sallied forth in search of a physician.

*

For several days after this painful scene Franz was very ill, ill almost beyond recovery. The physician declared him to be suffering from brain fever and said that the worst was to be feared. For nine long days the patient remained delirious; and Klaus, who was nursing him night and day with the solicitude of the tenderest mother, was horrified at the work of his own hands. For the first time since their acquaintance began, the old teacher, owing to the wild ravings of his pupils, was able to penetrate into the darkest corners of that weird, super- stitious, cold, and, at the same time, passionate nature; and – he trembled at what he discovered. For he saw that which he had failed to perceive before – Franz as he was in reality, and not as he seemed to superficial observers. Music was the life of the young man, and adulation was the air he breathed, without which that life became a burden; from the chords of his violin alone, Stenio drew his life and being, but the applause of men and even of gods was necessary to its support. He saw unveiled before his eyes a genuine, artistic, *earthly* soul, with its divine counterpart totally absent, a son of the Muses, all fancy and brain poetry, but without a heart. While listening to the ravings of that delirious and unhinged fancy Klaus felt as if he were for the first time in his long life exploring a marvellous and untravelled region, a human nature not of this world but of some incomplete planet. He saw all this, and shuddered. More than once he asked himself whether it would not be doing a kindness to his 'boy' to let him die before he returned to consciousness.

But he loved his pupil too well to dwell for long on such an idea. Franz had bewitched his truly artistic nature, and now old Klaus felt as though their two lives were inseparably linked together. That he could thus feel was a revelation to the old man; so he decided to save Franz, even at the expense of his own old and, as he thought, useless life.

The seventh day of the illness brought on a most terrible crisis. For twenty-four hours the patient never closed his eyes, nor remained for a moment silent; he raved continuously during the whole time. His visions were peculiar, and he minutely described each. Fantastic, ghastly figures kept slowly swimming out of the penumbra of his small, dark room, in regular and uninterrupted procession, and he greeted each by name as he might greet old acquaintances. He referred to himself as Prometheus, bound to the rock by four bands made of human intestines. At the foot of the Caucasian Mount the black waters of the River Styx were running ... They had deserted Arcadia, and were now endeavouring to encircle within a seven-fold embrace the rock upon which he was suffering ...

'Wouldst thou know the name of the Promethean rock, old man?' he roared into his adopted father's ear ... 'Listen then, ... its name is ... called ... Samuel Klaus ...

'Yes, yes! ...' the German murmured disconsolately. 'It is I who killed him, while seeking to console. The news of Paganini's magic arts struck his fancy too vividly ... Oh, my poor, poor boy!'

'Ha, ha, ha, ha!' The patient broke into a loud and discordant laugh. 'Aye, poor old man, sayest thou? ... So, so, thou art of poor stuff, anyhow, and wouldst look well only when stretched upon a fine Cremona violin! ...'

Klaus shuddered, but said nothing. He only bent over the poor maniac, and with a kiss upon his brow, a caress as tender and as gentle as that of a doting mother, he left the sick-room for a few instants, to seek relief in his own garret. When he returned, the ravings were following another channel. Franz was singing, trying to imitate the sounds of a violin.

Towards the evening of that day, the delirium of the sick man became perfectly ghastly. He saw spirits of fire clutching at his violin. Their skeleton hands, from each finger of which grew a flaming claw, beckoned to old Samuel ... They approached and surrounded the old master, and were preparing to rip him open ... him, 'the only man on this earth who loves me with an unselfish, holy love, and ... whose intestines can be of any good at all!' he went on whispering, with glaring eyes and demon laugh ...

By the next morning, however, the fever had disappeared, and by the end of the ninth day Stenio had left his bed, having no recollection of his illness, and no suspicion that he had allowed Klaus to read his inner thought. Nay; had he himself any knowledge that such a horrible idea as the sacrifice of his old master to his ambition had ever entered his mind? Hardly. The only immediate result of his fatal illness was, that as, by reason of his vow, his artistic passion could find no issue, another passion awoke, which might avail to feed his ambition and his insatiable fancy. He plunged headlong into the study of the occult arts, of alchemy, and of magic. In the practice of magic the young dreamer sought to stifle the voice of his passionate longing for his, as he thought, for-ever lost violin . . .

Weeks and months passed away, and the conversation about Paganini was never resumed between the master and the pupil. But a profound melancholy had taken possession of Franz, the two hardly exchanged a word, the violin hung mute, chordless, full of dust, in its habitual place. It was as the presence of a soulless corpse between them.

The young man had become gloomy and sarcastic, even avoiding the mention of music. Once, as his old professor, after long hesitation, took out his own violin from its dust-covered case and prepared to play, Franz gave a convulsive shudder, but said nothing. At the first notes of the bow, however, he glared like a madman, and rushing out of the house, remained for hours, wandering in the streets. Then old Samuel in his turn threw his instrument down, and locked himself up in his room till the following morning.

One night as Franz sat, looking particualrly pale and gloomy, old Samuel suddenly jumped from his seat, and after hopping about the room in a magpie pashion, approached his pupil, imprinted a fond kiss upon the young man's brow, and squeaked at the top of his shrill voice:

'Is it not time to put an end to all this?' . . .

Whereupon, starting from his usual lethargy, Franz echoed, as in a dream:

'Yes, it is time to put an end to this.'

Upon which the two separated, and went to bed.

On the following morning, when Franz awoke, he was astonished not to see his old teacher in his usual place to greet him. But he had greatly altered during the last few months, and he at first paid no attention to his absence, unusual as it was. He dressed and went into the adjoining room, a little parlour where they had their meals, and which separated their two bedrooms. The fire had not been lighted since the embers had died out on the previous night, and no sign was anywhere visible of the professor's busy hand in his usual housekeeping duties. Greatly puzzled, but in no way dismayed, Franz took his usual place at the corner of the now cold fireplace, and fell into an aimless reverie. As he stretched himself in his old armchair, raising both his hands to clasp them behind his head in a favourite posture of his, his hand came into contact with something on a shelf at his back; he knocked against a case, and brought it violently on the ground.

It was old Klaus' violin-case that came down to the floor with such a sudden crash that the case opened and the violin fell out of it, rolling to the feet of Franz. And then the chords, striking against the brass fender emitted a sound, prolonged, sad, and mournful as the sigh of an unrestful soul; it seemed to fill the whole room, and reverberated in the head and the very heart of the young man. The effect of that broken violin-string was magical.

'Samuel!' cried Stenio, with his eyes starting from their sockets, and an unknown terror suddenly taking possession of his whole being. 'Samuel! what has happened? ... My good, my dear old master!' he called out, hastening to the professor's little room, and throwing the door violently open. No one answered, all was silent within.

He staggered back, frightened at the sound of his own voice, so changed and hoarse it seemed to him at this moment. No reply came in response to his call. Naught followed but a dead silence ... that stillness which in the domain of sounds, usually denotes death. In the presence of a corpse, as in the lugubrious stillness of a tomb, such silence acquires a mysterious power, which strikes the sensitive soul with a nameless terror ... The little room was dark, and Franz hastened to open the shutters.

*

Samuel was lying on his bed, cold, stiff, and lifeless ... At the sight of the corpse of him who had loved him so well, and had been to him more than a father, Franz experienced a dreadful revulsion of feeling, a terrible shock. But the ambition of the fanatical artist got the better of the despair of the man, and smothered the feelings of the latter in a few seconds.

A note bearing his own name was conspicuously placed upon a table near the corpse. With trembling hand, the violinist tore open the envelope, and read the following:

My beloved son, Franz,

When you read this, I shall have made the greatest sacrifice, that your best and only friend and teacher could have accomplished for your fame. He, who loved you most, is now but an inanimate lump of clay. Of your old teacher there now remains but a clod of cold organic matter. I need not prompt you as to what you have to do with it. Fear not stupid prejudices. It is for your future fame that I have made an offering of my body, and you would be guilty of the blackest ingratitude were you now to render useless this sacrifice. When you shall have replaced the chords upon your violin, and these chords a portion of my own self, under your touch it will acquire the power of that accursed sorcerer, all the magic voices of Paganini's instrument. You will find therein my voice, my sighs and groans, my song of welcome, the prayerful sobs of my infinite and sorrowful sympathy, my love for you. And now, my Franz, fear nobody! Take your instrument with you, and dog the steps of him who filled our lives with bitterness and despair! ... Appear in every arena, where, hitherto, he has reigned without a rival, and bravely throw the gauntlet of defiance in his face. O Franz! then only wilt thou hear with what a magic power the full notes of unselfish love will issue forth from thy violin. Perchance, with a last caressing touch of its chords, thou wilt remember that they once formed a portion of thine old teacher, who now embraces and blesses thee for the last time.        Samuel

Two burning tears sparkled in the eyes of Franz, but

they dried up instantly. Under the fiery rush of passionate hope and pride, the two orbs of the future magician-artist, riveted to the ghastly face of the dead man, shone like the eyes of a demon.

Our pen refuses to describe that which took place on that day, after the legal inquiry was over. As another note, written with the view of satisfying the authorities, had been prudently provided by the loving care of the old teacher, the verdict was, 'Suicide from causes unknown'; after this the coroner and the police retired, leaving the bereaved heir alone in the death-room, with the remains of that which had once been a living man.

*

Scarcely a fortnight had elapsed from that day, ere the violin had been dusted, and four new, stout strings had been stretched upon it. Franz dared not look at them. He tried to play, but the bow trembled in his hand like a dagger in the grasp of a novice-brigand. He then determined not to try again, until the portentous night should arrive, when he should have a chance of rivalling, nay, of surpassing, Paganini.

The famous violinist had meanwhile left Paris, and was giving a series of triumphant concerts at an old Flemish town in Belgium.

*

One night, as Paganini, surrounded by a crowd of admirers, was sitting in the dining-room of the hotel at which he was staying, a visiting card, with a few words written on it in pencil, was handed to him by a young man with wild and staring eyes.

Fixing upon the intruder a look which few persons could bear, but receiving back a glance as calm and determined as his own, Paganini slightly bowed, and then dryly said:

'Sir, it shall be as you desire. Name the night. I am at your service.'

On the following morning the whole town was startled

120

by the appearance of bills posted at the corner of every street, and bearing the strange notice:

On the night of ... at the Grand Theatre of ... and for the first time, will appear before the public, Franz Stenio, a German violinist, arrived purposely to throw down the gauntlet to the world-famous Paganini and to challenge him to a duel – upon their violins. He purposes to compete with the great 'virtuoso' in the execution of the most difficult of his compositions. The famous Paganini has accepted the challenge. Franz Stenio will play, in competition with the unrivalled violinist, the celebrated 'Fantastic Caprice' of the latter, known as 'The Witches'.

The effect of the notice was magical. Paganini, who, amid his greatest triumphs, never lost sight of a profitable speculation, doubled the usual price of admission, but still the theatre could not hold the crowds that flocked to secure tickets for that memorable performance.

\*

At last the morning of the concert day dawned, and the 'duel' was in every one's mouth. Franz Stenio, who, instead of sleeping, had passed the whole long hours of the preceding midnight in walking up and down his room like an encaged panther, had, toward morning, fallen on his bed from mere physical exhaustion. Gradually he passed into a death-like and dreamless slumber. At the gloomy winter dawn he awoke, but finding it too early to rise he fell asleep again. And then he had a vivid dream – so vivid indeed, so life-like, that from its terrible realism he felt sure that it was a vision rather than a dream.

He had left his violin on a table by his bedside, locked in its case, the key of which never left him. Since he had strung it with those terrible chords he never let it out of his sight for a moment. In accordance with his resolution he had not touched it since his first trial, and his bow had never but once touched the human strings, for he had since always practised on another instrument. But now in his sleep he saw himself looking at the locked one. Something in it was attracting his attention, and he found himself incapable of detaching his eyes from it. Suddenly he saw the upper part of the case slowly rising, and within the chink thus produced, he perceived two small, phosphorescent green eyes – eyes but too familiar to him – fixing themselves on his, lovingly, almost beseechingly. Then a thin, shrill voice, as if issuing from these ghastly orbs – the voice and orbs of Samuel Klaus himself – resounded in Stenio's horrified ear, and he heard it say:

'Franz, my beloved boy ... Franz, I cannot, no, *I cannot* separate myself from ... *them!*'

And 'they' twanged piteously inside the case.

Franz stood speechless, horror-bound. He felt his blood actually freezing, and his hair moving and standing erect on his head ...

'It's but a dream, an empty dream!' he attempted to formulate in his mind.

'I have tried my best, Franzchen ... I have tried my best to sever myself from these accursed strings, without pulling them to pieces ...' pleaded the same shrill familiar voice. 'Wilt thou help me to do so? ...

Another twang, still more prolonged and dismal, resounded within the case, now dragged about the table in every direction, by some interior power, like some living, wriggling thing, the twangs becoming sharper and more jerky with every new pull.

It was not for the first time that Stenio heard those sounds. He had often remarked them before – indeed, ever since he had used his master's viscera as a footstool for his own ambition. But on every occasion a feeling of creeping horror had prevented him from investigating their cause, and he had tried to assure himself that the sounds were only a hallucination.

But now he stood face to face with the terrible fact, whether in dream or in reality he knew not, nor did he care, since the hallucination – if hallucination it were – was far more real and vivid than any reality. He tried to speak, to take a step forward; but, as often happens in nightmares, he could neither utter a word nor move a finger ... He felt hopelessly paralysed.

The pulls and jerks were becoming more desperate with each moment, and at last something inside the case snapped violently. The vision of his Stradivarius, devoid of its magical strings, flashed before his eyes, throwing him into a cold sweat of mute and unspeakable terror.

He made a superhuman effort to rid himself of the incubus that held him spell-bound. But as the last supplicating whisper of the invisible Presence repeated:

'Do, oh, do ... help me to cut myself off –'

Franz sprang to the case with one bound, like an enraged tiger defending its prey, and with one frantic effort breaking the spell.

'Leave the violin alone, you old fiend from hell!' he cried, in hoarse and trembling tones.

He violently shut down the self-raising lid, and while firmly pressing his left hand on it, he seized with the right a piece of rosin from the table and drew on the leather-covered top the sign of the six-pointed star – the seal used by King Solomon to bottle up the rebellious djins inside their prisons.

A wail, like the howl of a she-wolf moaning over her dead little ones, came out of the violin-case:

'Thou art ungrateful ... very ungrateful, my Franz!' sobbed the blubbering 'spirit-voice'. 'But I forgive ... for I still love thee well. Yet thou canst not shut me in ... boy. Behold!'

And instantly a greyish mist spread over and covered case and table, and rising upward formed itself first into an indistinct shape. Then it began growing, and as it grew, Franz felt himself gradually enfolded in cold and damp coils, slimy as those of a huge snake. He gave a terrible cry – awoke; but strangely enough, not on his bed, but near the table, just as he had dreamed, pressing the violin case desperately with both both his hands.

'It was but a dream. ... after all,' he muttered,

still terrified, but relieved of the load on his heaving breast.

With a tremendous effort he composed himself, and unlocked the case to inspect the violin. He found it covered with dust, but otherwise sound and in order, and he suddenly felt himself as cool and as determined as ever. Having dusted the instrument he carefully rosined the bow, tightened the strings and tuned them. He even went so far as to try upon it the first notes of 'The Witches'; first cautiously and timidly, then using his bow boldly and with full force.

The sound of that loud, solitary note – defiant as the war trumpet of a conqueror, sweet and majestic as the touch of a seraph on his golden harp in the fancy of the faithful – thrilled through the very soul of Franz. It revealed to him a hitherto unsuspected potency in his bow, which ran on in strains that filled the room with the richest swell of melody, unheard by the artist until that night. Commencing in uninterrupted *legato* tones, his bow sang to him of sun-bright hope and beauty, of moon-lit nights, when the soft and balmy stillness endowed every blade of grass and all things animate and inanimate with a voice and a song of love. For a few brief moments it was a torrent of melody, the harmony of which, 'tuned to soft woe', was calculated to make mountains weep, had there been any in the room, and to soothe

*. . even th' inexorable powers of hell,*

the presence of which was undeniably felt in this modest hotel room. Suddenly, the solemn *legato* chant, contrary to all laws of harmony, quivered, became *arpeggios*, and ended in shrill *staccatos*, like the notes of a hyena laugh. The same creeping sensation of terror, as he had before felt, came over him, and Franz threw the bow away. He had recognized the familiar laugh, and would have no more of it. Dressing, he locked the bedevilled violin securely in its case, and, taking it with him to the dining-room, determined to await quietly the hour of trial.

*

The terrible hour of the struggle had come, and Stenio was at his post -- calm, resolute, almost smiling.

The theatre was crowded to suffocation, and there was not even standing room to be got for any amount of hard cash or favouritism. The singular challenge had reached every quarter to which the post could carry it, and gold flowed freely into Paganini's unfathomable pockets, to an extent almost satisfying even to his insatiate and venal soul.

It was arranged that Paganini should begin. When he appeared upon the stage, the thick walls of the theatre shook to their foundations with the applause that greeted him. He began and ended his famous composition 'The Witches' amid a storm of cheers. The shouts of public enthusiasm lasted so long that Franz began to think his turn would never come. When, at last, Paganini, amid the roaring applause of a frantic public, was allowed to retire behind the scenes, his eye fell upon Stenio, who was tuning his violin, and he felt amazed at the serene calmness, the air of assurance, of the unknown German artist.

When Franz approached the footlights, he was received with icy coldness. But for all that, he did not feel in the least disconcerted. He looked very pale, but his thin white lips wore a scornful smile as response to this dumb unwelcome. He was sure of his triumph.

At the first notes of the prelude of 'The Witches' a thrill of astonishment passed over the audience. It was Paganini's touch – and it was something more. Some – and they were the majority – thought that never, in his best moments of inspiration, had the Italian artist himself, in executing that diabolical composition of his, exhibited such an extraordinary diabolical power. Under the pressure of the long muscular fingers of Franz, the chords shivered like the palpitating intestines of a disembowelled victim under the vivisector's knife. They moaned melodiously, like a dying child. The large blue

125

eye of the artist, fixed with a satanic expression upon the sounding-board, seemed to summon forth Orpheus himself from the infernal regions, rather than the musical notes supposed to be generated in the depths of the violin. Sounds seemed to transform themselves into objective shapes, thickly and precipitately gathering as at the evocation of a mighty magician, and to be whirling around him, like a host of fantastic, infernal figures, dancing the witches' 'goat dance'. In the empty depths of the shadowy background of the stage, behind the artist, a nameless phantasmagoria produced by the concussion of unearthly vibrations, seemed to form pictures of shameless orgies, of the voluptuous hymens of a real witches' sabbat ... A collective hallucination took hold of the public. Panting for breath, ghastly, and trickling with the icy perspiration of an inexpressible horror they sat spell-bound, and unable to break the spell of the music by the slightest motion. They experienced all the illicit enervating delights of the paradise of Mahommed, that come into the disordered fancy of an opium-eating Mussulman, and felt at the same time the abject terror, the agony of one who struggles against an attack of *delirium tremens* ... Many ladies shrieked aloud, others fainted, and strong men gnashed their teeth in a state of utter helplessness...

Then came the *finale*. Thundering uninterrupted applause delayed its beginning, expanding the momentary pause to a duration of almost a quarter of an hour. The bravos were furious, almost hysterical. At last, when after a profound and last bow, Stenio, whose smile was as sardonic as it was triumphant, lifted his bow to attack the famous *finale*, his eye fell upon Paganini, who, calmly seated in the manager's box, had been behind none in zealous applause. The small and piercing black eyes of the Genoese artist were riveted to the Stradivarius in the hands of Franz, but otherwise he seemed quite cool and unconcerned. His rival's face troubled him for one short instant, but he regained his self-possession and, lifting once more his bow, drew the first note.

Then the public enthusiasm reached its acme, and

soon knew no bounds. The listeners heard and saw indeed. The witches' voices resounded in the air, and beyond all the other voices, one voice was heard –

> *Discordant, and unlike to human sounds;*
> *It seem'd of dogs the bark, of wolves the howl;*
> *The doleful screechings of the midnight owl;*
> *The hiss of snakes, the hungry lion's roar;*
> *The sounds of billows beating on the shore;*
> *The groan of winds among the leafy wood,*
> *And burst of thunder from the rending cloud;*
> *'Twas these, all these in one ...*

The magic bow was drawing forth its last quivering sounds – famous among prodigious musical feats – imitating the precipitate flight of the witches before bright dawn; of the unholy women saturated with the fumes of their nocturnal Saturnalia, when – a strange thing came to pass on the stage. Without the slightest transition, the notes suddenly changed. In their aerial flight of ascension and descent, their melody was unexpectedly altered in character. The sounds became confused, scattered, disconnected ... and then – it seemed from the sounding-board of the violin – came out squeaking, jarring tones, like those of a street Punch, screaming at the top of a senile voice:

'Art thou satisfied, Franz, my boy?.. Have not I gloriously kept my promise, eh?'

The spell was broken. Though still unable to realize the whole situation, those who heard the voice and the *Punchinello*-like tones, were freed, as by enchantment, from the terrible charm under which they had been held. Loud roars of laughter, mocking exclamations of half-anger and half-irritation were now heard from every corner of the vast theatre. The musicians in the orchestra, with faces still blanched from weird emotion, were now seen shaking with laughter, and the whole audience rose, like one man, from their seats, unable yet to solve the enigma; they felt, nevertheless, too disgusted, too disposed to laugh to remain one moment longer in the building.

But suddenly the sea of moving heads in the stalls and the pit became once more motionless, and stood petrified as though struck by lightning. What all saw was terrible enough – the handsome though wild face of the young artist suddenly aged, and his graceful, erect figure bent down, as though under the weight of years; but this was nothing to that which some of the most sensitive clearly perceived. Franz Stenio's person was now entirely enveloped in a semi-transparant mist, cloud-like, creeping with serpentine motion, and gradually tightening round the living form, as though ready to engulf him. And there were those also who discerned in this tall and ominous pillar of smoke a clearly defined figure, a form showing the unmistakable outlines of a grotesque and grinning, but terribly awful-looking old man, whose viscera were protruding and the ends of the intestines stretched on the violin.

Within this hazy, quivering veil, the violinist was then seen, driving his bow furiously across human chords, with the contortions of a demoniac, as we see them represented on medeval cathedral paintings!

An indescribable panic swept over the audience, and breaking now, for the last time, through the spell which had again bound them motionless, every living creature in the theatre made one mad rush towards the door. It was like the sudden outburst of a dam, a human torrent, roaring amid a shower of discordant notes, idiotic squeakings, prolonged and whining moans, cacophonous cries of frenzy, above which, like the detonations of pistol shots, was heard the consecutive bursting of the four strings stretched upon the sound-board of that bewitched violin.

*

When the theatre was emptied of the last man of the audience, the terrified manager rushed on the stage in search of the unfortunate performer. He was found dead and already stiff, behind the footlights, twisted up into the most unnatural postures, with the 'catguts' wound curiously around his neck, and his violin shattered into a thousand fragments ...

When it became publicly known that the unfortunate would-be rival of Niccolo Paganini had not left a cent to pay for his funeral or his hotel bill, the Genoese, his proverbial meanness notwithstanding, settled the hotel bill and had poor Stenio buried at his own expense.

He claimed, however, in exchange, the fragments of the Stradivarius – as a memento of the strange event.

# NASTY

## by Frederic Brown

Walter Beauregard had been an accomplished and enthusiastic lecher for almost fifty years. Now, at the age of sixty-five, he was in danger of losing his qualifications for membership in the lecher's union. In danger of losing? Nay, let us be honest; he had *lost*. For three years now he had been to doctor after doctor, quack after quack, had tried nostrum. All utterly to no avail.

Finally he remembered his books on magic and necromancy. They were books he had enjoyed collecting and reading as part of his extensive library, but he had never taken them seriously. Until now. What did he have to lose?

In a musty, evil-smelling but rare volume he found what he wanted. As it instructed, he drew the pentagram, copied the cabalistic markings, lighted the candles, and read aloud the incantation.

There was a flash of light and a puff of smoke. And the demon. I won't describe the demon except to assure you that you wouldn't have liked him.

'What is your name?' Beauregard asked. He tried to make his voice steady but it trembled a little.

The demon made a sound somewhere between a shriek and a whistle, with overtones of a bull fiddle being played with a crosscut saw. Then he said, 'But you won't be able to pronounce that. In your dull language it would translate as Nasty. Just call me Nasty. I suppose you want the usual thing.'

'What's the usual thing?' Beauregard wanted to know.

'A wish of course. All right, you can have it. But not three wishes: that business about three wishes is sheer superstition. One is all you get and you won't like it.'

'One is all I want. And I can't imagine not liking it.'

'You'll find out. All right. I know what your wish is. And here is the answer to it.' Nasty reached into thin air and his hand vanished and came back holding a pair of silvery-looking swimming trunks. He held them out to Beauregard. 'Wear them in good health,' he said.

'What are they?'

'What do they look like? Swimming trunks. But they're special. The material is out of the future, a few millenniums from now. It's indestructible, they'll never wear out or tear or snag. Nice stuff. But the spell on them is a plenty old one. Try them on and find out.'

The demon vanished.

Walter Beauregard quickly stripped and put on the beautiful silvery swimming trunks. Immeditately he felt wonderful. Virility coursed through him, he felt as though he were a young man again, just starting his lecherous career.

Quickly he put on a robe and slippers. (Have I mentioned that he was a rich man? And that his home was a penthouse atop the swankiest hotel in Atlantic City? He was, and it was.) He went downstairs in his private elevator and outside to the hotel's luxurious swimming pool. It was, as usual, surrounded by gorgeous bikini-clad beauties showing off their wares under the pretence of acquiring sun-tans, while they waited for propositions from wealthy men like Beauregard.

He took time choosing. But not too much time.

Two hours later, still clad in the wonderful magic trunks, he sat on the edge of his bed and stared and sighed for the beautiful blonde who lay stretched out on the bed beside him, bikiniless – and sound asleep.

Nasty had been so right. And so well named. The miraculous trunks, the indestructible, untearable trunks worked perfectly. But if he took them off, or even let them down ...

# THE NEW PEOPLE

## by Charles Beaumont

If only he had told her right at the beginning that he didn't like the house, everything would have been fine. He could have manufactured some plausible story about bad plumbing or poor construction – something; anything! – and she'd have gone along with him. Not without a fight, maybe: he could remember the way her face had looked when they stopped the car. But he could have talked her out of it. Now, of course, it was too late.

For what? he wondered, trying not to think of the party and all the noise that it would mean. Too late for what? It's a good house, well built, well kept up, roomy. Except for that blood stain, cheerful. Anyone in his right mind . .

'Dear, aren't you going to shave?'

He lowered the newspaper gently and said, 'Sure.' But Ann was looking at him in that hurt, accusing way, and he knew that it was hopeless.

*Hank-what's-wrong*, he thought, starting towards the bathroom.

'Hank,' she said.

He stopped but did not turn. 'Uh-huh?'

'What's wrong?'

'Nothing,' he said.

'Honey. Please.'

He faced her. The pink chiffon dress clung to her body, which had the firmness of youth; her face was unblemished, the lipstick and powder incredibly perfect; her hair, cut long, was soft on her white shoulders: in seven years Ann hadn't changed.

Resentfully, Prentice glanced away. And was ashamed. You'd think that in this time I'd get accustomed to it, he thought. *She* is. Damn it!

'Tell me,' Ann said.

'Tell you what? Everything is okay,' he said.

She came to him and he could smell the perfume, he could see the tiny freckles that dotted her chest. He wondered what it would be like to sleep with her. Probably it would be very nice.

'It's about Davey, isn't it?' she said, dropping her voice to a whisper. They were standing only a few feet from their son's room.

'No,' Prentice said; but, it was true – Davey was part of it. For a week now Prentice had ridden on the hope that getting the locomotive repaired would change things. A kid without a train, he'd told himself, is bound to act peculiar. But he'd had the locomotive repaired and brought it home and Davey hadn't even bothered to set up the track.

'He appreciated it, dear,' Ann said. 'Didn't he thank you?'

'Sure, he thanked me.'

'Well?' she said. 'Honey, I've *told* you: Davey is going through a period, that's all. Children do. Really.'

'I know.'

'And school's been out for almost a month.'

'I know,' Prentice said, and thought: *Moving to a neighbourhood where there isn't another kid in the whole damn block for him to play with, that might have something to do with it, too!*

'Then,' Ann said, 'it's me.'

'No, no, no.' He tried a smile. There wasn't any sense in arguing: they'd been through it a dozen times, and she had an answer for everything. He could recall the finality in her voice ... 'I love the house, Hank. And I love the neighbourhood. It's what I've dreamed of all my life, and I think I deserve it. Don't you?' (It was the first time she'd ever consciously reminded him.) 'The trouble is, you've lived in dingy little apartments so long you've come to *like* them. You can't adjust to a really *decent* place – and Davey's no different. You're two of a kind:

little old men who can't stand a change, even for the better! Well, I can. I don't care if *fifty* people committed suicide here, I'm happy. You understand, Hank? Happy.'

Prentice had understood, and had resolved to make a real effort to like the new place. If he couldn't do that, at least he could keep his feelings from Ann – for they were, he knew, foolish. Damned foolish. Everything she said was true, and he ought to be grateful.

Yet, somehow, he could not stop dreaming of the old man who had picked up a razor one night and cut his his throat wide open . . .

Ann was staring at him.

'Maybe,' he said, 'I'm going through a period too.' He kissed her forehead, lightly. 'Come on, now; the people are going to arrive any second, and you look like Lady Macbeth.'

She held his arm for a moment. 'You are getting settled in the house, aren't you?' she said. 'I mean, it's becoming more like home to you, isn't it?'

'Sure,' Prentice said.

His wife paused another moment, then smiled. 'Okay, get the whiskers off. Rhoda is under the impression you're a handsome man.'

He walked into the bathroom and plugged in the electric shaver. Rhoda, he thought. First names already and we haven't been here three weeks.

'Dad?'

He looked down at Davey, who had slipped in with nine-year-old stealth. 'Yo.' According to ritual, he ran the shaver across his son's chin.

Davey did not respond. He stepped back and said, 'Dad, is Mr Ames coming over tonight?'

Prentice nodded. 'I guess so.'

'And Mr Chambers?'

'Uh-huh. Why?'

Davey did not answer.

'What do you want to know for?'

'Gee.' Davey's eyes were red and wide. 'Is it okay if I stay in my room?'

'Why? You sick?'

'No. Kind of.'

'Stomach? Head?'

'Just sick,' Davey said. He pulled at a thread in his shirt and fell silent again.

Prentice frowned. 'I thought maybe you'd like to show them your train,' he said.

'Please,' Davey said. His voice had risen slightly and Prentice could see tears gathering. 'Dad, please don't make me come out. Leave me stay in my room. I won't make any noise, I promise, and I'll go to sleep on time.'

'Okay, okay. Don't make such a big deal out of it!' Prentice ran the cool metal over his face. Anger came and went, swiftly. Stupid to get mad. 'Davey, what'd you do, ride your bike on their lawn or something? Break a window?'

'No.'

'Then why don't you want to see them?'

'I just don't.'

'Mr Ames likes you. He told me so yesterday. He thinks you're a fine boy, so does Mr Chambers. They –'

'*Please*, Dad!' Davey's face was pale; he began to cry. 'Please, please, please. Don't let them get me!'

'What are you talking about? Davey, cut it out. Now!'

'I saw what they were doing there in the garage. And they know I saw them, too. They know. And –'

'Davey!' Ann's voice was sharp and loud and resounding in the tile-lined bathroom. The boy stopped crying immediately. He looked up, hesitated, then ran out. His door slammed.

Prentice took a step.

'No, Hank. Leave him alone.'

'He's upset.'

'Let him be upset.' She shot an angry glance towards the bedroom. 'I suppose he told you that filthy story about the garage?'

'No,' Prentice said, 'he didn't. What's it all about?'

'Nothing. Absolutely nothing. Honestly, I'd like to meet Davey's parents!'

'We're his parents,' Prentice said, firmly.

'All right, all right. But he got that imagination of his from *some*body, and it wasn't from us. You're going to have to speak to him, Hank. I mean it. Really.'

'About what?'

'These wild stories. What if they got back to Mr Ames? I'd – well, I'd die. After he's gone out of his way to be nice to Davey, too.'

'I haven't heard the stories,' Prentice said.

'Oh, you will.' Ann undid her apron and folded it, furiously. 'Honestly! Sometimes I think the two of you are trying to make things just as miserable as they can be for me.'

The doorbell rang, stridently.

'Now make an effort to be pleasant, will you? This is a *house*warming, after all. And do hurry.'

She closed the door. He heard her call, Hi!' and heard Ben Roth's baritone booming: 'Hi!'

Ridiculous, he told himself, plugging the razor in again. Utterly goddam ridiculous. No one complained louder than I did when we were tripping over ourselves in that little upstairs coffin on Friar. *I'm* the one who kept moaning for a house, not Ann.

So now we've got one.

He glanced at the tiny brownish blood stain that wouldn't wash out of the wallpaper, and sighed.

Now we've got one.

'Hank!'

'Coming!' He straightened his tie and went into the living room.

The Roths, of course, were there. Ben and Rhoda. Get it right, he thought, because we're all going to be pals. 'Hi, Ben.'

'Thought you'd deserted us. boy,' said the large, pink man, laughing.

'No. Wouldn't do that.'

'Hank,' Ann signalled. 'You've met Beth Cummings, haven't you?'

The tall, smartly dressed woman giggled and extended

her hand. 'We've seen each other,' she said. 'Hello.'

Her husband, a pale man with white hair, crushed Prentice's fingers. 'Fun and games,' he said, tightening his grip and wheezing with amusement. 'Yes, sir.'

Trying not to wince, Prentice retrieved his hand. It was instantly snatched up by a square, bald man in a double-breasted brown suit. 'Reiker,' the man said. 'Call me Bud. Everyone does. Don't know why; my name is Oscar.'

'*That's* why,' a woman said, stepping up. 'Ann introduced us but you probably don't remember, if I know men. I'm Edna.'

'Sure,' Prentice said. 'How are you?'

'Fine. But then, I'm a woman: I *like* parties!'

'How's that?'

'Hank!'

Prentice excused himself and walked quietly into the kitchen. Ann was holding up a package.

'Honey, look what Rhoda gave us!'

He dutifully handled the salt and pepper shakers and set them down again. 'That's real nice.'

'You turn the rooster's head,' Mrs Roth said, 'and it grinds your pepper.'

'Wonderful,' Prentice said.

'And Beth gave us this lovely salad bowl, see? And we've needed *this* for *cen*turies!' She held out a grey tablecloth with gold bordering. 'Plastic!'

'Wonderful,' Prentice said. Again, the doorbell rang. He glanced at Mrs Roth, who had been staring thoughtfully at him, and returned to the living room.

'How you be, Hank?' Lucian Ames walked in, rubbing his hands together briskly. 'Well! The gang's all here, I see. But where's that boy of yours?'

'Davey? Oh,' Prentice said, 'he's sick.'

'Nonsense! Boys that age are never sick. Never!'

Ann laughed nervously from the kitchen. 'Just something he ate!'

'Not the candy we sent over, I hope.'

'Oh, no.'

'Well, tell him his Uncle Lucian said hello.'

A tan elf of man, with sparkling eyes and an ill fitting moustache, Ames reminded Prentice somewhat of those clerks who used to sit silently on high wooden stools, posting infintesimal figures in immense yellow ledgers. He was, however, the head of a nationally famous advertizing agency.

His wife Charlotte provided a remarkable contrast. She seemed to belong to the era of the twenties, with her porcelain face, her thin, delicately angular body, her air of fragility.

Nice, Prentice told himself.

He removed coats and hung them in closets. He shook hands and smiled until his face began to ache. He looked at presents and thanked the women and told them they shouldn't have. He carried out sandwiches. He mixed drinks.

By eight-thirty, everyone in the block had arrived. The Johnsons, the Ameses, the Roths, the Reikers, the Klementaskis, the Chamberses; four or five others whose names Prentice could not remember, although Ann had taken care to introduce them.

What it is, he decided, looking at the people, at the gifts they had brought, remembering their many kindnesses and how, already, Ann had made more friends than she'd ever had before, is, I'm just an anti-social bastard.

After the third round of whiskys and martinis, someone turned on the FM and someone else suggested dancing. Prentice had always supposed that one danced only at New Year's Eve parties, but he said the hell with it, finally, and tried to relax.

'Shall we?' Mrs Ames said.

He wanted to say no, but Ann was watching. So he said, 'Sure, if you've got strong toes,' instead.

Almost at once he began to perspire. The smoke, the drinks, the heat of the crowded room, caused his head to ache; and as usual, he was actutely embarrassed at having to hold a strange woman so closely.

But, he continued to smile.

Mrs Ames danced well, she followed him with unerring instinct; and within moments she was babbling freely into his ear. She told him about old Mr Thomas, the man who had lived here before, and how surprised everyone had been at what had happened; she told him how curious they'd all been about The New People and how relieved they were to find him and Ann so very nice; she told him he had strong arms. Ann was being twirled about by Herb Johnson. She was smiling.

An endless, slow three-step came on, then, and Mrs Ames put her cheek next to Prentice's. In the midst of a rambling sentence, she said, suddenly, in a whisper: 'You know, I think it was awfully brave of you to adopt little Davey. I mean, considering.'

'Considering what?'

She pulled away and looked at him. 'Nothing,' she said. 'I'm awfully sorry.'

Blushing with fury, Prentice turned and strode into the kitchen. He fought his anger, thinking, God, God, is she telling strangers about it now? Is it a topic for back fence gossip? *'My husband is impotent, you know. Is yours?'*

He poured whisky into a glass and drank it fast. It made his eyes water, and when he opened them, he saw a figure standing next to him.

It was – who? Dystal. Matthew Dystal; bachelor; movie writer or something; lives down the block. Call him Matt.

'Miserable, isn't it?' the man said, taking the bottle from Prentice's hand.

'What do you mean?'

'Everything,' the man said. He filled his glass and drained it smartly. 'Them. Out there.' He filled the glass again.

'Nice people,' Prentice forced himself to say.

'You think so?'

The man was drunk. Clearly, very drunk. And it was only nine-thirty.

'You think so?' he repeated.

'Sure. Don't you?'

'Of course. I'm one of them, aren't I?'

Prentice peered at his guest closely, then moved towards the living room.

Dystal took his arm. 'Wait,' he said. 'Listen. You're a good guy. I don't know you very well, but I like you, Hank Prentice. So I'm going to give you some advice.' His voice dropped to a whisper. 'Get out of here,' he said.

'What?'

'Just what I said. Move away, move away to another city.'

Prentice felt a quick ripple of annoyance, checked it. 'Why?' he asked, smiling.

'Never mind that,' Dystal said. 'Just do it. Tonight. Will you?' His face was livid, clammy with perspiration; his eyes were wide.

'Well, I mean, Matt, that's a heck of a thing to say. I thought you said you liked us. Now you want to get rid of us.'

'Don't joke,' Dystal said. He pointed at the window. 'Can't you see the moon? You bloody idiot, can't you –'

'Hey, hey! Unfair!'

At the sound of the voice, Dystal froze. He closed his eyes for a moment and opened them, slowly. But he did not move.

Lucian Ames walked into the kitchen. 'What's the story here,' he said, putting his arm on Dystal's shoulder, 'you trying to monopolize our host all night?'

Dystal did not answer.

'How about a refill, Hank?' Ames said, removing his hand.

Prentice said, 'Sure,' and prepared the drink. From the corner of his eye, he saw Dystal turn and walk stiffly out of the room. He heard the front door open and close.

Ames was chuckling. 'Poor old Matt,' he said. 'He'll be hung over tomorrow. It seems kind of a shame, doesn't it? I mean, you know, of all people, you'd think a big Hollywood writer would be able to hold his liquor. But not Matt. He gets loaded just by staring at the labels.'

Prentice said, 'Huh.'

'Was he giving you one of his screwball nightmares?'

'What? No – we were just sort of talking. About things.'

Ames dropped an ice cube into his drink. 'Things?' he said.

'Yeah.'

Ames took a sip of the whisky and walked to the window, looking lithe, somehow, as well as small. After what seemed a long time, he said, 'Well, it's a fine night, isn't it. Nice and clear, nice fine moon.' He turned and tapped a cigarette out of a red package, lighted the cigarette. 'Hank,' he said, letting the grey smoke gush from the corners of his mouth, 'tell me something. What do you do for excitement?'

Prentice shrugged. It was an odd question, but then everything seemed odd to him tonight. 'I don't know,' he said. 'Go to a movie once in a while. Watch TV. The usual.'

Ames cocked his head. 'But – don't you get bored?' he asked.

'Sure, I guess. Every so often. Being a C.P.A., you know, that isn't exactly the world's most fascinating job.'

Ames laughed sympathetically. 'It's awful, isn't it?'

'Being a C.P.A.?'

'No. Being bored. It's about the worst thing in the world, don't you agree? Someone once remarked they thought it was the only real sin a human could commit.'

'I hope not,' Prentice said.

'Why?'

'Well, I mean – everybody gets bored, don't they?'

'Not,' Ames said, 'if they're careful.'

Prentice found himself becoming increasingly irritated at the conversation. 'I suppose it helps,' he said, 'if you're the head of an advertizing agency.'

'No, not really. It's like any other job: interesting at first, but then you get used to it. It becomes routine. So you go fishing for other diversions.'

'Like what?'

'Oh ... anything. Everything.' Ames slapped Prentice's

arm good-naturedly. 'You're all right, Hank,' he said.

'Thanks.'

'I mean it. Can't you tell how happy we all are that you moved here.'

'No more than we are!' Ann walked unsteadily to the sink with a number of empty glasses. 'I want to apologize for Davey again, Lucian. I was telling Charlotte, he's been a perfect beast, lately. He should have thanked you for fixing the seat on his bike.'

'Forget it,' Ames said, cheerfully. 'The boy's just upset because he doesn't have any playmates.' He looked at Prentice. 'Some of us elders have kids, Hank, but they're all practically grown. You probably know that our daughter, Ginnie, is away at college. And Chris and Beth's boy lives in New York. But, you know, I wouldn't worry. As soon as school starts, Davey'll straighten out. You watch.'

Ann smiled. 'I'm sure you're right, Lucian. But I apologize, anyway.'

'Nuts.' Ames returned to the living room and began to dance with Beth Cummings.

Prentice thought then of asking Ann what the devil she meant by blabbing about their personal life to strangers, but decided not to. This was not the time. He was too angry, too confused.

The party lasted another hour. Then Beth Roth said, 'Better let these good folks get some sleep!' and, slowly, the people left.

Ann closed the door. She seemed to glow with contentment, looking younger and prettier than she had for several years. 'Home,' she said, softly, and began picking up ash trays and glasses and plates. 'Let's get all this out of the way so we won't have to look at it in the morning,' she said.

Prentice said, 'All right,' in a neutral tone. He was about to move the coffee table back into place when the telephone rang.

'Yes?'

The voice that answered was a harsh whisper, like a

rush of wind through leaves. 'Prentice, are they gone?'

'Who is this?'

'Matt Dystal. Are they gone?'

'Yes.'

'All of them? Ames? Is he gone?'

'Yes. What do you want, Dystal? It's late.'

'Later than you might think, Prentice. He told you I was drunk, but he lied. I'm not drunk. I'm –'

'Look, what is it you want?'

'I've got to talk with you,' the voice said. 'Now. To-night. Can you come over?'

'At eleven o'clock?'

'Yes. Prentice, listen to me. I'm not drunk and I'm not kidding. This is a matter of life and death. Yours. Do you understand what I'm saying?'

Prentice hesitated, confused.

'You know where my place is – fourth house from the corner, right-hand side. Come over now. But listen, care-fully: go out the back door. The back door. Prentice, are you listening?'

'Yes,' Prentice said.

'My lights will be off. Go around to the rear. Don't bother to knock, just walk in – but be quiet about it. They mustn't see you.'

Prentice heard a click, then silence. He stared at the receiver for a while before replacing it.

'Well?' Ann said. 'Man talk?'

'Not exactly.' Prentice wiped his palms on his trousers. 'That fellow Matt Dystal, he's apparently sick. Wants me to come over.'

'Now?'

'Yeah. I think I better; he sounded pretty bad. You go on to sleep, I'll be back in a little while.'

'Okay, honey. I hope it isn't anything serious. But it *is* nice to be doing something for *them* for a change, isn't it?'

Prentice kissed his wife, waited until the bathroom door had closed; then he went outside, into the cold night.

He walked along the grass verge of the alleyway, across the small lawns, up the steps to Dystal's rear door.

He deliberated with himself for a moment, then walked in.

'Prentice?' a voice hissed.

'Yes. Where are you?'

A hand touched his arm in the darkness and he jumped; nervously. 'Come into the bedroom.'

A dim lamp went on. Prentice saw that the windows were covered by heavy tan drapes. It was chilly in the room, chilly and moist.

'Well?' Prentice said, irritably.

Matthew Dystal ran a hand through his rope-coloured hair. 'I know what you're thinking,' he said. 'And I don't blame you. But it was necessary, Prentice. It was necessary. Ames has told you about my "wild nightmares" and that's going to stick with you, I realize; but get this straight.' His hand became a fist. 'Everything I'm about to say is true. No matter how outlandish it may sound, it's *true* – and I have proof. All you'll need. So keep still, Prentice, and listen to me. It may mean your life: yours and your wife's and your boy's. And, maybe, mine . . .' His voice trailed off; then, suddenly, he said, 'You want a drink?'

'No.'

'You ought to have one. You're only on the outskirts of confusion, my friend. But, there are worse things than confusion. Believe me.' Dystal walked to a bookcase and stood there for almost a full minute. When he turned, his features were slightly more composed. 'What do you know,' he asked, 'about the house you're living in?'

Prentice shifted uncomfortably. 'I know that a man killed himself in it, if that's what you mean.'

'But do you know why?'

'No.'

'Because he lost,' Dystal said, giggling. 'He drew the short one. How's that for motivation?'

'I think I'd better go,' Prentice said.

'Wait.' Dystal took a handkerchief from his pocket and

tapped his forehead. 'I didn't mean to begin that way. It's just that I've never told this to anyone, and it's difficult. You'll see why. Please, Prentice, promise you won't leave until I've finished!'

Prentice looked at the wiry, nervous little man and cursed the weakness that had allowed him to get himself into this miserably uncomfortable situation. He wanted to go home. But he knew he could not leave now.

'All right,' he said. 'Go on.'

Dystal sighed. Then, staring at the window, he began to talk. 'I built this house,' he said, 'because I thought I was going to get married. By the time I found out I was wrong, the work was all done. I should have sold it, I know, I see that, but I was feeling too lousy to go through the paper work. Besides, I'd already given up my apartment. So I moved in.' He coughed. 'Be patient with me, Prentice: this is the only way to tell it, from the beginning. Where was I?'

'You moved in.'

'Yes! Everybody was very nice. They invited me to their homes for dinner, they dropped by, they did little favours for me; and it helped, it really did. I thought, you know, what a hell of a great bunch of neighbours. Regular. *Real*. That was it: they were real. Ames, an advertising man; Thomas, a lawyer; Johnson, paint company; Chambers, insurance; Reiker and Cummings, engineers – I mean, how average can you get?' Dystal paused; an ugly grin appeared on his face, disappeared. 'I liked them,' he said. 'And I was really delighted with things. But, of course, you know how it is when a woman gives you the business. I was still licking my wounds. And I guess it showed, because Ames came over one evening. Just dropped by, in a neighbourly way. We had some drinks. We talked about the ways of the female. Then, bang, out of nowhere, he asked me the question. Was I bored?' --

Prentice stiffened.

'Well, when you lost your girl, you lost a lot of your ambition. I told him yes, I was plenty bored. And he said,

145

"I used to be." I remember his exact words. "I used to be," he said. "The long haul to success, the fight, the midnight oil: it was over. I'd made it," he said. "Dough in the bank. Partnership in a toy agency. Daughter grown and away to school. I was ready to be put out to pasture, Matt. But the thing was, I was only fifty-two! I had maybe another twenty years left. And almost everybody else in the block was the same way – Ed and Ben and Oscar, all the same. You know: they fooled around with their jobs, but they weren't interested any more – not really. Because the jobs didn't *need* them any more. They were bored." ' Dystal walked to the nightstand and poured himself a drink. 'That was five years ago,' he murmured. 'Ames, he pussy-footed around the thing for a while – feeling me out, testing me; then he told me that he had decided to do something about it. About being bored. He'd organized everyone in the block. Once a week, he explained, they played games. It was real Group Activity. Community effort. It began with charades, but they got tired of that in a while. Then they tried cards. To make it interesting, they bet high. Everybody had his turn at losing. Then Ames said, someone suggested making the game even *more* interesting, because it was getting to be a drag. So they experimented with strip poker one night. Just for fun, you understand, Rhoda lost. Next time it was Charlotte. And it went that way for a while, until finally, Beth lost. Everyone had been waiting for it. Things became anticlimatic after that, though, so the stakes changed again. Each paired off with another's wife; lowest scoring team had to –' Dystal tipped the bottle. 'Sure you won't have a bracer?'

Prentice accepted the drink without argument. It tasted bitter and powerful, but it helped.

'Well,' Dystal went on, 'I had one hell of a time believing all that. I mean, you know: *Ames*, after all – a little book-keeper type with grey hair and glasses ... Still, the way he talked, I knew – somehow, I *knew* – it was the truth. Maybe because I didn't feel that a guy like Ames could make it all up! Anyway: when they'd tried all the possible combinations, things got dull again. A few of the women wanted to stop, but, of course, they were in too deep already. During one particular Fun Night, Ames had taken photographs. So, they had to keep going. Every week, it was something new. Something different. Swapsies occupied them for a while, Ames told me: Chambers took a two-week vacation with Jacqueline, Ben and Beth went to Acapulco, and that sort of thing. And that is where I came into the picture.' Dystal raised his hand. 'I know, you don't need to tell me, I should have pulled out. But I was younger then. I was a big writer, man of the world. Training in Hollywood. I couldn't tell him I was shocked: it would have been betraying my craft. And he figured it that way, too: that's why he told me. Besides, he knew I'd be bound to find out everything eventually. They could hide it from just about everybody, but not someone right in the block. So, I played along. I accepted his invitation to join the next Group Activity – which is what he calls them.

'Next morning, I thought I'd dreamed the whole visit, I really did. But on Saturday, sure enough, the phone rings and Ames says, "We begin at eight, sharp." When I got to his house, I found it packed. Everybody in the neighbourhood. Looking absolutely the same as always too. Drinks; dancing; the whole bit. After a while, I started to wonder if the whole thing wasn't an elaborate gag. But at ten, Ames told us about the evening's surprise.' Dystal gave way to a shudder. 'It was a surprise, all right,' he said. 'I told them I wanted nothing to do with it, but Ames had done something to my drink. I didn't seem to have any control. They led me into the bedroom, and ...

Prentice waited, but Dystal did not complete his sentence. His eyes were dancing now.

'Never mind,' he said. 'Never mind what happened! The point is, I was drunk, and – well, I went through with it. I *had* to. You can see that, can't you?'

Prentice said that he could see that.

'Ames pointed out to me that the only sin, the *only*

one. was being bored. That was his justification, that was his incentive. He simply didn't want to sin, that was all. So the Group Activities went on. And they got worse. Much worse. One thing, they actually plotted a crime and carried it off: the Union bank robbery, maybe you read about it: 1953. I drove the car for them. Another time, they decided it would ward off ennui by setting fire to a warehouse down by the docks. The fire spread. Prentice – do you happen to remember that DC-7 that went down between here and Detroit?'

Prentice said, 'Yes, I remember.'

'Their work,' Dystal said. 'Ames planned it. In a way, I think he's a genius. I could spend all night telling you the things we did, but there isn't time. I've got to skip.' He placed his fingers over his eyes. 'Joan of Arc,' he said, 'was the turning point. Ames had decided that it would be diverting to re-enact famous scenes from literature. So he and Bud went down to Main Street, I think it was, and found a beat doll who thought the whole thing would be fun. They gave her twenty-five dollars, but she never got a chance to spend it. I remember that she laughed right up to the point where Ames lit the pile of oil-soaked rags ... Afterwards, they re-enacted other scenes. The execution of Marie Antoinette. The murder of Hamlet's father. You know *The Man in the Iron Mask*? They did that one. And a lot more. It lasted quite a while, too, but Ames began to get restless.' Dystal held out his hands suddenly and stared at them. 'The next game was a form of Russian roulette. We drew straws. Whoever got the short one had to commit suicide – in his own way. It was understood that if he failed, it would mean something much worse – and Ames had developed some damned interesting techniques, like the nerve clamps, for instance. Thomas lost the game, anyway. They gave him twelve hours to get it over with.'

Prentice felt a cold film of perspiration over his flesh. He tried to speak, but found that it was impossible. The man, of course, was crazy. Completely insane. But – he had to hear the end of the story. 'Go on,' he said.

Dystal ran his tongue across his lower lip, poured another drink and continued. 'Cummings and Chambers got scared then,' he said. 'They argued that some stranger would move into the house and then there'd be all sorts of trouble. We had a meeting at Reiker's, and Chris came out with the idea of us all chipping in and buying the place. But Ames didn't go for it. "Let's not be so darned exclusive," he said. "After all, the new people might be bored, too. Lord knows we could use some fresh blood in the Group." Cummings was pessimistic. He said, "What if you're wrong? What if they don't want to join us?" Ames laughed it off. "I hope," he said, "that you don't think we're the only ones. Why, every city has its neighbourhoods just like ours. We're really not that unique." And then he went on to say that if the new people didn't work out, he would take care of the situation. He didn't say how.'

Dystal looked out the window again.

'I can see that he's almost ready to give you an invitation, Prentice. Once that happens, you're finished. It's join them or accept the only alternative.'

Suddenly the room was very quiet.

'You don't believe me, do you?'

Prentice opened his mouth.

'No, of course you don't. It's a madman's ravings. Well, I'm going to prove it to you, Prentice.' He started for the door. 'Come on. Follow me; but don't make any noise.'

Dystal walked out the back door, closed it, moved soundlessly across the soft, black grass.

'They're on a mystic kick right now,' he whispered to Prentice. 'Ames is trying to summon the devil. Last week we slaughtered a dog and read the Commandments backward; the week before, we did some chants out of an old book that Ben found in the library; before that it was orgies –' He shook his head. 'It isn't working out, though. God knows why. You'd think the devil would be so delighted with Ames that he'd sign him up for the team.'

Prentice followed his neighbour across the yards, walking carefully, and wondering why. He thought of his neat

149

little office on Harmon Street, old Mrs Gleason, the clean, well-lighted restaurant where he had his lunch and read newspaper headlines; and they seemed terribly far away.

Why, he asked himself, am I creeping around back-yards with a lunatic at midnight?

Why?

'The moon is full tonight, Prentice. That means they'll be trying again.'

Silently, without the slightest sound, Matthew Dystal moved across the lawns, keeping always to the shadows. A minute later he raised his hand and stopped.

They were at the rear of the Ameses' house.

It was dark inside.

'Come on,' Dystal whispered.

'Wait a minute.' Somehow, the sight of his own living room, still blazing with light, reassured Prentice. 'I think I've had enough for this evening.'

'Enough?' Dystal's face twisted grotesquely. He bunched the sleeve of Prentice's jacket in his fist. 'Listen,' he hissed, 'listen, you idiot. I'm risking my life to help you. Don't you understand yet? If they find out I've talked ...' He released the sleeve. 'Prentice, *please*. You have a chance now, a chance to clear out of this whole stinking mess; but you won't have it long – believe me!'

Prentice sighed. 'What do you want me to do?' he said.

'Nothing. Just come with me, quietly. They're in the basement.'

Breathing hard now, Dystal tiptoed around to the side of the house. He stopped at a small, earth-level window.

It was closed.

'Prentice. *Softly*. Bend down and keep out of view.'

In invisible, slow movements, Dystal reached out and pushed the window. It opened a half inch. He pushed it again. It opened another half inch.

Prentice saw yellow light stream out of the crack. Instantly his throat felt very dry, very painful.

There was a noise. A low, murmurous sound; a susurrous, like distant humming.

'What's that?'

Dystal put a finger to his lips and motioned: 'Here.'

Prentice knelt down at the window and looked into the light.

At first he could not believe what his eyes saw.

It was a basement, like any other basements in old houses, with a large iron furnace and a cement floor and heavy beams. This much he could recognize and understand. The rest, he could not.

In the centre of the floor was a design, obviously drawn in coloured chalks. It looked a bit, to Prentice, like a Star of David, although there were other designs around and within it. They were not particularly artistic, but they were intricate. In the middle was a large cup, similar to a salad bowl, vaguely familiar, empty.

'There,' whispered Dystal, withdrawing.

Slightly to the left were drawn a circle and a pentagram, its five points touching the circumference equally.

Prentice blinked and turned his attention to the people.

Standing on a block of wood, surrounded by men and women, was a figure in a black robe and a serpent-shaped crown.

It was Ames.

His wife, Charlotte, dressed in a white gown, stood next to him. She held a brass lamp.

Also in robes and gowns were Ben and Rhoda Roth, Bud Reiker and his wife, the Cummingses, the Chambereses, the Johnsons –

Prentice shook away his sudden dizziness and shaded his eyes.

To the right, near the furnace, was a table with a white sheet draped across it. And two feet away, an odd, six-sided structure with black candles burning from a dozen apertures.

'Listen,' Dystal said.

Ames' eyes were closed. Softly, he was chanting:

*All degradation, all sheer infamy,*
*Thou shalt endure. Thy head beneath the mire.*

*And dung of worthless women shall desire*
*As in some hateful dream, at last to lie;*
*Woman must trample thee till thou respire*
*That deadliest fume;*
*The vilest worms must crawl, the loathliest vampires*
*gloom . . .*

'The Great Beast,' chuckled Dystal.

'I,' said Ames, 'am Ipsissimus,' and the others chanted, 'He is Ipsissimus.'

'I have read the books, dark Lord. *The Book of Sacred Magic of Abra-Melin the Mage* I have read, and I reject it!'

'We reject it!' murmured the Roths.

'The power of Good shall be served by the power of Darkness, always.'

He raised his hands. 'In Thy altar is the stele of Ankf-f-n-Khonsu; there, also, *The Book of the Dead* and *The Book of the Law*, six candles to each side, my Lord, Bell, Burin, Lamen, Sword, Cup, and the Cakes of Life . . .'

Prentice looked at the people he had seen only a few hours ago in his living room, and shuddered. He felt very weak.

'We, your servants,' said Ames, singing the words, 'beseech your presence, Lord of Night and of Life Eternal, Ruler of the Souls of men in all Thy vast dominion . . .'

Prentice started to rise, but Dystal grasped his jacket. 'No,' he said. 'Wait. Wait another minute. This is something you ought to see.'

'. . . we live to serve you; grant us . . .'

'He's begging the devil to appear,' whispered Dystal.

'. . . tonight, and offer the greatest and most treasured gift. Accept our offering!'

'Accept it!' cried the others.

'What the hell is this, anyway?' Prentice demanded, feverishly.

Then Ames stopped talking, and the rest were silent. Ames raised his left hand and lowered it. Chris Cummings and Bud Reiker bowed and walked backwards into the shadows where Prentice could not see them.

Charlotte Ames walked to the six-sided structure with the candles and picked up a long, thin object.

She returned and handed this to her husband.

It was a knife.

'*Killnotshaltthou!*' screamed Ed Chambers, and he stepped across the pentagram to the sheet-shrouded table.

Prentice rubbed his eyes.

'Shhh.'

Bud Reiker and Chris Cummings returned to the centre of light then. They were carrying a bundle. It was wrapped in blankets.

The bundle thrashed and made peculiar muffled noises. The men lifted it on to the table and held it.

Ames nodded and stepped down from the block of wood. He walked to the table and halted, the long-bladed butcher knife glittering in the glow of the candles.

'To Thee, O Lord of the Underground, we make this offering! To Thee, the rarest gift of all!'

'What is it?' Prentice asked. 'What is this gift?'

Dystal's voice was ready and eager. 'A virgin,' he said.

Then they removed the blanket.

Prentice felt his eyes bursting from their sockets, felt his heart charging the walls of his chest.

'Ann,' he said, in a choked whisper. 'Ann!'

The knife went up.

Prentice scrambled to his feet and fought the dizziness. 'Dystal,' he cried. 'Dystal, for God's sake, what are they doing? Stop them. You hear me? Stop them!'

'I can't,' said Matthew Dystal, sadly. 'It's too late. I'm afraid your wife said a few things she shouldn't have, Prentice. You see – we've been looking for a real one for such a long time ...'

Prentice tried to lunge, but the effort lost him his balance. He fell to the ground. His arms and legs were growing numb, and he remembered, suddenly, the bitter taste of the drink he'd had.

'It really couldn't have been avoided, though,' Dystal said. 'I mean, the boy knew, and he'd have told you eventually. And you'd have begun investigating, and – oh, you understand. I told Lucian we should have bought the place, but he's so obstinate; he thinks he knows *every-thing*! Now, of course, we'll have to burn it, and that does seem a terrible waste.' He shook his head from side to side. 'But don't you worry,' he said. 'You'll be asleep by then and, I promise, you won't feel a thing. Really.'

Prentice turned his eyes from the window and screamed silently for a long time.

# IN THE VALLEY OF THE SORCERESS

## by Sax Rohmer

Condor wrote to me three times before the end (said Neville, Assistant-Inspector of Antiquities, staring vaguely from his open window at a squad drilling before the Kasr-en-Nîl Barracks). He dated his letters from the camp at Deir-el-Bahari. Judging from these, success appeared to be almost within his grasp. He shared my theories, of course, respecting Queen Hatasu, and was devoting the whole of his energies to the task of clearing up the great mystery of Ancient Egypt which centres around that queen.

For him, as for me, there was a strange fascination about those defaced walls and roughly obliterated inscriptions. That the queen under whom Egyptian art came to the apogee of perfection should thus have been treated by her successors; that no perfect figure of the wise, famous, and beautiful Hatasu should have been spared to posterity; that her very cartouche should have been ruthlessly removed from every inscription upon which it appeared, presented to Condor's mind a problem only second in interest to the immortal riddle of Gîzeh.

You know my own views upon the matter? My monograph, 'Hatasu, the Sorceress', embodies my opinion. In short, upon certain evidences, some adduced by Theodore Davis, some by poor Condor, and some resulting from my own inquiries, I have come to the conclusion that the source – real or imaginary – of this queen's power was an intimate acquaintance with what nowadays we term, vaguely, magic. Pursuing her studies beyond the limit which is lawful, she met with a certain end, not uncommon, if the old writings are to be believed, in the case of those who penetrate too far into the realms of the Borderland.

For this reason – the practice of black magic – her statues were dishonoured, and her name erased from the monuments. Now, I do not propose to enter into any discussion respecting the reality of such practices; in my monograph I have merely endeavoured to show that, according to contemporary belief, the queen was a sorceress. Condor was seeking to prove the same thing; and when I took up the inquiry, it was in the hope of completing his interrupted work.

He wrote to me early in the winter of 1908, from his camp by the Rock Temple. Davis's tomb, at Bibân el-Mulûk, with its long, narrow passage, apparently had little interest for him; he was at work on the high ground behind the temple, at a point one hundred yards or so due west of the upper platform. He had an idea that he should find there the mummies of Hatasu – and another; the latter, a certain Sen-Mût, who appears in the inscriptions of the reign as an architect high in the queen's favour. The archaeological points of the letter do not concern us in the least, but there was one odd little paragraph which I had cause to remember afterwards.

'A girl belonging to some Arab tribe,' wrote Condor, 'came racing to the camp two nights ago to claim my protection. What crime she had committed, and what punishment she feared, were far from clear; but she clung to me, trembling like a leaf, and positively refused to depart. It was a difficult situation, for a camp of fifty native excavators, and one highly respectable European enthusiast, affords no suitable quarters for an Arab girl – and a very personable Arab girl. At any rate, she is still here; I have had a sort of lean-to rigged up in a little valley east of my own tent, but it is very embarrassing.'

Nearly a month passed before I heard from Condor again; then came a second letter, with the news that on the eve of a great discovery – as he believed – his entire native staff – the whole fifty – had deserted one night in a body! 'Two days' work,' he wrote, 'would have seen the tomb opened – for I am more than ever certain that my plans are accurate. Then I woke up one morning to find every man Jack of my fellows missing! I went down into the village where a lot of them live, in a towering rage, but not one of the brutes was to be found, and their relations professed entire ignorance respecting their whereabouts. What caused me almost as much anxiety as the check in my work was the fact that Mahâra – the Arab girl – had vanished also. I am wondering if the thing has any sinister significance.'

Condor finished with the statement that he was making tremendous efforts to secure a new gang. 'But,' said he, 'I shall finish the excavation, if I have to do it with my own hands.'

His third and last letter contained even stranger matters than the two preceding it. He had succeeded in borrowing a few men from the British Archaeological camp in the Fáyûm. Then, just as the work was restarting, the Arab girl, Mahâra turned up again, and entreated him to bring her down the Nile, 'at least as far as Dendera. For the vengeance of her tribesmen,' stated Condor, 'otherwise would result not only in her own death, but in mine! At the moment of writing I am in two minds about what to do. If Mahâra is to go upon this journey, I do not feel justified in sending her alone, and there is no one here who could perform the duty,' etc.

I began to wonder, of course; and I had it in mind to take the train to Luxor merely in order to see this Arab maiden, who seemed to occupy so prominent a place in Condor's mind. However, Fate would have it otherwise; and the next thing I heard was that Condor had been brought into Cairo, and was at the English hospital.

He had been bitten by a cat – presumably from the neighbouring village; and although the doctor at Luxor dealt with the bite at once, travelled down with him, and placed him in the hands of the Pasteur man at the hospital, he died, as you remember, on the night of his arrival, raving mad; the Pasteur treatment failed entirely.

I never saw him before the end, but they told me that

his howls were horribly like those of a cat. His eyes changed in some way, too, I understand; and, with his fingers all contracted, he tried to *scratch* everyone and everything within reach.

They had to strap the poor beggar down, and even then he tore the sheets into ribbons.

Well, as soon as possible, I made the necessary arrangements to finish Condor's inquiry. I had access to his papers, plans, etc., and in the spring of the same year I took up my quarters near Deir-el-Bahari, roped off the approaches to the camp, stuck up the usual notices, and prepared to finish the excavation, which, I gathered, was in a fairly advanced state.

My first surprise came very soon after my arrival, for when, with the plan before me, I started out to find the shaft, I found it, certainly, but only with great difficulty.

It had been filled in again with sand and loose rock right to the very top!

*

All my inquiries availed to nothing. With what object the excavation had been thus closed I was unable to conjecture. That Condor had not reclosed it I was quite certain, for at the time of his mishap he had actually been at work at the bottom of the shaft, as inquiries from a native of Suefee, in the Fáyûm, who was his only companion at the time, had revealed.

In his eagerness to complete the inquiry, Condor, by lantern light, had been engaged upon a solitary night-shift below, and the rabid cat had apparently fallen into the pit; probably in a frenzy of fear, it had attacked Condor, after which it had escaped.

Only this one man was with him, and he, for some reason that I could not make out, had apparently been sleeping in the temple – quite a considerable distance from Condor's camp. The poor fellow's cries had aroused him, and he had met Condor running down the path and away from the shaft.

This, however, was good evidence of the existence of

the shaft at the time, and as I stood contemplating the tightly packed rubble which alone marked its site, I grew more and more mystified, for this task of reclosing the cutting represented much hard labour.

Beyond perfecting my plans in one or two particulars, I did little on the day of my arrival. I had only a handful of men with me, all of whom I knew, having worked with them before, and beyond clearing Condor's shaft I did not intend to excavate farther.

Hatasu's Temple presents a lively enough scene in the daytime during the winter and early spring months, with the streams of tourists constantly passing from the white causeway to Cook's Rest House on the edge of the desert. There had been a goodly number of visitors that day to the temple below, and one or two of the more curious and venturesome had scrambled up the steep path to the little plateau which was the scene of my operations. None had penetrated beyond the notice boards, however, and now, with the evening sky passing through those innumerable shades which defy palette and brush, which can only be distinguished by the trained eye, but which, from palest blue melt into exquisite pink, and by some magical combination form that deep violet which does not exist to perfection elsewhere than in the skies of Egypt, I found myself in the silence and the solitude of 'the Holy Valley'.

I stood at the edge of the plateau, looking out at the rosy belt which marked the course of the distant Nile, with the Arabian hills vaguely sketched beyond. The rocks stood up against that prospect as great black smudges, and what I could see of the causeway looked like a grey smear upon a drab canvas. Beneath me were the chambers of the Rock Temple, with those wall paintings depicting events in the reign of Hatasu which rank among the wonders of Egypt.

Not a sound disturbed my reverie, save a faint clatter of cooking utensils from the camp behind me – a desecration of that sacred solitude. Then a dog began to howl in the neighbouring village. The dog ceased, and faintly to my ears came the note of a reed pipe. The breeze died away, and with it the piping.

I turned back to the camp, and having partaken of a frugal supper, turned in upon my campaigner's bed, thoroughly enjoying my freedom from the routine of official life in Cairo, and looking forward to the morrow's work pleasureably.

Under such circumstances a man sleeps well; and when, in an uncanny grey half-light, which probably heralded the dawn, I awoke with a start, I knew that something of an unusual nature alone could have disturbed my slumbers.

Firstly, then, I identified this with a concerted howling of the village dogs. They seemed to have conspired to make night hideous; I have never heard such an eerie din in my life. Then it gradually began to die away, and I realized, secondly, that the howling of the dogs and my own awakening might be due to some common cause. This idea grew upon me, and as the howling subsided, a sort of disquiet possessed me, and, despite my efforts to shake it off, grew more urgent with the passing of every moment.

In short, I fancied that the thing which had alarmed or enraged the dogs was passing from the village through the Holy Valley, upward to the Temple, upward to the plateau, and was approaching *me*.

I have never experienced an identical sensation since, but I seemed to be audient of a sort of psychic patrol, which, from a remote *pianissimo*, swelled *fortissimo*, to an intimate but silent clamour, which beat in some way upon my brain, but not through the faculty of hearing, for now the night was deathly still.

Yet I was persuaded of some *approach* – of the coming of something sinister, and the suspense of waiting had become almost insupportable, so that I began to accuse my Spartan supper of having given me nightmare, when the tent-flap was suddenly raised, and, outlined against the paling blue of the sky, with a sort of reflected elfin light playing upon her face, I saw an Arab girl looking in at me!

By dint of exerting all my self-control I managed to restrain the cry and upward start which this apparition prompted. Quite still, with my fists tightly clenched, I lay and looked into the eyes which were looking into mine.

The style of literary work which it has been my lot to cultivate fails me in describing that beautiful and evil face. The features were severely classical and small, something of the Bishârîn type, with a cruel little mouth and a rounded chin, firm to hardness. In the eyes alone lay the languor of the Orient; they were exceedingly – indeed, excessively – long and narrow. The ordinary ragged, picturesque finery of a desert girl bedecked this midnight visitant, who, motionless, stood there watching me.

I once read a work by Pierre de l'Ancre, dealing with the Black Sabbaths of the Middle Ages, and now the evil beauty of this Arab face threw my memory back to those singular pages, for, perhaps owing to the reflected light which I have mentioned, although the explanation scarcely seemed adequate, those long, narrow eyes shone catlike in the gloom.

Suddenly I made up my mind. Throwing the blanket from me, I leapt to the gound, and in a flash had gripped the girl by the wrists. Confuting some lingering doubts, she proved to be substantial enough. My electric torch lay upon a box at the foot of the bed, and, stooping, I caught it up and turned its searching rays upon the face of my captive.

She fell back from me, panting like a wild creature trapped, then dropped upon her knees and began to plead – began to plead in a voice and with a manner which touched some chord of consciousness that I could swear had never spoken before, and has never spoken since.

She spoke in Arabic, of course, but the words fell from her lips as liquid music in which lay all the beauty and all the deviltry of the 'Sirens' Song'. Fully opening her astonishing eyes, she looked up at me, and, with her free hand pressed to her bosom, told me how she had fled from an unwelcome marriage; how, an outcast and a pariah, she had hidden in the desert places for three days and three nights, sustaining life only by means of a few dates which she had brought with her, and quenching her thirst with stolen water-melons.

'I can bear it no longer, *effendim*. Another night out in the desert, with the cruel moon beating, beating, beating upon my brain, with creeping things coming out from the rocks, wriggling, wriggling, their many feet making whisperings in the sand – ah, it will kill me! And I am for ever outcast from my tribe, from my people. No tent of all the Arabs, though I fly to the gates of Damascus, is open to me, save I enter in shame, as a slave, as a play-thing, as a toy. My heart' – furiously she beat upon her breast – 'is empty and desolate, *effendim*. I am meaner than the lowliest thing that creeps upon the sand; yet the God that made that creeping thing made me also – and you, you, who are merciful and strong, would not crush any creature because it was weak and helpless.'

I had relaeased her wrist now, and was looking down at her in a sort of stupor. The evil which at first I had seemed to perceive in her was effaced, wiped out as an artist wipes out an error in his drawing. Her dark beauty was speaking to me in a language of its own; a strange language, yet one so intelligible that I struggled in vain to disregard it. And her voice, her gestures, and the witch-fire of her eyes were whipping up my blood to a fever heat of passionate sorrow – of despair. Yes, incredible as it sounds, despair!

In short, as I see it now, this siren of the wilderness was playing upon me as an accomplished musician might play upon a harp, striking this string and that at will, and sounding each with such full notes as they had rarely, if ever, emitted before.

Most damnable anomaly of all, I – Edward Neville, archaeologist, most prosy and matter-of-fact man in Cairo, perhaps – *knew* that this nomad who had burst into my tent, upon whom I had set eyes for the first time scarce three minutes before, held me enthralled; and yet, with her wondrous eyes upon me, I could summon up no resentment, and could offer but poor resistance.

'In the Little Oasis, *effendim*, I have a sister who will admit me into her household, if only as a servant. There I can be safe, there I can rest. O *Inglisi*, at home in England you have a sister of your own! Would you see her pursued, a hunted thing from rock to rock, crouching for shelter in the lair of some jackal, stealing that she might live – and flying always, never resting, her heart leaping for fear, flying, flying, with nothing but dishonour before her?'

She shuddered and clasped my left hand in both her own convulsively, pulling it down to her bosom.

'There can be only one thing, *effendim*,' she whispered. 'Do you not see the white bones bleaching in the sun?'

Throwing all my resolution into the act, I released my hand from her clasp, and, turning aside, sat down upon the box which served me as chair and table, too.

A thought had come to my assistance, had strengthened me in the moment of my greatest weakness; it was the thought of that Arab girl mentioned in Condor's letters. And a scheme of things, an incredible scheme, that embraced and explained some, if not all, of the horrible circumstances attendant upon his death, began to form in my brain.

Bizarre it was, stretching out beyond the realm of things natural and proper, yet I clung to it, for there, in the solitude, with this wildly beautiful creature kneeling at my feet, and with her uncanny powers of fascination yet enveloping me like a cloak, I found it not so improbable as inevitably it must have seemed at another time.

I turned my head, and through the gloom sought to look into the long eyes. As I did so they closed and appeared as two darkly luminous slits in the perfect oval of the face.

'You are an impostor!' I said in Arabic, speaking firmly and deliberately. 'To Mr Condor' – I could have sworn that she started slightly at sound of the name – 'you called yourself Mahâra. I know you, and I will have nothing to do with you.'

But in saying it I had to turn my head aside, for the strangest, maddest impulses were bubbling up in my brain in response to the glances of those half-shut eyes.

I reached for my coat, which lay upon the foot of the bed, and, taking out some loose money, I placed fifty piastres in the nerveless brown hand.

'That will enable you to reach the Little Oasis, if such is your desire,' I said. 'It is all I can do for you, and now – you must go.'

The light of the dawn was growing stronger momentarily, so that I could see my visitor quite clearly. She rose to her feet, and stood before me, a straight, slim figure, sweeping me from head to foot with such a glance of passionate contempt as I had never known or suffered.

She threw back her head magnificently, dashed the money on the ground at my feet, and, turning, leapt out of the tent.

For a moment I hesitated, doubting, questioning my humanity, testing my fears; then I took a step forward, and peered out across the plateau. Not a soul was in sight. The rocks stood up grey and eerie, and beneath lay the carpet of the desert stretching unbroken to the shadows of the Nile Valley.

\*

We commenced the work of clearing the shaft at an early hour that morning. The strangest ideas were now playing in my mind, and in some way I felt myself to be in opposition to definite enmity. My excavators laboured with a will, and, once we had penetrated below the first three feet or so of tightly packed stone, it became a mere matter of shovelling, for apparently the lower part of the shaft had been filled up principally with sand.

I calculated that four days' work at the outside would see the shaft clear to the base of Condor's excavation. There remained, according to his own notes, only another six feet or so; but it was solid limestone – the roof of the passage, if his plans were correct, communicating with the tomb of Hatasu.

With the approach of night, tired as I was, I felt little inclination for sleep. I lay down on my bed with a small Browning pistol under the pillow, but after an hour or so of nervous listening drifted off into slumber. As on the night before, I awoke shortly before the coming of dawn.

Again the village dogs were raising a hideous outcry, and again I was keenly conscious of some ever-nearing menace. This consciousness grew stronger as the howling of the dogs grew fainter, and the sense of *approach* assailed me as on the previous occasion.

I sat up immediately with the pistol in my hand, and, gently raising the tent flap, looked out over the darksome plateau. For a long time I could perceive nothing; then, vaguely outlined against the sky, I detected something that moved above the rocky edge.

It was so indefinite in form that for a time I was unable to identify it, but as it slowly rose higher and higher, two luminous eyes – obviously feline eyes, since they glittered greenly in the darkness – came into view. In character and in shape they were the eyes of a cat, but in point of size they were larger than the eyes of any cat I had ever seen. Nor were they jackal eyes. It occurred to me that some predatory beast from the Sudan might conceivably have strayed thus far north.

The presence of such a creature would account for the nightly disturbance amongst the village dogs; and, dismissing the superstitious notions which had led me to associate the mysterious Arab girl with the phenomenon of the howling dogs, I seized upon this new idea with a sort of gladness.

Stepping boldly out of the tent, I strode in the direction of the gleaming eyes. Although my only weapon was the Browning pistol, it was a weapon of considerable power, and, moreover, I counted upon the well-known cowardice of nocturnal animals. I was not disappointed in the result.

The eyes dropped out of sight, and as I leapt to the

edge of rock overhanging the temple a lithe shape went streaking off in the greyness beneath me. Its colouring appeared to be black, but this appearance may have been due to the bad light. Certainly it was no cat, was no jackal; and once, twice, thrice my Browning spat into the darkness.

Apparently I had not scored a hit, but the loud reports of the weapon aroused the men sleeping in the camp, and soon I was surrounded by a ring of inquiring faces.

But there I stood on the rock-edge, looking out across the desert in silence. Something in the long, luminous eyes, something in the sinuous, flying shape had spoken to me intimately, horribly.

Hassan es-Sugra, the headman, touched my arm, and I knew that I must offer some explanation.

'Jackals,' I said shortly. And with no other word I walked back to my tent.

The night passed without further event, and in the morning we addressed ourselves to the work with such a will that I saw, to my satisfaction, that by noon of the following day the labour of clearing the loose sand would be completed.

During the preparation of the evening meal I became aware of a certain disquiet in the camp, and I noted a disinclination on the part of the native labourers to stray far from the tents. They hung together in a group, and whilst individually they seemed to avoid meeting my eye, collectively they watched me in a furtive fashion.

A gang of Moslem workmen calls for delicate handling, and I wondered if, inadvertently, I had transgressed in some way their iron-bound code of conduct. I called Hassan es-Sugra aside.

'What ails the men?' I asked him. 'Have they some grievance?'

Hassan spread his palms eloquently.

'If they have,' he replied, 'they are secret about it, and I am not in their confidence. Shalll I thrash three or four of them in order to learn the nature of this grievance?'

'No, thanks all the same,' I said, laughing at this characteristic proposal. 'If they refuse to work tomorrow, there will be time enough for you to adopt those measures.'

On this, the third night of my sojourn in the Holy Valley by the Temple of Hatasu, I slept soundly and uninterruptedly. I had been looking forward with the keenest zest to the morrow's work, which promised to bring me within sight of my goal, and when Hassan came to awaken me, I leapt out of bed immediately.

Hassan es-Sugra, having performed his duty, did not, as was his custom, retire; he stood there, a tall, angular figure, looking at me strangely.

'Well?' I said.

'There is trouble,' was his simple reply. 'Follow me, Neville Effendi.'

Wondering greatly, I followed him across the plateau and down the slope to the excavation. There I pulled up short with a cry of amazement.

Condor's shaft was filled in to the very top, and presented, to my astonished gaze, much the same aspect that had greeted me upon my first arrival!

'The men –' I began.

Hassan es-Sugra spread wide his palms.

'Gone!' he replied. 'Those Coptic dogs, those eaters of carrion, have fled in the night.'

'And this' – I pointed to the little mound of broken granite and sand – 'is their work?'

'So it would seem,' was the reply; and Hasan sniffed his sublime contempt.

I stood looking bitterly at this destruction of my toils. The strangeness of the thing at the moment did not strike me, in my anger; I was only concerned with the outrageous impudence of the missing workmen, and if I could have laid hands upon one of them it had surely gone hard with him.

As for Hassan es-Sugra, I believe he would cheerfully have broken the necks of the entire gang. But he was a man of resource.

'It is so newly filled in,' he said, 'that you and I, in

three days, or in four, can restore it to the state it had reached when those nameless dogs, who regularly prayed with their shoes on, those devourers of pork, began their dirty work.'

His example was stimulating. *I* was not going to be beaten, either.

After a hasty breakfast, the pair of us set to work with pick and shovel and basket. We worked as those slaves must have worked whose toil was directed by the lash of the Pharaoh's overseer. My back acquired an almost permanent crook, and every muscle in my body seemed to be on fire. Not even in the midday heat did we slacken or stay our toils; and when dusk fell that night a great mound had arisen beside Condor's shaft, and we had excavated to a depth which it had taken our gang double the time to reach.

When at last we threw down our tools in utter exhaustion, I held out my hand to Hassan, and wrung his brown fist enthusiastically. His eyes sparkled as he met my glance.

'Neville Effendi,' he said, 'You are a true Moslem!'

And only the initiated can know how high was the compliment conveyed.

That night I slept the sleep of utter weariness, yet it was not a dreamless sleep, or perhaps it was not so deep as I supposed, for blazing cat-eyes encircled me in my dreams, and a constant feline howling seemed to fill the night.

When I awoke the sun was blazing down upon the rock outside my tent, and, springing out of bed, I perceived, with amazement, that the morning was far advanced. Indeed, I could hear the distant voices of the donkey-boys and other harbingers of the coming tourists.

Why had Hassan es-Sugra not awakened me?

I stepped out of the tent and called him in a loud voice. There was no reply. I ran across the plateau to the edge of the hollow.

Condor's shaft had been reclosed to the top!

Language fails me to convey the wave of anger, amazement, incredulity, which swept over me. I looked across to the deserted camp and back to my own tent; I looked down at the mound, where but a few hours before had been a pit, and seriously I began to question whether I was mad or whether madness had seized upon all who had been with me. Then, pegged down upon the heap of broken stones, I perceived, fluttering, a small piece of paper.

Dully I walked across and picked it up. Hassan, a man of some education, clearly was the writer. It was a pencil scrawl in doubtful Arabic, and not without difficulty, I deciphered it as follows:

'Fly, Neville Effendi! This is a haunted place!'

Standing there by the mound, I tore the scrap of paper into minute fragments, bitterly casting them from me upon the ground. It was incredible; it was insane.

The man who had written that absurd message, the man who had undone his own work, had the reputation of being fearless and honourable. He had been with me before a score of times, and had quelled petty mutinies in the camp in a manner which marked him a born over-seer. I could not understand; I could scarcely believe the evidence of my own senses.

What did I do?

I suppose there are some who would have abandoned the thing at once and for always, but I take it that the national traits are strong within me. I went over to the camp and prepared my own breakfast; then, shouldering pick and shovel, I went down into the valley and set to work. What ten men could not do, what two men had failed to do, one man was determined to do.

It was about half an hour after commencing my toils, and when, I suppose, the surprise and rage occasioned by the discovery had begun to wear off, that I found myself making comparisons between my own case and that of Condor. It became more and more evident to me that events – mysterious events – were repeating themselves.

The frightful happenings attendant upon Condor's death were marshalling in my mind. The sun was blazing down upon me, and distant voices could be heard in the desert stillness. I knew that the plain below was dotted with pleasure-seeking tourists, yet nervous tremors shook me. Frankly, I dreaded the coming of the night.

Well, tenacity or pugnacity conquered, and I worked on until dusk. My supper despatched, I sat down on my bed and toyed with the Browning.

I realized already that sleep, under existing conditions, was impossible. I perceived that on the morrow. I must abandon my one-man enterprise, pocket my pride, in a sense, and seek new assistants, new companions.

The fact was coming home to me conclusively that a menace, real and not mythical, hung over that valley. Although, in the morning sunlight and filled with indignation, I had thought contemptuously of Hassan es-Sugra, now, in the mysterious violet dusk so conducive to calm consideration, I was forced to admit that he was at least a brave a man as I. And he had fled! What did that night hold in keeping for me?

*

I will tell you what occurred, and it is the only explanation I have to give of why Condor's shaft, said to communicate with the real tomb of Hatasu, to this day remains unopened.

There, on the edge of my bed, I sat far into the night, not daring to close my eyes. But physical weariness conquered in the end, and, although I have no recollection of its coming, I must have succumbed to sleep, since I remember – can never forget – a repetition of the dream, or what I had assumed to be a dream, of the night before.

A ring of blazing green eyes surrounded me. At one point this ring was broken, and in a kind of nightmare panic I leapt at that promise of safety, and found myself outside the tent.

Lithe, slinking shapes hemmed me in – cat shapes, ghoul shapes, veritable figures of the pit. And the eyes, the shapes, although they were the eyes and shapes of cats, sometimes changed elusively, and became the wicked eyes and the sinuous, writhing shapes of women. Always the ring was incomplete, and always I retreated in the only direction by which retreat was possible. I retreated from those cat-things.

In this fashion I came at last to the shaft, and there I saw the tools which I had left at the end of my day's toil.

Looking around me, I saw also, with such a pang of horror as I cannot hope to convey to you, that the ring of green eyes was now unbroken about me.

And it was closing in.

Nameless feline creatures were crowding silently to the edge of the pit, some preparing to spring down upon me where I stood. A voice seemed to speak in my brain; it spoke of capitulation, telling me to accept defeat, lest, resisting, my fate be the fate of Condor.

Peals of shrill laughter rose upon the silence. The laughter was mine.

Filling the night with this hideous, hysterical merriment, I was working feverishly with pick and with shovel filling in the shaft.

The end? The end is that I awoke, in the morning, lying, not on my bed, but outside on the plateau, my hands torn and bleeding and every muscle in my body throbbing agonizingly. Remembering my dream – for even in that moment of awakening I thought I had dreamed – I staggered across to the valley of the excavation.

Condor's shaft was reclosed to the top.

# THE DEVIL'S DEBT

## by James Platt

Somewhere about the Middle Ages – somewhere in a medieval town – there lived a man who walked always on the shady side of the way. None of his neighbours could have assigned a reason why he should only tread where the lapse of time leaves no trace on the dial, yet so it was. None had ever seen him in sunshine.

This man was known by the name of Porphyro, though we may reasonably doubt if it was given to him in baptism. For he belonged to a class that baptised toads by night at their Sabbaths in mockery of the baptism of babes by day. In a word, Porphyro was a wizard, and for one circumstance (which will presently be mentioned) was perhaps better known among his like than any practiser of the Black Art before or since.

There was, and likely enough still is, in Europe a University of the occult sciences, buried underground, carved out of the roots of mountains, far from the hum of men. Here taught weird professors – eerie, eldritch, elflocked. Here came weird students to tread the intoxicating winepress of magical study. Your true wizard is set apart from birth by some particularity which bespeaks his vocation. To the University came representatives of every class which felt this call. Here was the demoniac and the stigmatic, the abortion and the albino, the hermaphrodite and the changeling, the hag-ridden and the pixy-led, sleepwalker, Cesarean, Sunday-child, seventh son, and he that is born with the caul. This motley crew was of as many hues as there are ends of the earth. Many'tongued as Mithridates, all wrote their notes by common consent in the *lingua angelorum*.

The University boasted a laboratory of at least a hundred paces in length and proportionately broad and high. A mock sun gave it cold light by day, and a mock moon by night. Here experiments in exorcism were conducted, of course under the strictest supervision of the principals. Here the students learned that the ghosts of dead men (having always some of the old Adam that was unpurged from them), are easier to call back to us than elemental spirits can be wrenched from their eternal spheres. The most trivial task (and therefore that of the junior classes), was to re-incarnate some suicide, set in four cross roads, whose soul still hovered like a noxious gas about the only body where it could hope to find toleration. The pupils were very properly forbidden to incur the danger of repeating these experiments in private. Nevertheless something of the kind went on under the nose. As a rule the novices (and these were after all the lucky ones), ignominiously failed in their attempts to storm the outworks of hell. They knew how to call spirits from the vasty deep, but the spirits refused to come when they did call them. One youth, however, boasted that he had raised the devil, or at any rate, a devil. He described him to his bosom friends as nearly as follows:

'A great and full stature, soft and phlegmatic, of colour like a black obscure cloud, having a swollen countenance, with eyes red and full of water, a bald head, and teeth like a wild boar.'

One of the listeners, doubtless jealous, attempted to cheapen this success of his companion, by remarking that an exorcist, if worth his salt, should be able to make the spirit appear in what guise he chose.

'Then, by the belt of Venus,' swore a third, 'I would command it to appear as a lovely girl, with longer hair and smaller feet than any on this top which the Almighty set spinning and dubbed earth.'

Another poor fellow appears to have been so inflamed with the suggestion of this rustler, that he tried to bring it into the sphere of practical politics. He was never seen alive again. Not answering to his name at the roll-call next morning, his bedroom was visited, and a thin trickle of blood found oozing under the door. One of the search party put a pistol to the lock and fired. The door flew open. A cry burst from all present, and some of the youngest, covering their faces with their hands, fled. The body of the devoted wretch who had played with unholy fire, was scattered parcel meal about the room. The lopped limbs were twisted round into spirals as if boneless. One of stronger stomach than the rest of the onlookers, and who examined them more closely, declared that the bone had melted and run out under some incredible heat. One of the teachers opined that if the demon had only breathed upon the bone, it would have been enough to fuse it. There were no more experiments in students' rooms.

Apart from such accidental deaths, the Academy paid a regular yearly rent of one living soul to hell, and woe unto teachers and taught had they lapsed into arrear one day. The victim who was to suffer, that the rest might live and learn, was selected in the following traditional manner. The whole of the pupils toed a line at one extreme end of the hall, and, at a given signal, raced to the opposite door. There was, as may be imagined, a terrible struggle to pass through the hangings. The last to cross the threshold was hugged to hell by the awaiting fiend. It was on such an occasion that Porphyro earned the unique distinction, alluded to above, of having successfully cozened the Prince of Darkness himself. Strain as he might, he was the last to touch the winning post. His competitors, who now breathed themselves in safety in the lobby, had given him up for lost. But no piercing shriek of disolution stabbed the air, no fiendish laughter made horrible the echoes. Instead, voices were heard, until presently their comrade rejoined those who had already mourned him. Amid a scene of the wildest excitement, he was dragged into the light. Something unprecedented must obviously have occurred. His hair had turned snowy white. Those fell back who looked first into his eyes, for they saw in them reflected the face of hell himself. The tale which Porphyro told them was in substance this, that when he arrived last at the curtains, and already felt the breath of punishment upon his cheek, there occurred to him one loophole of escape. He turned desperately at bay, like hunted quarry, and roundly told the scrutineer that all he could claim by the letter of his bond was Porphyro's shadow. That was the last living thing which passed out of the lists; and not Porphyro, who proceeded it. Strange as it may seem, after a few heated words, the justice of this quibble was acknowledged by the father of all such juggleries. He bore off the shadow with a sort of smile, that was more terrible than men's frown, and lo and behold! when the schoolfellows, with one accord, looked down at the feet of him who had so miraculously escaped the infernal maw, they saw that Porphyro was, as he ever afterwards remained, shadowless. And now our readers can guess why our hero walked away on the shady side of the way.

Nothing had ever been known (even in circles like this) so successfully daring as this piece of evasion. Round and round the whole round globe, by means only known to wizards, the news sped very fast to all the wizard world. It was proclaimed at every Sabbath, from Blockula to the Brocken. The Lapland witch whispered it to the Finland witch, as they sat tying up wind after wind in knots for their seafaring customers. The Druids of Carnac knew it, and the Persian devil-worshippers. The Shamans of Siberia made a song of it and beat their magic drums thereto. The magicians of Egypt pictured it in their mirrors of ink. The African Obi men washed their great fetish in the blood of a thousand virgins, and sent it as a present over the desert sands, to Porphyro. Even the medicine men heard of it, in the heart of an undiscovered continent, and emblazoned it upon the walls of their medicine lodge. Everyone forsaw a brilliant career for Porphyro. They fully expected him to disembowel hell. The reverse was what really happened. Instead of swinging himself at once to the top round of the ladder, he showed no disposition to trouble himself at all. He opened a private office in the town referred to at the beginning of our story, and carried on a private business in magic of the whitest kind. For him no monster evocations, with a million demons at his beck and call, like the Sicilian whom Benvenuto Cellini employed to conjure for him in the Coliseum. Porphyro refused in the most stiff-necked manner to exorcise on any terms for anyone. He confined himself solely to pettyfogging business, such as writing talismans, and reckoning magic squares, drawing horoscopes, and casting schemes of geomancy, poisoning rivals for lovers, or close-fisted relatives for spendthrift heirs. Need we state in black and white the reason (concealed from everyone else), why he held his hand from higher things? Oh, the humiliation of it! He was afraid! Yes, Porphyro was afraid, even he, who had plucked a hair from the devil's beard: for that very reason he was afraid. He had saved his soul alive, losing only a shadow of little moment to him, but in return, he had incurred the eternal enmity of one whose grudge had once shaken the high heavens. The general adversary of all mankind was first and beyond all things most ferociously Porphyro's adversary. Unhappy Porphyro, who had already given seisin to hell, Porphyro with one half of him already in the living devil's clutch, who never slept but he dreamed of the tortures his poor shadow suffered at the hands of those that lovingly work evil! Tortures, which were but foreshadowings of his own! No wonder Porphyro dared not invoke even the least of spirits. He knew too well that the mightiest of them would appear with no greater calling than a word.

But there was one antidote which wrestled with the nightshade in his cup, one star of the right colour appeared above his horizon. There was a woman in his town (one only for him), a princess and the ward of a king, an exquisite beauty. From the first time he saw her, he loved her with a passion which reproached his meaner self. She fed upon his sighs, without knowing that the air she breathed was full of them. In any case, he would never have dared to speak to her. It was sufficient daily bread to him to see her move. He hung upon her footsteps. He kept pace with her in her rides, running ever in the shadow because he himself had no shadow to call his own. Yet he forgot while looking at her this one great fact of his life. Even in his dreams she presently held his hand while he suffered. And he dreamed of her thus till he set his teeth in his pillow. Gradually her little mouth sucked up all the breath of his body. He wrote poems about his princess and swallowed them. Often he took no other food for days. He made philtres which would infallibly have caused her to love him, had he not ruthlessly thrown them all away as soon as made. He constructed an image of her in wax, and worshipped it five times daily. It was this which wrought his downfall. Certain of his clients (they had not paid him) denounced him as a sorcerer. Without notice he received a domiciliary visit from the authorities. Apart from other evidence which the house contained, the wax image of the princess was discovered, and he was at once charged with intending to make away with her life. Oh, the irony of fate – he who would have cheerfully laid down his own for her! Being forcibly removed from his house, the secret he had so long kept was discovered, and this shadowlessness, though accounted for in a hundred ways, all wide of the truth, was added at once to the long list of crimes in his indictment. At the preliminary examination, he would confess nothing. He was accordingly imprisoned pending the preparation of tortures to shake his resolution. With the aid of these refinements he might be made to confess anything, even that he had attempted the life of his best beloved. The scaffold loomed before him. And oh, that her name should be bandied about in such context.

Meanwhile Porphyro sat, body and soul in darkness. He saw none but the jailer, who brought him food once daily, with a finger ever on his lips. Rats there were, and such small deer, but with these he could hold no converse, although in his youth he had met with men who professed to teach their languages. Porphyro was fain to chatter constantly to himself that he might have no time to think. He played his school games over again, rehearsed his school tasks to imaginary masters, held imaginary conversations with clients and with his parents long dead, and with his princess who was more than parent, and more than dead to him. He wooed her in a thousand ways; now as an emperor, raising her to his level; now as the meanest of her grooms, to whom she sweetly condescended; now he was a soldier, better used to red lips of wounds than red lips which wound; now he was a scholar, who forgot all wisdom save hers; now he was a miser, who came like Jupiter in a shower of gold. Thus riotous reigned carnival before his coming Lent.

And now comes the strangest part of all this strange eventful history. He fancied once or twice that he was replied to as he spoke. Again and again he groped all over the blind prison, and felt no one. Yet there was of a surety a tongue which answered him. And the weirdness of it was that, turn though he might, it always spoke from behind him. Again he searched the litter of the dungeon, and again without result. The voice was at first unintelligible, like the murmur of the sea, yet with a cadence which soon struck his ear as strangely familiar. He had heard it only once before, but it had been in that cock-pit underground where he had fought a main which had coloured his whole life. He was bound up with the memory of it like a poor prisoner whom men fetter to a corpse. It was the still small voice which dominates the brawl of hell.

His hair could grow no whiter, else it had done so. He listened with all his ears and began to catch syllables and afterwards words, till at last he made out that the Tempter was proposing terms of peace with him.

Right well knew Porphyro (none better) the price that must be paid for such a truce. His soul must feed the quick of hell. It seemed hard to yield up at last that immortal henchman which he had once so gloriously saved from these same talons. Yet what chance had he? On the one hand, if he maintained his feud with the Evil One, the halter was weaving which must strangle love and life. On the other part, if he surrendered his soul to the Exile, he could at any rate make what terms he pleased. And there were terms he pictured himself exacting which made ultimate payment of the highest price seem easy to the blood which had once stood face to face with Satan, and given him better than he gave. Porphyro still continued to argue *pro* and *con*, though his decision was a foregone conclusion. At last he formulated his demands to the spirit. He must marry the Princess. He must be her husband, were it but for a single night.

The walls of the dungeon suddenly became bright with a kind of phosphorescent glow. Porphyro (still alone, or, at any rate, he seemed so) saw a table standing in front of him, bearing a bond already drawn and the materials for signing it. The terms set forth were those he had himself proposed. He signed, sealed, and delivered it, and was plunged into darkness again as his finger left the parchment. A sense of infernal laughter pervaded the air, though nothing was to be heard. Porphyro fell full length to the ground in a fainting fit.

When he recovered his jailer was standing over him, come (as he thought) to bring him food, but he was soon disabused of any such notion by the man himself. He, who had refused on all prior occasions to hold converse with his prisoner, now spoke voluntarily to tell him the sands of his captivity had run out. At first the dazed cage bird (who had forgotten for the moment his compact) believed that he was on the point of expiating his crimes, real and imaginary, upon the scaffold. But the jailer, not without difficulty, made it clear to him that all captives received pardon on the joyous occasion of the marriage of their Princess, which was fixed for that day. Then Porphyro remembered all, and swooned again.

When he revived, our hero was sitting in the open air upon the steps which led from the jail. He caught the smell of oxen roasting whole in the market-place. The sky was red with the fires. The streets as far as he could see them, were paved with flowers and decorated with triumphal arches. The citizens were bustling about in holiday attire. Music seemed to be playing everywhere. Occasionally some exuberant person fired off a gun. Porphyro rubbed his eyes and wondered whether this could really be his wedding day. He had faith in the boundless powers of the banner under which he had enrolled himself. And yet was it possible? But his faith was amply justified. An equerry suddenly rode up, parting the spectators to right and left, leading a spare horse magnificently caparisoned, and followed in the distance by a brilliant retinue. He doffed his cap to Porphyro and sprang to the ground, and with a profound obeisance, said in tones of deep respect:

'I trust your Highness has recovered from your indisposition. I have brought the horse as your Highness commanded.'

Porphyro dimly understood that some potent influence was at work on his behalf. With the assistance of his squire he took to the saddle. The latter then, with another bow, remounted his own horse, scattered a handful of gold to each side to break up the crowd, and with the rest of the train (which had caught up to them) they galloped to the Cathedral. Porphyro noted with stupid surprise that all the fountains spouted wine, whereto certain of the citizens, judging by the hiccups which mingled with their cheers, had already applied themselves, not wisely but too well. But our hero was in a state of so great fog himself as to feel his heart warm more towards these than to the soberer ones, whose salutations he clumsily returned. By the time the Cathedral was reached, he was rolling in his saddle. He could not have dismounted without help. The incense made him dizzy. He could not get the ringing of the bells out of his ears. The candles danced before his eyes. Of all the service he heard one word, and that was uttered by one who stood beside him, and whom alone he saw (and that through a mist) of all that gay asembly. It was the Princess. He pressed her hand as if he would never part with it.

The service over, he had no idea how, or in what order they reached the castle, and the banquet which followed was more or less of a blank to him. The wines, of which he partook liberally, could make him no more drunk, nor all the compliments of all the fulsome speeches (had he heard them) raise by one degree his pride. He soared empyrean high in the thought that he had won the right to crush into one cup, one moment, all the eternal delirium of all the heavens.

That moment of fruition had come at last. Porphyro stood in that holy of holies, his princess's chamber. A guard of soldiers was ranged along the four walls of this dainty nest. Each leaned with one arm upon a pike, while with the other hand he held aloft a blazing torch. Great personages were also present, both courtiers and noble dames, and at last the bride herself was brought in by her women. While complimentary discourse passed from mouth to mouth, Porphyro longed with his whole bartered soul to be alone with her. He was burning with internal fire which he could hold in little longer. At last he approached one that appeared to act as master of the ceremonies.

'When is this rigmarole going to end?' he muttered between his teeth.

'Whenever your Highness pleases to draw your sword and lay it in the middle of the bed, the Princess will take up her place upon one side of it, while you occupy the other,' was the reply.

Porphyro started. He surely recognized that voice. The official kept his face averted, but it was undoubtedly the demon.

'What mean you be this gabble of naked swords between me and her?' thundered Porphyro, unheeding who might hear. 'Damned posture master, is she not my wife?'

'Your wife yes, but only be letters of procuration,' and there was a note of triumph in that voice.

'God of the Judgement! What is that you say?'

'I say you must be dreaming not to remember that you are only temporarily united to the Princess in your character of proxy for his Imperial Majesty, the Holy Roman Emperor.'

'Alas the while! Then I am dreaming, indeed!'

'These soldiers,' continued the demon, 'will remain here all night. These ladies and gentlemen will also attend here till morning, to entertain you and your bride of an hour through your somewhat tedious spell of lying fully dressed together.'

'Death and the Pit! Is this true?'

'True as death, assured as the pit. Tomorrow you will sheathe your sword, and depart from her for ever.'

Porphyro pressed his hands to his temples. He thought his brain would burst. He saw it all now. He was the dupe of the fiend who had once been his dupe. His place in this pageant had been contrived with infernal subtlety, only to wring the uttermost pang from his heart strings. He who sups with the devil (they say) must needs have a very long spoon. No help was possible. The Evil One was reaping his revenge. And now he was assured his victim had at last grasped the situation, he threw off the mask, and showed himself in his true colours. He raised his eyes for the first time from the ground, those brimming lakes of bottomless hate which Porphyro had fronted once before in the underground hall. It was his turn now to quail.

'Ha! ha!' laughed the fallen angel. 'By mine ancient seat in Heaven (and that is an oath I never lightly take as you may guess), confess, have I not bested you, friend Porphyro? He laughs best who laughs the last; is it not so?'

'But what about that bond registered between us in Hell's chancery?' cried Porphyro, in a voice which would have melted triple brass.

'Your bond,' shrieked Beelzebub. 'Do you remind me of your bond; you who once outfaced me that a bond should be read by the letter, and not by the spirit? I have come round to your views, and I now fling word back in your teeth. You have had your bond to the letter, and now go and kill yourself, for there is nothing more for you to do.'

Porphyro bent like a broken reed. He had found his over-mastering fate. His hopes were ash. He breathed in gasps. He staggered to the window, and threw open the casement. A great pitiful star looked in, but to his eyes it appeared red and bloodshot. He turned round again to the room. He wished to see once more before he died that mistress of his soul for whose sake he had flung it away. But the figure of his master had swelled, and was swelling so rapidly in size that it seemed to fill every available corner of the room. Porphyro raised his hands to heaven, and called upon his lady's name. Three times he called it, and then sprang out of the window. The Princess who had grasped nothing of what had passed, ran to the shutter, and looked out just in time to hear the splash of his body as it fell into the moat. It was the first sign of interest in him which she had shown.

# THE HAND OF GLORY

## by Seabury Quinn

### 1. *The Shrieking Woman*

'Th' tip o' th' marnin' to yez, gintlemen.' Officer Collins touched the vizor of his cap as Jules de Grandin and I rounded the corner with none too steady steps. The night was cold, and our host's rum punch had a potency peculiarly its own, which accounted for our decision to walk the mile or so which stretched between us and home.

'*Holà, mon brave,*' responded my companion, now as ever ready to stop and chat with any member of the gendarmerie. 'It is morning, you say? *Ma foi*, I had not thought it much past ten o'clock.'

Collins grinned appreciatively. 'Arrah, Doctor de Grandin, sor,' he answered, 'wid a bit o' th' crayter th' likes o' that ye've had, 'tis meself as wouldn't be bodderin' wid th' time o' night ayther, fer –'

His witticism died birth-strangled, for, even as he paused to guffaw at the intended thrust, there came stabbing through the pre-dawn calm a cry of such thin-edged, unspeakable anguish as I had not heard since the days when as an intern I rode an ambulance's tail and amputations often had to be performed without the aid of anaesthesia.

'*Bon Dieu!*' de Grandin cried, dropping my elbow and straightening with the suddenness of a coiled spring released from its tension. 'What is that, in pity's gracious name?'

His answer followed fast upon his question as a pistol's crack succeeds the powder-flash, for round the shoulder of the corner building came a girl on stumbling, fear-hobbled feet, arms spread, eyes wide, mouth opened for a

184

scream which would not come, a perfect fantasm of terror.

'Here, here, now, phwat's up?' demanded Collins gruffly, involuntary fright lending harshness to his tones. ''Tis a foin thing ye're afther doin', runnin' through th' strates in yer nighties, scarin' folks out o' their sivin senses, an' –'

The woman paid him no more heed than if he'd been a shadow, for her dilated eyes were blinded by extremity of fear, as we could see at a glance, and had de Grandin not seized her by the shoulder she would have passed us in her headlong, stumbling flight. At the touch of the Frenchman's hand she halted suddenly, swayed uncertainly a moment; then, like a marionette whose strings are cut, she buckled suddenly, fell half kneeling, half sprawling to the sidewalk and lifted trembling hands to him beseechingly.

'It was afire!' she babbled thickly. 'Afire – blazing, I tell you – and the door flew open when they held it out. They – they – *aw-wah-wahl* –' her words degenerated into unintelligible syllables as the tautened muscles of her throat contracted with a nervous spasm, leaving her speechless as an infant, her thin face a white wedge of sheer terror.

'D.T.'s sor?' asked Collins cynically, bending for a better view of the trembling woman.

'Hysteria,' denied de Grandin shortly. Then, to me:

'Assist me, Friend Trowbridge, she goes into the paroxysmal stage.' As he uttered the sharp warning, the woman sank face-downwards to the pavement, lay motionless, then trembled with convulsive shudders, the shudders becoming twitches and the twitches going into wild, abandoned gestures, horribly reminiscent of the reflex contortionists of a decapitated fowl.

'Good Lord, I'll call th' wagon,' Collins offered; but:

'A cab, and quickly, if you please,' de Grandin countermanded. 'This is no time for making of arrests, my friend; this poor one's sanity may depend upon our ministrations.'

Luckily, a cruising taxi hove in sight even as he spoke, and with a hasty promise to inform police headquarters of the progress of the case, we bundled our patient into the vehicle and rushed at breakneck speed towards my office.

'Morphine, quickly, if you please,' de Grandin ordered as he bore the struggling woman to my surgery, thrust her violently upon the examination table and drew up the sleeve of her georgette pajama jacket, baring the white flesh for the caress of the mercy-bearing needle.

Swabbing the skin with alcohol, I pinched the woman's trembling arm, inserted the hypo point into the folded skin and thrust the plunger home, driving a full three-quarter grain dose into her system; then, with refilled syringe, stood in readiness to repeat the treatment if necessary.

But the opiate took effect immediately. Almost instantly the clownish convulsions ceased, within a minute the movements of her arms and legs had subsided to mere tremblings, and the choking, anguished moans which had proceeded from her throat died to little, childish whimpers.

'Ah, so,' de Grandin viewed the patient with satisfaction. 'She will be better now, I think. Meantime, let us prepare some stimulant for the time of her awakening. She has been exposed, and we must see that she does not take cold.'

Working with the speed and precision of one made expert by long service in the war's field hospitals, he draped a steamer rug across the back of an easy-chair in the study, mixed a stiff dose of brandy and hot water and set it by the open fire; then, calm-eyed but curious, resumed his station beside the unconscious girl upon the table.

We had not long to wait. The opiate had done its work quickly, but almost as quickly had found its antidote in the intensely excited nervous system of the patient. Within five minutes her eyelids fluttered, and her head rolled from side to side, like that of a troubled sleeper. A little moan, half of discomfort, half involuntary protest at re-

186

turning consciousness, escaped from her.

'You are in the office of Doctor Samuel Trowbridge, Mademoiselle,' de Grandin announced in a low, calm voice, anticipating the question which nine patients out of every ten propound when recovering from a swoon. 'We found you in the street in a most deplorable condition and brought you here for treatment. You are better now? *Permettez-moi.*'

Taking her hands in his, he raised her from the table, eased her to the floor and, his arms about her waist, guided her gently to the study, where, with the adeptness of a deck steward, he tucked the steamer rug about her feet and knees, placed a cushion at her back and before she had a chance to speak, held the glass of steaming toddy to her lips.

She drank the torrid liquid greedily, like a starving child gulping at a goblet of warm milk; then, as the potent draft raced through her, leaving a faint flush on her dead-pale cheeks, gave back the glass and viewed us with a pathetic, drowsy little smile.

'Thank you,' she murmured. 'I – oh, I remember now!' Abruptly her half-somnolent manner vanished and her hands clutched claw-like at the chair-arms. 'It was afire!' she told us in a hushed, choking voice. 'It was blazing, and –'

'Mademoiselle! You will drink this, if you please!' Sharply, incisively, the Frenchman's command cut through her fearful utterance as he held forward a cordial glass half full of cloudy liquid.

Startled, but docile, she obeyed, and a look of swift bewilderment swept across her pale, peaked features as she finished drinking. 'Why' – she exclaimed – 'why –' Her voice sank lower, her lids closed softly and her head fell back against the cushion at her shoulders.

'*Voilà*, I feared that recollection might unsettle her and had it ready,' he announced. 'Do you go up to bed, my friend. Me, I shall watch beside her, and should I need you I shall call. I am inured to sleeplessness and shall not mind the vigil; but it is well that one of us has rest, for tomorrow – *eh bien*, this poor once's case has the smell of herring on it and I damn think we shall have more sleepless nights than one before we see the end of it.'

Murmuring, I obeyed. Delightful companion, thoughtful friend, indefatigable co-worker that he was, Jules de Grandin possessed a streak of stubbornness beside which the most refractory mule ever sired in the State of Missouri was docility personified, and I knew better than to spend the few remaining hours of darkness in fruitless argument.

## 2. *The Hand of Glory*

A gentle murmur of voices sounded from the study when I descended from my room after something like four hours' sleep. Our patient of the night before still sat swathed in rugs in the big wing chair, but something approximating normal colour had returned to her lips and cheeks, and though her hands fluttered now and again in tremulous gesticulation as she talked, it required no second glance to tell me that her condition was far from bordering on nervous collapse. 'Taut, but not stretched dangerously near the snapping-point,' I diagnosed as I joined them. De Grandin reclined at ease across the fire from her, a pile of burned-out cigarettes in the ash-tray beside him, smoke from a freshly lighted 'Maryland' slowly spiralling upwards as he waved his hand back and forth to emphasize his words.

'What you tell is truly interesting, Mademoiselle,' he was assuring her as I entered the study.

'Trowbridge, *mon vieux*, this is Mademoiselle Wickwire. Mademoiselle, my friend and colleague, Doctor Samuel Trowbridge. Will you have the goodness to repeat your story to him? I would rather that he had it from your own lips.'

The girl turned a wan smile towards me, and I was struck by her extreme slenderness. Had her bones been larger, she would have been distressfully thin; as it was, the covering of her slight skeletal structure was so scanty as to make her almost as ethereal as a sprite. Her hair was fair, her eyes of an indeterminate shade somewhere between true blue and amethyst, and their odd coloration was picked up and accentuated by a chaplet of purple stones about her slender throat and the purple settings of the rings she wore upon the third finger of each hand. Limbs and extremities were fine-drawn as silver wire and elongated to an extent which was just short of grotesque, while her profile was robbed of true beauty by its excessive clarity of line. Somehow, she reminded me more of a statuette carved from crystal than of a flesh-and-blood woman, while the georgette pajamas of sea-green trimmed with amethyst and the absurd little boudoir cap which perched on one side of her fair head helped lend her an air of tailor's-dummy unreality.

I bowed acknowledgement of de Grandin's introduction and waited expectantly for her narrative, prepared to cancel ninety per cent of all she told me as the vagary of an hysterical young woman.

'Doctor de Grandin tells me I was screaming that "it was burning" when you found me in the street last night,' she began without preamble. 'It was.'

'Eh?' I ejaculated, turning a quick glance of inquiry on de Grandin. 'What?'

'The hand.'

'Bless my soul! The *what*?'

'The hand,' she returned with perfect aplomb. Then: 'My father is Joseph Wickwire, former Horner Professor of Orientology and Ancient Religion at De Puy University. You know his book, *The Cult of the Witch in Assyria*?'

I shook my head, but the girl, as though anticipating my confession of ignorance, went on without pause:

'I don't understand much about it, for Father never troubled to discuss his studies with me, but from some things he's told me, he became convinced of the reality of ancient witchcraft – or magic – some years ago, and gave up his chair at De Puy to devote himself to private research. While I was at school he made several trips to the Near East and last year spent four months in Mesopotamia, supervizing some excavations. He came home with two big cases – they looked more like casket-boxes than anything else – which he took to his study, and since then no one's been allowed in the room, not even I or Fanny, our maid. Father won't permit anything, not even so much as a grain of dust to be taken from that room; and one of the first things he did after receiving those boxes was to have an iron-plated door made for the study and have heavy iron bars fitted to all the windows.

'Lately he's been spending practically all his time at work in the study, sometimes remaining there for two or three days at a time, refusing to answer when called to meals or to come out for rest or sleep. About a month ago something happened which upset him terribly. I think it was a letter he received, though I'm not sure, for he wouldn't tell me what it was; but he seemed distracted, muttering constantly to himself and looking over his shoulder every now and then as though he expected some one, or something to attack him from behind. Last week he had some workmen come and reinforce all the doors with inch-wide strips of cast iron. Then he had special combination locks fitted to the outside doors and Yale locks to all the inside ones, and every night, just at dusk, he sets the combinations, and no one may enter or leave the house till morning. It's been rather like living in prison.'

'More like a madhouse,' I commented mentally, looking at the girl's thin face with renewed interest. 'Delusions of persecution on the part of the parent might explain abnormal behaviour on the part of the offspring, if –'

The girl's recital broke in on my mental diagnosis: 'Last night I couldn't sleep. I'd gone to bed about eleven and slept soundly for an hour or so; then suddenly I sat up, broad awake, and nothing I could do would get me back to sleep. I tried bathing the back of my neck with cologne, turning my pillows, even taking ten grains of allonal; nothing was any good, so finally I gave up trying and went down to the library. There was a copy of Hallam's *Constitutional History of England* there, and I picked that out as being the dullest reading I could find, but I read over a hundred pages without the slightest sign of drowsiness. Then I decided to take the book upstairs. Possibly, I thought, if I tried reading it in bed I might drop off without realizing it.

'I'd gotten as far as the second floor – my room's on the third – and was almost in front of Father's study when I heard a noise at the front door. "Any burglar who tries breaking into this house will be wasting his talents," I remember saying to myself, when just as though they were being turned by an invisible hand, the dials of the combination lock started to spin. I could see them in the light of the hall ceiling-lamp, which Father insists always be kept burning, and they were turned not slowly, but swiftly, as though being worked by one who knew the combination perfectly.

'At the same time the queerest feeling came over me. It was like one of those dreadful nightmares people sometimes have, when they're being attacked or pursued by some awful monster, and can't run or cry out, or even *move*. There I stood, still as a marble image, every faculty alert, but utterly unable to make a sound or move a finger – or even wink an eye.

'And as I watched in helpless stillness, the front door swung back silently and two men entered the hall. One carried a satchel or suitcase or some sort, the other' – she paused and caught her breath like a runner nearly spent, and her voice sank to a thin, harsh whisper – 'the other was holding *a blazing hand* in front of him!'

'A *what*?' I demanded incredulously. There was no question in my mind that the delusions of the sire were ably matched by the hallucinations of the daughter.

'A blazing hand,' she answered, and again I saw the shudder of a nervous chill run through her slender frame. 'He held it forward, like a candle, as though to light his way; but there was no need of it for light, for the hall lamp has a hundred-watt bulb, and its luminance reached up the stairs and made everything in the upper passage plainly visible. Besides, the thing burned with more fire than light. There seemed to be some sort of wick attached to each of the fanned-out fingers, and these burned with a clear, steady blue flame, like blazing alcohol. It –'

'But my dear young lady,' I expostulated, 'that's impossible.'

'Of course it is,' she agreed with unexpected calmness. 'So is this: As the man with the blazing hand mounted the stairs and paused before my father's study, I heard a distinct *click*, and the door swung open, unlocked. Through the opening I could see Father standing in the middle of the room, the light from an unshaded ceiling-lamp making everything as clear as day. On a long table was some sort of object which reminded me of one of those little marble stones they put over soldiers' graves in national cemeteries, only it was grey instead of white, and a great roll of manuscript lay beside it. Father had risen and stood facing the door with one hand resting on the table, the other reaching towards a sawed-off shotgun which lay beside the stone and manuscript. But he was paralysed – frozen in the act of reaching for the gun as I had been in the act of walking down the hall. His eyes were wide and set with surprise – no, not quite that, they were more like the painted eyes of a window-figure in a store, utterly expressionless – and I remember wondering, in that odd way people have of thinking of inconsequential things in moments of intense excitement, whether mine looked the same.

'I saw it all. I saw them go through the study's open door, lift the stone off the table, bundle up Father's manuscript and stuff everything into the bag. Then, the man with the burning hand going last, walking backwards and holding the thing before him, they left as silently as they came. The doors swung to behind them without being touched. The study door had a Yale snap-lock in addition to its combination fastenings, so it was fastened when it closed, but the bolts of the safe lock on the front door didn't fly back in place when it closed.

'I don't know how long that strange paralysis held me after the men with the hand had gone; but I remember suddenly regaining my power of motion and finding myself with one foot raised – I'd been overcome in the act of stepping and had remained helpless, balanced on one foot, the entire time. My first act, of course, was to call Father, but I could get no response, even when I beat and kicked on the door.

'Then panic seized me. I didn't quite know what I was doing, but something seemed urging me to get away from that house as though it had been haunted, and the horrifying memory of that blazing hand with those combination-locked doors flying open before it came down on me like a cloud of strangling, smothering gas. The front door was still unfastened, as I've told you, and I flung it open, fighting for a breath of fresh outdoors air, and ran screaming into the street. You know the rest.'

'You see?' asked Jules de Grandin.

I nodded understandingly. I saw only too well. A better symptomatized case of dementia praecox it had never been my evil fortune to encounter.

There was a long moment of silence, broken by de Grandin. '*Eh bien, mes amis*, we make no progress here,' he announced. 'Grant me fifteen small minutes for my toilette, Madamoiselle, and we shall repair to the house of your father. There, I make no doubt, we shall learn something of interest concerning last night's so curious events.'

He was as good as his promise, and within the stipulated time had rejoined us, freshly shaved, washed and brushed, a most agreeable odour of bath salts and dusting powder emanating from his spruce, diminutive person.

'Come, let us go,' he urged, assisting our patient to her feet and wrapping the steamer rug about her after the manner of an Indian's blanket.

## 3. *The House of the Magician*

The front entrance of Professor Wickwire's house was closed, but unfastened, when we reached our destination, and I looked with interest at the formidable iron reinforcements and combination locks upon the door. Thus far the girl's absurd story was borne out by facts, I was forced to admit, as we mounted the stairs to the upper floor where Wickwire had his barricaded sanctum.

No answer coming to de Grandin's peremptory summons, Miss Wickwire tapped lightly on the iron-bound panels. 'Father, it is I, Diane,' she called.

Somewhere beyond the door we heard a shuffling step and a murmuring voice, then a listless fumbling at the locks which held the portal fast.

The man who stood revealed as the heavy door swung back looked like a Fundamentalist cartoonist's caricature of Charles Darwin. The pate was bald, the jaw bearded, the brows heavy and prominent, but where the great evolutionist's forehead bulged with an intellectual swell, this man's skull slanted back obliquely, and the temples were flat, rather than concave. Also, it required no second glance to tell us that the full beard covered a soft, receding chin, and the eyes beneath the shaggy brows were weak with a weakness due to more that mere poor vision. He looked to me more like the sort of person who would spend spare time reading books on development of will-power and personality than poring over ponderous tomes on Assyriology. And though he seemed possessed of full dentition, he mumbled like a toothless ancient as he stared at us, feeble eyes blinking owlishly behind the pebbles of his horn-rimmed spectacles.

'*Magna Mater ... trismegistus ... salve ...*' we caught the almost unintelligible Latin of his mumbled incantation.

'Father!' Diane Wickwire exclaimed in distress. 'Father, here are –'

The man's head rocked insanely from side to side, as

194

though his neck had been a flaccid cord, and *'Magna Mater..* he began again with a whimpering persistence.

*'Monsieur*! Stop it. I command it, and I am Jules de Grandin!' Sharply the little Frenchman's command rang out; then, as the other goggled at him and began his muttered prayer anew, de Grandin raised his small gloved hand and dealt him a stinging blow across the face. *'Parbleu*, I will be obeyed, me!' he snorted wrathfully. 'Save your conjurations for another time, Monsieur; at present we would talk with you.'

Brutal as his treatment was, it was efficacious. The blow acted like a douche of cold water on a swooning person, and Wickwire seemed for the first time to realize we were present.

'These gentlemen are Doctors Trowbridge and de Grandin,' his daughter introduced. 'I met them when I ran for help last night, and they took me with them. Now, they are here to help you –'

Wickwire stopped her with uplifted hand. 'I fear there's no help for me – or you, my child,' he interrupted sadly. 'They have the Sacred Meteorite, and it is only a matter of time till they find the Word of Power, then –'

*'Nom d'un coq*, Monsieur, let us have things logically and in decent order, if you please,' de Grandin broke in sharply. 'This sacred meteorite, this word of powerfulness, this so mysterious "they" who have the one and are about to have the other, in Satan's name, who and what are they? Tell us from the start of the beginning. We are intrigued, we are interested; *parbleu*, we are consumed with the curiosity of a dying cat!'

Professor Wickwire smiled at him, the weary smile a tired adult might give a curious child. 'I fear you wouldn't understand,' he answered softly.

'By blue, you do insult my credulity, Monsieur!' the Frenchman rejoined hotly. 'Tell us your tale, all – every little so small bit of it – and let us be the judges of what we shall believe. Me, I am an occultist of no small ability, and this so strange adventure of last night assuredly has the flavour of the superphysical. Yes, certainly.'

Wickwire brightened at the other's words. 'An occult-ist?' he echoed. 'Then perhaps you can assist me. Listen carefully, if you please, and ask me anything which you may not understand:

'Ten years ago, while assembling data for my book on witchcraft in the ancient world, I became convinced of the reality of sorcery. If you know anything at all of medieval witchcraft, you realize that Diana was the pat-roness of the witches, even in that comparatively late day. Burchard, Bishop of Worms, writing of sorcery, heresy, and witchcraft in Germany in the year 1000 says: "Cer-tain wretched women, seduced by the sorcery of demons, affirm that during the night they ride with Diana, god-dess of the heathens, and a host of other women, and that they traverse immense spaces."

'Now, Diana, whom most moderns look upon as a clean-limbed goddess of chastity, was only one name for the great Female Principle among the pantheon of ancient days. Artemis, or Diana, is typified by the moon, but there is also Hecate, goddess of the black and fearful night, queen of magic, sorcery, and witchcraft, deity of goblins and the underworld, and guardian of crossroads; she was another attribute of the same night-goddess whom we know best today as Diana.

'But back of all the goddesses of night, whether they be styled Diana, Artemis, Hecate, Rhea, Astarte, or Ishtar, is the Great Mother – *Magna Mater*. The origin of her cult is so ancient that recorded history does not even touch it, and even oral tradition tells of it only by indirection. Her worship is so old that the Anatolian meteorite brought to Rome in 204 B.C. compares to it as Christian Science or New Thought compare in age with Buddhism.

'Piece by piece I traced back the chain of evidence of her worship and finally became convinced that it was not in Anatolia at all that her mother-shrine was located, but in some obscure spot, so many centuries forgotten as to be no longer named, near the site of the ancient city of Uruck. An obscure Roman legionary mentions the temple where the goddess he refers to by the Syro-Phoenician name of Astarte was worshipped by a select coterie of adepts, both men and women, to whom she gave dominion over earth and sea and sky – power to raise tempests or to quiet them, to cause earthquakes, to cause fertility or sterility in men and beasts, or cause the illness or death of an enemy. They were also said to have the power of levitation, or flying through the air for great distances, or even to be seen in several places at the same time. This, you see, is about the sum total of all the powers claimed for witches and wizards in medieval times. In fine, this obscure goddess of our nameless centurion is the earliest ascertainable manifestation of the female divinity who governed witchcraft in the ancient world, and whose place has been usurped by the devil in Christian theology.

'But this was only the beginning: The Roman chronicler stated definitely that her idol was a 'stone from heaven, wrapped in an envelope of earth, and that no man durst break the tegument of the celestial stone for far of rousing Astarte's wrath; yet to him who had the courage to do so would be given the *Verbum Magnum*, or Word of Power – an incantation whereby all majesty, might, power, and dominion of all things visible and invisible would be put into his hands, so that he who knew the word would be, literally, Emperor of the Universe.

'As I said before, I became convinced of the reality of witchcraft, both ancient and modern, and the deeper I delved into the records of the past the more convinced I was that the greatest claims made by latter-day witches were mere childish nonsense compared to the mighty powers actually possessed by the wizards of olden times. I spent my health and bankrupted myself seeking that nameless temple of Astarte – but at last *I found it.* I found the very stone of which the Roman wrote and brought it back to America – here.'

Wickwire paused, breathing in laboured gasps, and his pale eyes shone with the quenchless ardour of the enthusiast as he looked triumphantly from one of us to the other.

'*Bien*, Monsieur, this stone of the old one is brought here; what then?' de Grandin asked as the professor showed no sign of proceeding further with his narrative.

'Eh? Oh, yes.' Once more Wickwire lapsed into semi-somnolence. 'Yes, I brought it back, and was preparing to unwrap it, studying my way carefully, of course, in order to avoid being blasted by the goddess' infernal powers when I broke the envelope, but – but they came last night and stole it.'

'*Bon sang d'un bon poisson*, must we drag information from you bit by little bit, Monsieur?' blazed the exasperated Jules de Grandin. 'Who was it pilfered your unmentionable stone?'

'Kraus and Steinert stole it.' Wickwire answered tonelessly. 'They are German *illuminati*, Hanoverians whose researches paralleled mine in almost every particular, and who discovered the approximate location of the mystic meteorite shortly after I did. Fortunately for me their data were not so complete as mine, and they lost some time trying to locate the ancient temple. I had dug up the stone and was on my way home when they finally found the place.

'Can you imagine what it would mean to any mortal man to be suddenly translated into godhood, to sway the destinies of nations – of all mankind – as a wind sways a wheatfield? If you can, you can imagine what those two adepts in black magic felt when they arrived and found the key to power gone and on its way to America in the possession of a rival. They sent astral messengers after me, first offering partnership, then, when I laughed at them, making all manner of threats. Several times they attempted my life, but my magic was stronger than theirs, and each time I beat their spirit-messengers off.

'Lately, though, their emissaries have been getting stronger. I began to realize this when I found myself weaker and weaker after each encounter. Whether they have found new sources of strength, or whether it is because two of them work against me I do not know, but I began to realize we were becoming more evenly matched and it was only a matter of time before they would master me. Yet there was much to be done before I dared remove the envelope from that stone; to attempt it unprepared would be foolhardy. Such forces as would be unleashed by the cracking of that wrapping are beyond the scope of human imagining, and every precaution had to be taken. Any dunce can blow himself up handling gunpowder carelessly; only the skilled artillerist can harness the explosive and make it drive a projectile to a given target.

'While I was perfecting my spiritual defences I took all physical precautions, also, barring my windows and so securing my doors that if my enemies gave up the battle of magic in disgust and fell back upon physical force, I should be more than a match for them. Then, because I thought myself secure, for a little time at least, I overlooked one of the most elementary forms of sorcery, and last night they entered my house as though there had been no barriers and took away the magic stone. With that in their possession I shall be no match for them; they will work their will on me, then overwhelm the world with the forces of their wizardry. If only –'

'Excuse me, Professor,' I broke in, for, wild as his story was, I had become interested despite myself; 'what was the sorcery these men resorted to in order to force entrance? Your daughter told us something of a blazing hand, but –'

'It was a hand of glory,' he returned, regarding me with something of the look a teacher might bestow upon a backward schoolboy, 'one of the oldest, simplest bits of magic known to adepts. A hand – preferably the sinister – is cut from the body of an executed murderer, and five locks of hair are clipped from his head. The hand is smoked over a fire of juniper wood until it becomes dry and mummified; after this the hair is twisted into wicks which are affixed to the finger tips. If the proper invocations are recited while the hand and wicks are being prepared and the words of power pronounced when the wicks are lighted, no lock can withstand the light cast by the blazing glory hand, and –'

'*Ha*, I remember him,' de Grandin interrupted delightedly. 'Your so droll Abbé Barham tells of him in his exquisitely humorous poem:

> *Now open lock to the dead man's knock,*
>    *Fly bolt and bar and band;*
> *Nor move nor swerve joint, muscle or nerve,*
>    *At the spell of the dead man's hand.*
> *Sleep all who sleep, wake all who wake,*
>    *But be as the dead for the dead man's sake.*

Wickwire nodded grimly. 'There's a lot of truth in those doggerel rimes,' he answered. 'We laugh at the fairy-story of Bluebeard today, but it was no joke in fifteenth century France when Bluebeard was alive and making black magic.'

'*Tu parles, mon vieux*,' agreed de Grandin, 'and –'

'Exuse me, but you've spoken several times of removing the envelope from this stone, Professor,' I broke in again. 'Do you mean that literally, or –'

'Literally,' Wickwire responded. 'In Babylonia and Assyria, you know, all "documents" were clay tablets on which the cuneiform characters were cut while they were still moist and soft, and which were afterwards baked in a kiln. Tablets of special importance, after having been once written upon and baked, were covered with a thin coating of clay upon which an identical inscription was impressed, and the tablets were once more baked. If the outer writing were then defaced by accident or altered by design, the removal of the outer coating would at once show the true text. Such a clay coating has been wrapped about the mystic meteorite of the Great Mother-Goddess, but even in the days of the Roman historian most of the inscription had been obliterated by time. When I found it I could distinguish only one or two characters, such as the double triangle, signifying the moon, and the eight-pointed asterisks meaning the lord of lords and god of gods, or lady of ladies and goddess of goddesses. These, I may add, were not in the Assyrian cuneiforms of 700 B.C. or even the archaic characters dating back to 2500, but the early, primitive cuneiform, which was certainly not used later than 4500 B.C., probably several centuries earlier.'

'And how did you propose removing this clay integument without hurt to yourself, Monsieur?' de Grandin asked.

Wickwire smiled, and there was something devilish, callous, in his expression as he did so. 'Will you be good enough to examine my daughter's rings?' he asked.

Obedient to his nodded command, the girl stretched forth her thin, frail hands, displaying the purple settings of the circlets which adorned the third finger of each. The stones were smoothly polished, though not very bright, and each was deeply incised with this inscription:

'It's the ancient symbol of the Mother-Goddess,' Wickwire explained, 'and signifies "Royal Lady of the Night, Ruler of the Lights of Heaven, Mother of Gods, Men and Demons." Diane would have cracked the envelope for me, for only the hands of a virgin adorned with rings of amethyst bearing the Mother-Goddess' signet can wield the hammer which can break that clay – and the maid must do the act without fear or hesitation; otherwise she will be powerless.'

'U'm?' de Grandin twisted fiercely at his little blond moustache. 'And what becomes of this ring-decorated virgin, Monsieur?'

Again that smile of fiendish indifference transformed

Wickwire's weak face into a mask of horror. 'She would die,' he answered calmly. 'That, of course, is certain, but' – some lingering light of parental sanity broke through the look of wild fanaticism – 'unless she were utterly consumed by the tremendous forces liberated when the envelope was cracked, I should have power to restore her to life, for all power, might, dominion, and majesty in the world would have been mine; death should bow before me, and life should exist only by my sanction. I –'

'You are a scoundrel and a villain and a most unpleasant species of a malodorous camel,' cut in Jules de Grandin. 'Mademoiselle, you will kindly pack a portmanteau and come with us. We shall esteem it a privilege to protect you till danger from those *sales bêtes* who invaded your house last night is past.'

Without a word, or even a glance at the man who would have sacrificed her to his ambition, Diane Wickwire left the room, and we heard the clack-clack of her bedroom mules as she ascended to her chamber to procure a change of clothing.

Professor Wickwire turned a puzzled look from de Grandin to me, then back to the Frenchman. That we could not understand and sympathize with his ambition and condone his willingness to sacrifice his daughter's life never seemed to enter his mad brain. 'But me – what's to become of me?' he whimpered.

'*Eh bien*, one wonders,' answered Jules de Grandin. 'As far as I am concerned, Monsieur, you may go to the devil, nor need you delay your departure in anywise out of consideration for my feelings.'

'Mad,' I diagnosed. 'Mad as hatters, both of 'em. The man's a potential homicidal maniac; only heaven knows how long it will be before we have to put the girl under restraint.'

De Grandin looked cautiously about; then, satisfied that Diane Wickwire was still in the chamber to which she had been conducted by Nora McGinnis, my efficient housefold factotum, he replied: 'You think that story of the glory hand was madness, *hein?*'

'Of course it was,' I answered. 'What else could it be?'

'*Le bon Dieu* knows, not I,' he countered; 'but I would that you read this item in today's *Journal* before consigning her to the madhouse.' Picking up a copy of the morning paper he indicated a boxed item in the centre of the first page:

Police are seeking the ghouls who broke into James Gibson's funeral parlor, 1037 Ludlow St, early last night and stole the left hand from the body of José Sanchez, which was lying in the place awaiting burial today. Sanchez had been executed Monday night at Trenton for the murder of Robert Knight, caretaker in the closed Stephens iron foundry, last summer, and relatives had commissioned Gibson to bring the body to Harrisonville for interment.

Gibson was absent on a call in the suburbs last night, and as his assistant, William Lowndes, was confined to bed at home by unexpected illness, had left the funeral parlour unattended, having arranged to have any telephone calls switched to his residence in Winthrop St. On his return he found a rear door of his establishment had been jimmied and the left hand of the executed murderer severed at the wrist.

Strangely enough, the burglars had also shorn a considerable amount of hair from the corpse's head. A careful search of the premises failed to disclose anything else had been taken, and a quantity of money lying in the unlocked safe was untouched.

'Well!' I exclaimed, utterly nonplussed; but:

'Non,' he denied shortly. 'It is not all well, my friend, it is most exceedingly otherwise. It is fiendish, it is diabolical; it is devilish. These are determined miscreants against whom we have set ourselves, and I damn think that we shall lose some sleep ere all is done. Yes.'

## 4. *The Sending*

However formidable Professor Wickwire's rivals might have been, they gave no evidence of ferocity that I could see. Diane settled down comfortably in our midst, fitting perfectly into the quiet routine of the household, giving no trouble and making herself so generally agreeable that I was heartily glad of her presence. There is something comforting about the pastel shades of filmy dresses and white arms and shoulders gleaming softly in the candlelight at dinner. The melody of a well-modulated feminine voice, punctuated now and again with little rippling notes of quiet laughter, is more than vaguely pleasant to the bachelor ear, and as the time of our companionship lengthened I often found myself wondering if I should have had a daughter such as this to sit at table or before the fire with me if fate had willed it otherwise and my sole romance had ended elsewhere than an ivy-covered grave with low white headstone in St Stephen's churchyard. One night I said as much to Jules de Grandin, and the pressure of his hand on mine was good to feel.

'*Bien*, my friend,' he whispered, 'who are we to judge the ways of heaven? The grass grows green above the lips you used to kiss – me, I do not know if she I loved is in the world or gone away. I only know that never may I stand beside her grave and look at it, for in that cloistered cemetery no man may come, and – *eh*, what is that? *Un chaton*?' Outside the window of the drawing-room, scarce heard above the shrieking of the boisterous April wind, there sounded a plaintive mew, as though some feline wanderer begged entrance and a place before our fire.

Crossing the room, I drew aside the casement curtain, straining my eyes against the murky darkness. Almost level with my own, two eyes of glowing green looked through the pane, and another pleading miaul implored my charity.

'All right, Pussy, come in,' I invited, drawing back the sash to permit an entrance for the little waif, and through the opening jumped a plump, soft-haired angora cat, black as Erebus, jade-eyed, velvet-pawed. For a moment it stood at gaze, as though doubtful of the worthiness of my abode to house one of its distinction; then, with a satisfied little cat-chuckle, it crossed the room, furry tail waving jauntily, came to halt before the fire and curled up on the hearth rug, where, with paws tucked demurely in and tail curled about its body, it lay blinking contentedly at the leaping flames and purring softly. A saucer of warm milk further cemented cordial relations, and another member was added to our household personnel.

The little cat, on which we had bestowed the name of Eric Brighteyes, at once attached himself to Diane Wickwire, and could hardly be separated from her. Towards de Grandin and me it showed disdainful tolerance. For Nora McGinnis it had supreme contempt.

It was the twenty-ninth of April, a raw, wet night when the thermometer gave the lie to the calendar's assertion that spring had come. Three of us, de Grandin, Diane, and I, sat in the drawing-room. The girl seemed vaguely nervous and distrait, toying with her coffee cup, puffing at her cigarette, grinding out its fire against the ash-tray, then lighting another almost instantly. Finally she went to the piano and began to play. For a time she improvised softly, white fingers straying at random over the white keys; then, as though led by some subconscious urge for the solace of ecclesiastical music, she began the opening bars of Gounod's *Sanctus*:

> *Holy, Holy, Holy,*
> *Lord God of Hosts,*
> *Heaven and earth are full of Thy Glory ...*

The music ended on a sharply dissonant note and a gasp of horrified surprise broke the echoing silence as the player lifted startled fingers from the keys. We turned towards the piano, and:

'*Mon Dieu!*' exclaimed de Grandin. 'Hell is unchained against us!'

The cat, which had been contentedly curled up on the piano's polished top, had risen and stood with arched back, bristling tail and gaping, blood-red mouth, gazing from blazing ice-green eyes at Diane with such a look of murderous hate as made the chills of sudden blind, unreasoning fear run rippling down my spine.

'Eric – Eric Brighteyes!' Diane extended a shaking hand to soothe the menacing beast, and in a moment it was its natural, gentle self again, its back still arched, but arched in seeming playfulness, rubbing its fluffy head against her fingers and purring softly with contented friendliness. 'And did the horrid music hurt its eardrums? Well, Diane won't play it any more,' the girl promised, taking the jet-black ball of fur into her arms and nursing it against her shoulder. Shortly afterwards she said good-night, and, the cat still cuddled in her arms, went up to bed.

'I hardly like the idea of her taking that brute up with her,' I told de Grandin. 'It's always seemed so kind and gentle, but – well' – I laughed uneasily – 'when I saw it snarling at her just now I was heartily glad it wasn't any bigger.'

'U'm,' returned the Frenchman, looking up from silent study of the fire, 'one wonders.'

'Wonders what?'

'Much, by blue. Come, let us go.'

'Where?'

'Upstairs, *cordieu*, and let us step softly while we are about it.'

De Grandin in the lead, we tiptoed to the upper floor and paused before the entrance to Diane's chamber. From behind the white-enamelled panels came the sound of something like a sob; then, in a halting, faltering voice:

'Amen. Evil from us deliver but temptation into not us

lead, and us against trespass who those forgive we as . . .'

'*Grand Dieu – la prière renversée!*' de Grandin cried, snatching savagely at the knob and dashing back the door.

Diane Wickwire knelt beside her bed, purple-ringed hands clasped before her, tears streaming down her cheeks, while slowly, haltingly, like one wrestling with the vocables of an unfamiliar tongue, she painfully repeated the Lord's Prayer backwards.

And on the counterpane, its black muzzle almost forced against her face, crouched the black cat. But now its eyes were not the cool jade-green which we had known; they were red as embers of a dying fire when blown to life by some swift draft of air, and on its feline face, in hellish parody of humanity, there was a *grin*, a smile as cold and menacing, yet wicked and triumphant as any medieval artist ever painted on the lips of Satan!

We stood immovable a moment, taking in the tableau with a quickening gaze of horror; then:

'Say it, *Mademoiselle*, say it after me – *properly*!' commanded Jules de Grandin, raising his right hand to sign the cross above the girl's bowed head and beginning slowly and distinctly: 'Our Father, which art in Heaven, hallowed by Thy name . . .'

A terrifying screech, a scream of unsupportable agony, as though it had been plunged into a blazing fire, broke from the cowering cat-thing on the bed. Its reddened eyes flashed savagely, and its gaping mouth showed gleaming, knife-sharp teeth as it turned its gaze from Diane Wickwire and fixed it on de Grandin. But the Frenchman paid no heed.

'. . . and lead us not into temptation, but deliver us from evil. Amen,' he finished the petition.

And Diane prayed with him. Catching her cue from his slowly spoken syllables, she repeated the prayer word by painful word, and at the end collapsed, a whimpering, flaccid thing, against the bedstead.

But the cat? It was gone. As the girl and Frenchman reached 'Amen' the beast snarled savagely, gave a final spiteful hiss, and whirled about and bolted through the open window, vanishing into the night from which it had come a week before, leaving but the echo of its menacing sibilation and the memory of its dreadful transformation as mementoes of its visit.

'In heaven's name, what was it?' I asked breathlessly.

'A spy,' he answered. 'It was a sending, my old one; an emissary from those evil ones to whom we stand opposed.'

'A – a sending?'

'Perfectly. Assist me with Mademoiselle Diane and I shall elucidate.'

The girl was sobbing bitterly, trembling like a wind-shaken reed, but not hysterical, and a mild sedative was sufficient to enable her to sleep. Then, as we once more took our seats before the fire, de Grandin offered:

'I did not have suspicion of the cat, my friend. He seemed a natural animal, and as I like cats, I was his friend from the first. Indeed, it was not until tonight, when he showed aversion for the sacred music that I first began to realize what I should have known from the beginning. He was a sending.'

'Yes, you've said that before,' I reminded him, 'but what the devil is a "sending"?'

'The crystallized, physicallized desires and passions of a sorcerer or wizard,' he returned. 'Somewhat as the medium builds a semi-physical, semi-spiritual body out of that impalpability which we call psychoplasm or ectoplasm, so the skilled adept in magic can evoke a physical-seeming entity out of his wicked thoughts and send it where he will, to do his bidding and work his evil purposes. These ones against whom we are pitted, these burglar-thieves who entered Monsieur Wickwire's house with their accursed glory hand and stole away his unnamable stone of power are no good, my friend. No, certainly. On the contrary, they are all bad. They are drunk with lust for the power which they think will come into their hands when they have stripped the wrapping off that unmentionable stone. They know also, I should say, that Wickwire – may he eat turnips and drink water throughout eternity! – had ordained his daughter for the sacrifice, had chosen her for the rôle of envelope-stripper-off for that stone, and they accordingly desire to avail themselves of her services. To that end they evoke that seeming-cat and send it here, and it did work their will – conveyed their evil suggestions to the young girl's mind. She, who is all innocent of any knowledge of witchery or magic-mongering, was to be perverted; and right well the work was done, for tonight when she knelt to say her prayers she could not frame to pronounce them aright, but was obliged perforce to pray witch-fashion.'

'Witch-fashion?'

'But certainly. Of course. Those who have taken the vows of witchhood and signed their names in Satan's book of blackness are unable to pray like Christians from that time forward; they must repeat the holy words in reverse. Mademoiselle Diane, she is no professed witch, but I greatly fear she is infected by the virus. Already she was unable to pray like others, though when I said the prayer aright, she was still able to repeat it after me. Now –'

'Is there any way we can find these scoundrels and free Diane,' I interrupted. Not for a moment did I grant his premises, but that the girl was suffering some delusion I was convinced; possibly it was long-distance hypnotic suggestion, but whatever its nature, I was determined to seek out the instigators and break the spell.

For a moment he was silent, pinching his little pointed chin between a thoughtful thumb and forefinger and gaz-ing pensively into the fire. At length: 'Yes,' he answered. 'We can find the place where they lair, my friend; she will lead us to them.'

'She? How –'

'*Exactement.* Tomorrow is May Eve, Witch-Night – Walpurgis-Nacht. Of all the nights which go to make the year, they are most likely to try their deviltry then. It was not for nothing that they sent their spy into this house and established rapport with Mademoiselle Diane. Oh no. They need her in their business, and I think that all unconsciously she will go to them some time tomorrow evening. Me, I shall make it my especial duty to keep in touch with her, and where she goes, there will I go also.'

'I, too,' I volunteered, and we struck hands upon it.

## 5. *Walpurgis-Nacht*

Covertly, but carefully, we noted every movement the girl made next day. Shortly after luncheon de Grandin looked in at the consulting-room and nodded significantly. 'She goes; so do I,' he whispered, and was off.

It was nearly time for the evening meal when Diane returned, and a moment after she had gone upstairs to change for dinner I heard de Grandin's soft step in the hall.

'Name of a name,' he ejaculated, dropping into the desk-side chair and lighting a cigarette, 'but it is a merry chase which she has led me today, that one!'

I raised interrogative brows, and:

'From pharmacy to pharmacy she has gone, like a hypochondriac seeking for a cure. Consider what she bought' – he checked the items off upon his fanned-out fingers – 'aconitum, belladonna, solanin, mandragora officinalis. Not in any one, or even any two places did she buy these things. No, she was shrewd, she was clever, by blue, but she was subtle! Here she bought a flacon of perfume, there a box of powder, again, a cake of scented soap, but mingled with her usual purchases would be occasionally one of these strange things which no young lady can possibly be supposed to want or need. What think you of it, my friend?'

'H'm, it sounds like some prescription from the medieval pharmacopoeia,' I returne'd.

'Well said, my old astute one!' he answered. 'You have hit the thumb upon the nail, my Trowbridge. That is exactly what it is, a prescription from the *Pharmacopoeia Maleficorum* – the witches' book of recipes. Every one of those ingredients is stipulated as a necessary part of the witch's ointment –'

'The what?'

'The unguent with which those about to attend a sabbat, or meeting of a coven of witches, anointed themselves. If you will stop and think a moment, you will realize that nearly every one of those ingredients is a hypnotic or sedative. One thoroughly rubbed with a concoction of them would to a great degree lose consciousness, or, at the least, a sense of true responsibility.'

'Yes? And –'

'Quite yes. Today foolish people think of witches as rather amiable, sadly misunderstood and badly persecuted old females. That is quite as silly as the vapid modern belief that fairies, elves, and goblins are a set of well-intentioned folk. The truth is that a witch or wizard was – and is – one who by compact with the powers of darkness attains to power not given to the ordinary man, and uses that power for malevolent purposes; for a part of the compact is that he shall love evil and hate good. Very well. *Et puis?* Just as your modern gunmen of America and the *apaches* of Paris drug themselves with cocaine in order to stifle any flickering remnant of morality and remorse before committing some crime of monstrous ruthlessness, so did – and do – the witch and wizard drug themselves with this accursed ointment that they might utterly forget the still small voice of conscience urging them to hold their hands from evil unalloyed. It was not merely magic which called for this anointing, it was practical psychology and physic which prescribed it, my friend.'

'Yes; well –'

'By damn,' he hurried on, heedless of my interruption, 'I think that we have congratulated ourselves all too soon. Mademoiselle Diane is not free from the wicked influence of those so evil men; she is very far from free, and tonight, unconsciously and unwillingly, perhaps, but nevertheless surely, she will anoint herself with this witch-prescription, and her body shining like something long dead and decomposing, will go to them.'

'But what are we to do? Is there anything –'

'But yes; of course. You will please remain here, as close as may be to her door, and if she leaves the house, you follow her. Me, I have important duties to perform, and I shall do them quickly. Anon I shall return, and if she has not gone by then, I shall join you in your watch. If –'

'Yes, that's just it. Suppose she leaves while you're away,' I broke in. 'How am I to get in touch with you? How will you know where to come?'

'Call this number on the 'phone,' he answered, scratching a memorandum on a card. 'Say but "She is gone and I go with her", and I shall come at once. For safety's sake I would suggest that you take a double pocketful of rice, and scatter it along your way. I shall see the small white grains and follow hard upon your trail as though you were a hare and I a hound.'

Obedient to his orders, I mounted to the second floor and took my station where I could see the door of Diane's room. Half an hour or more I waited in silence, feeling decidedly foolish, yet fearing to ignore his urgent request. At length the soft creaking of hinges brought me alert as a fine pencil of light cut through the darkened hall. Walking so softly that her steps were scarcely audible, Diane Wickwire came from her room. From throat to insteps she was muffled in a purple cloak, while a veil or scarf of some dark-coloured stuff was bound about her head, concealing the bright beacon of her glowing golden hair. Hoping desperately that I should not lose her in the delay, I dialled the number which de Grandin had given me and as a man's voice challenged 'Hello?' repeated the formula he had stipulated:

'She goes, and I go with her.'

Then, without waiting for reply, I clashed the monophone back into its hooks, snatched up my hat and topcoat, seized a heavy blackthorn cane and crept as silently as possible down the stairs behind the girl.

She was fumbling at the front door lock as I reached the stairway's turn, and I flattened myself against the wall, lest she descry me; then as she let herself through the portal, I dashed down the stairs, stepped soft-footedly across the porch, and took up the pursuit.

She hastened onward through the thickening dusk, her muffled figure but a faint shade darker than the surrounding gloom, led me through one side street to another, gradually bending her way towards the old East End of town where ramshackle huts of squatters, abandoned factories, unofficial dumping-grounds and occasional tumbledown and long-vacated dwellings of the better sort disputed for possession of the neighbourhood with weed-choked fields of yellow clay and partly inundated swamp land – the desolate backwash of the tide of urban growth which every city has as a memento of its early settlers' bad judgement of the path of progress.

Where field and swamp and desolate tin-can-and-ash-strewn dumping-ground met in dreary confluence, there stood the ruins of a long-abandoned church. Immediately after the Civil War, when rising Irish immigration had populated an extensive shanty town down on the flats, a young priest, more ambitious than practical, had planted a Catholic parish, built a brick chapel with funds advanced by sympathetic co-religionists from the richer part of town, and attempted to minister to the spiritual needs of the newcomers. But prosperity had depopulated the mean dwellings of his flock who, offered jobs on the railway or police force, or employment in the mills then being built on the other side of town, had moved their humble household gods to new locations, leaving him a shepherd without sheep. Soon he, too, had gone and the church stood vacant for two-score years or more, time and weather and ruthless vandalism taking toll of it till now it stood amid the desolation which surrounded it like a lich amid a company of sprawling skeletons, its windows broken out, its doors unhinged, its roof decayed and fallen in, naught but its crumbling walls and topless spire remaining to bear witness that it once had been a house of prayer.

The final grains of rice were trickling through my fingers as I paused before the barren ruin, wondering what my next move was to be. Diane had entered through the doorless portal at the building's front, and the darkness of the black interior had swallowed her completely. I had a box of matches in my pocket, but they, I knew would scarcely give me light enough to find my way about the ruined building. The floors were broken in a dozen places, I was sure, and where they were not actually displaced they were certain to be so weakened with decay that to step on them would be courting swift disaster. I had no wish to break a leg and spend the night, and perhaps the next day and the next, in an abandoned ruin where the chances were that anyone responding to my cries for help would only come to knock me on the head and rob me.

But there was no way out but forward. I had promised Jules de Grandin that I'd keep Diane in sight, and so, with a sigh which was half a prayer to the God of Foolish Men, I grasped my stick more firmly and stepped across the threshold of the old, abandoned church.

Stygian darkness closed about me as waters close above the head of one who dives, and like foul, greasy water, so it seemed to me, the darkness pressed upon me, clogging eyes and nose and throat, leaving only the sense of hearing – and of apprehension – unimpaired. The wind soughed dolefully through the broken arches of the nave and whistled with a sort of mocking ululation among the rotted cross-beams of the transept. Drops of moisture accumulated on the studdings of the broken roof fell dismally from time to time. The choir and sanctuary were invisible, but I realized they must be at the farther end of the building, and set a cautious foot forward, but drew it quickly back, for only empty air responded to the pressure of my probing boot. 'Where was the girl? Had she fallen through an opening in the floor, to be precipitated on the rubble in the basement?' I asked myself.

'Diane? Oh, Diane?' I called softly.

No answer.

I struck a match and held the little torch aloft, its feeble light barely staining the surrounding blackness with the faintest touch of orange, then gasped involuntarily.

Just for a second, as the match-head kindled into flame, I saw a vision. Vision, perhaps, is not the word for it; rather, it was like one of those phosphenes or subjective sensations of light which we experience when we press our fingers on our lowered eyelids, not quite perceived, vague, dancing, and elusive, yet, somehow, definitely *felt*. The moulding beams and uprights of the church, long denuded of their pristine coat of paint and plaster, seemed to put on new habiliments, or to have been mysteriously metamorphosed; the bare brick walls were sheathed in stone, and I was gazing down a long and narrow colonnaded corridor, agleam with glowing torches, which terminated in a broad, low flight of steps leading to a marble platform. A giant statue dominated all, a figure hewn from stone and representing a tall and bearded being with high, virgin, female breasts, clothed below the waist in woman's robes, a sceptre tipped with an acorn-like ornament in the right hand, a new-born infant cradled in the crook of the left elbow. Music, not heard, but rather felt, filled the air until the senses swooned beneath its overpowering pressure, and a line of girls, birth-nude, save for the veilings of their long and flowing hair, entered from the right and left, formed twos and stepped with measured, mincing tread in the direction of the statue. With them walked shaven-headed priests in female garb, their weak and beardless faces smirking evilly.

Brow-down upon the tessellated pavement dropped the maiden priestesses, their hands, palm forwards, clasped above their heads while they beat their foreheads softly on the floor and the eunuch priests stood by impatiently.

And now the grovelling women rose and formed a circle where they stood, hands crossed above their breasts, eyes cast demurely down, and four shaven-pated priests came marching in, a gilded litter on their shoulders. On it, garlanded in flowers, but otherwise unclothed, lay a young girl, eyes closed, hands clasped as if in prayer, slim ankles crossed. They put the litter on the floor before the statue of the monstrous hermaphroditic god-thing; the circling maidens clustered round; a priest picked up a golden knife and touched the supine girl upon the insteps. There was neither fear nor apprehension on the face of her upon the litter, but rather an expression of ecstatic longing and anticipation as she uncrossed her feet. The flaccid-faced, emasculated priest leant over her, gloating...

As quickly as it came the vision vanished. A drop of gelid moisture fell from a rafter overhead, extinguishing the quivering flame of my match, and once more I stood in the abandoned church, my head whirling, my senses all but gone, as I realized that through some awful power of suggestion I had seen a tableau of the worship of the great All-Mother, the initiation of a virgin priestess to the ranks of those love-slaves who served the worshippers of the goddess of fertility, Diana, Milidath, Astarte, Cobar, or by whatever name men knew her in differing times and places.

But there was naught of vision in the flickering lights which now showed in the ruined sanctuary-place. Those spots of luminance were torches in the hands of living, mortal men, men who moved soft-footedly across the broken floor and set up certain things – a tripod with a brazen bowl upon its top, a row of tiny brazen lamps which flickered weakly in the darkness, as though they had been votive lamps before a Christian altar. And by their faint illumination I saw an odd-appearing thing stretched east and west upon the spot where the tabernacle had been housed, a grey-white, leprous-looking thing which might have been a sheeted corpse or lichened tombstone, and before it the torch-bearers made low obeisance, genuflecting deeply, and the murmur of their chant rose above the whispering reproaches of the wind.

It was an obscene invocation. Although I could not understand the words, or even classify the language which was used, I felt that there was something wrong about it. It was something like a phonographic record played in reverse. Syllables which I knew instinctively should be sonorously noble were oddly turned and twisted in pronounciation ... 'diuq sirairolg'. With a start I found the key. It was Latin – spoken backwards. They were intoning the fifty-second Psalm: '*Quid gloriaris* ... why boastest thou thyself ... whereas the goodness of God endureth yet daily?'

A stench, as of burning offal, stole through the building as the incense pot upon the tripod began to belch black smoke into the air.

And now another voice was chanting. A woman's rich contralto. '*Oitanimulli sunimod* ...' I strained my ears and bent my brows in concentration, and at last I had the key. It was the twenty-seventh Psalm recited in reverse Latin: 'The Lord is my light and my salvation ...'

From the shadows Diane Wickwire came, straight and supple as a willow wand, unclothed as for the bath, but smeared from soles to hairline with some luminous concoction, so that her slim, nude form stood out against the blackness like a spirit out of purgatory visiting the earth with the incandescence of the purging fires still clinging to it.

Silently, on soft-soled naked feet, she stepped across the long-deserted sanctuary and paused before the object lying there. And as her voice mingled with the chanting of the men I seemed to see a monstrous form take shape against the darkness. A towering, obscene, freakish form, bearded like a hero of the *Odyssey*, its pectoral region thick-hung with multiple mammae, its nether limbs encased in a man's chiton, a lingam-headed sceptre and a child held in its hands.

I shuddered. A chill not of the storm-swept night, but colder than any physical cold, seemed creeping through the air, as the ghostly, half-defined form seemed taking solidarity from the empty atmosphere. Diane Wickwire paused a moment, then stepped forwards, a silver hammer gleaming in the lambent light rays of the little brazen lamps.

But suddenly, like a draft of clear, fresh mountain breeze cutting through the thick, mephitic vapours of a swamp, there came another sound. Out of the darkness it came, yet not long was it in darkness, for, his face picked out by candlelight, a priest arrayed in full canonicals stepped from the shadows, while beside him, clothed in cassock and surplice, a lighted taper in his hand, walked Jules de Grandin.

They were intoning the office of exorcism. 'Remember not, Lord, our offences nor the offences of our forefathers, neither take Thou vengeance of our sins . . .'

As though struck dumb by the singing of the holy chant, the evocators ceased their sacrilegious intonation, and stared amazed as de Grandin and the cleric approached. Abreast of them, the priest raised the aspergillum which he bore and sprinkled holy water on the men, the woman, and the object of their veneration.

The result was cataclysmic. Out went the light of every brazen lamp, vanished was the hovering horror from the air above the stone, the luminance on Diane's body faded as though wiped away, and from the sky's dark vault there came the rushing of a mighty wind.

It shook the ancient ruined church, broke joists and timbers from their places, toppled tattered edges of brick walls into the darkened body of the rotting pile. I felt the floor swaying underneath my feet, heard a woman's wild, despairing scream, and the choking, suffocated roar of something in death-agony, as though a monster strangled in its blood; then:

'Trowbridge, *mon brave*; Trowbridge, *mon cher*, do you survive? are you still breathing?' I heard de Grandin's hail, as though from a great distance.

I sat up gingerly, his arm behind my shoulders. 'Yes, I

think so,' I answered doubtfully. 'What was it, an earthquake?'

'Something very like it,' he responded with a laugh. 'It might have been coincidence – though I do not think it was – but a great wind came from nowhere and completed the destruction which time began. That ruined church will never more give sanctuary to wanderers of the night. It is only debris, now.'

'Diane –' I began, and:

'She is yonder,' he responded, nodding towards an indistinct figure lying on the ground a little distance off. 'She is still unconscious, and I think her arm is broken, but otherwise she is quite well. Can you stand?'

With his assistance I rose and took a few tottering steps, then, my strength returning, helped him lift the swooning girl and bear her to a decrepit Ford which was parked in the muddy apology for a road beside the marshy field. '*Mon Père*,' de Grandin introduced, 'this is the good physician, Doctor Trowbridge, of whom I told you, he who led us to this place. Friend Trowbridge, this is Father Ribet of the French Mission, without whom we should – *eh bien*, who can say what we should have done?'

The priest, who, like most members of his calling, drove well but furiously, took us home, but declined to stay for refreshment, saying he had much to do the next day.

We put Diane to bed, her fractured arm carefully set and bandaged. De Grandin sponged her with a Turkish cloth, drying her as deftly as an trained hospital nurse could have done; then, when we'd put her night-clothes on her and tucked her in between the sheets, he bore the basin of bath-water to the sink, poured it out and followed it with a liberal libation of carbolic antiseptic. 'See can you withstand that, vile essence of the old one?' he demanded as the strong scent of phenol filled the room.

'Well, I'm listening,' I informed him as we lighted our cigars. 'What's the explanation, if any?'

He shrugged his shoulders. 'Who can say?' he answered. 'You know from what I told you that Mademoiselle Diane prepared to go to them; from what you did observe yourself, you know she went.

'To meet their magic with a stronger counter-agent, I had recourse to the good Père Ribet. He is a Frenchman, therefore he was sympathetic when I laid the case before him, and readily agreed to go with me and perform an exorcism of the evil spirit which possessed our dear Diane and was ruled by those vile miscreants. It was his number which I bade you call, and fast we followed on your message, tracing you by the trail of rice you left and making ready to perform our office when all was ready. We waited till the last safe minute; then, while they were chanting their so blasphemous inverted Psalms, we broke in on them and –'

'What was that awful, monstrous thing I saw forming in the air just before you and Father Ribet came in?' I interrupted.

'*Tiens*, who can say?' he answered with another shrug. 'Some have called it one thing, some another. Me, I think it was the visible embodiment of the evil thing which man worshipped in the olden days and called the Mother Principle. These things, you know, my friend, were really demons, but their strength was great, for they drew form and substance from the throngs which worshipped them. But demons they were and are, and so are subject to the rite of exorcism, and accordingly, when good Père Ribet did sprinkle –'

'D'ye mean you actually believe a few phrases of ecclesiastical Latin and a few drops of holy water could dissipate that dreadful thing?' I asked incredulously.

He puffed slowly at his cigar; then: 'Have it this way, if you prefer,' he answered. 'The power of evil which this thing we call the *Magna Mater* for want of a better name possesses comes from her – or its – worshippers. Generation after superstitious generation of men worshipped it, pouring out daily praise and prayer to it, *believing* in it. Thereby they built up a very great psychological power, a very exceedingly great power, indeed; make no doubt about that.

'But the olden gods died when Christianity came. Their worshippers fell off; they were weakened for very lack of psychic nourishment. Christianity, the new virile faith, upon the other hand, grew strong apace. The office of exorcism was developed by the time-honoured method of trial and error, and finally it was perfected. Certain words – certain sounds, if you prefer – pronounced in certain ways, produced certain ascertainable effects, precisely as a note played upon a violin produces a responsive note from a piano. You have the physical explanation of that? Good; this is a spiritual analogy. Besides, generations of faithful Christians have believed, firmly believed that exorcism is effective. *Voilà*; it is, therefore, effective. A psychological force of invincible potency has been built up for it.

'And so, when Père Ribet exorcised the demon goddess in that old ruined church tonight – *tiens*, you saw what happened.'

'What became of those men?' I asked.

'One wonders,' he responded. 'Their bodies I can vouch for. They are broken and buried under tons of fallen masonry. Tomorrow the police emergency squad will dig them out, and speculation as to who they were, and how they met their fate will be a nine days' wonder in the newspapers.'

'And the stone?'

'Crushed, my friend. Utterly crushed and broken. Père Ribet and I beheld it, smashed into a dozen fragments. It was all clay, not clay surrounding a meteorite, as the poor deluded Wickwire believed. Also –'

'But look here, man,' I broke in. 'This is all the most fantastic lot of balderdash I've ever heard. D'ye think I'm satisfied with any such explanation as this? I'm willing to concede part of it, of course, but when it comes to all that stuff about the *Magna Mater* and –'

'*Ah bah,*' he cut me off, 'as for those explanations, they satisfy me no more than they do you. There *is* no expla-

nation for these happenings which will meet a scientific
or even logical analysis, my friend. Let us not be too
greatly concerned with whys and wherefores. The hour
grows late and I grow very thirsty. Come, let us take a
drink and go to bed.'